CLOSE

BEAUTIFUL ORDINARY BOOK ONE

S.A. MCEWEN

CLOSE

BEAUTIFUL ORDINARY BOOK ONE

S.A. MCEWEN

ALSO BY THE AUTHOR

Romantic Suspense

Perfect (Beautiful Ordinary #2)

Ruined (Beautiful Ordinary Book 3)

Domestic Thrillers

The Good Daughter

The Lost Boy

Good Girl Bad

Sister in Trouble

Please Note: *Ruined* and *The Good Daughter* are a steamy and non-steamy version of the same book

For Steph and Sarah—
Your friendship makes my world go round.

PROLOGUE

Lucas

June 2016

When my mother showed me a picture of his body, the thing that struck me first was not how grey he looked, how at odds with his habitual golden glow.

Nor was it how small he looked—his six-foot frame and broad chest somehow diminished. Childlike and vulnerable. Rendered irrelevant by death.

It wasn't even the feelings—the tsunami of feelings that would rush in later and blindside me. Given that I had barely seen him in years and had never been close to him to begin with, the feelings were surprisingly ferocious.

Those things came later. They came and hit me—less like the proverbial sledgehammer and more like a subtle self-combustion. Invisible to an observer. But damaging nonetheless. Suffocating me. Crushing me from the inside out.

But not then. Not at first.

The thing that struck me initially was that she had coolly snapped a picture. As though this was another moment in time to capture for posterity. More striking because what other mothers might have captured, she had never bothered with.

First tooth. No snap.

First step. No snap.

First birthday. No snap. No cake, either, for that matter.

But first death?

Snap, snap, snap.

1

CLARA

January 2017

"Naughty, naughty boys!"

Sapphire is prancing and squealing, tossing back her long blonde hair as she leans forward, ass grasped firmly in her hands, exposing her butt crack as she mimes words with her ass cheeks.

It's busy and loud—a normal Thursday night.

As normal as you can get when your colleague is pretending to talk out of her butt to scold grown businessmen.

"Now, which naughty boys would like to see my titties?" she continues to talk with her butt cheeks, coyly looking over her shoulder at the half-embarrassed, half-titillated men mulling around behind her.

She's petite and slim and sweet-looking. I'm pretty sure that at first glance, inside or outside the club, no one would ever imagine her talking to businessmen with her butt.

Several dances down already, I'd just sat at the bar to rest after my five minutes on the podium when she had beckoned me flirtatiously, grabbing my hand and whispering conspiratorially, tickling my cleavage with fresh, fragrant blonde hair as she leaned close, close, closer. Then she smacked my bottom and giggled.

I roll my eyes, but she just bought her first house outright at nineteen, so I probably should watch and learn instead of judging. Sweet-looking or not, she knows how to relieve a man of his cash. Fast.

"What about Zefi's titties?" she continues, winking at me. "Lots of titties here, plenty for everyone!"

I gathered quickly it was a bachelor party, and a raft of girls descended on the group of men to ensure everyone felt attended to, desired. Within moments we had each of them paired with bright girls sporting skimpy underwear and big smiles. It used to surprise me how this occurred without language, girls scattering like mercury amongst newcomers and pairing off within moments. No time to lose. Time was money, and seconds weren't wasted. The girls decided who went with whom, and at times like this, we were Team Money.

When the pickings were scarce, it wasn't so smooth. Competitiveness threatened. Podium times were watched like rocket launches, down to the second. A few seconds over and you might miss being first to a potential dance. Lateness was not tolerated.

But tonight, there was a steady stream of clients, and they were easy with their fifties.

Chad was mine. Enormous. His shirt clung to him perfectly, his stomach and abs delectable underneath. But while it's nice to get a pretty, young thing to play with for a change, I don't pay too much attention. I'm not here to meet men. I come, I dance, I bank the cash.

Chad looks awkward, avoiding eye contact, mumbling his name. This isn't unusual for a buck's night. There's always one or two who are verging on mortified. At the other end of the scale there's often drunken whooping and crowing, a pack mentality that prefers watching in groups to one-on-one dances. But the dances are where the money is, and we try to lure the guys apart, whispering brash promises with shiny lips, pressing pert butts against all number of places.

It's easy work, most of the time.

I press my barely covered breasts against his torso, my hot breath in his ear, imploring him to follow me somewhere private, pushing him gently to sit in a secluded booth, where plush red velour could rise all around him, protect us from prying eyes, giving the illusion of intimacy.

"One song for twenty, three for fifty," I say, tugging suggestively at a bra strap, peeking out through thick lashes from lowered eyes—coquettish.

Wordlessly, he hands me a fifty and I start my routine. My stiletto against his leg, I deftly fold the fifty around a shoe strap with a rubber band, alongside all the others. It has been a good night.

I'm not like this in my private life. That's the attraction, in part, I suppose. I can be anyone here. I can be someone different every night. Try out various personas, fool around with them. Amuse myself.

I'm tired now though. It's nearly 4 a.m. It's harder to keep up the façade when I'm tired; sometimes I almost slip into my ordinary, introverted, self-protective self.

Not very helpful in a strip club.

Taking a deep breath, I try to focus on the job at hand.

I spin around against the seat opposite me, running my hands slowly down the back of my stay-ups to my ankles, slowly letting my dark locks snake and swivel to the floor, keeping my eyes to the front, legs spread an alluring but not indecent distance. The song is sexy, throbbing, and slow, and I move my ass slowly from side to side with straight legs, giving Chad plenty of privacy to enjoy the view. Too much eye contact is a mistake. It lets reality or self-consciousness loom too large. Let them look at what they came for. Escape, fantasy? Fantasy certainly makes more dough.

Slowly I run one hand back up a leg, letting my forefinger linger tantalisingly on the elastic of my g-string. There's barely anything there, but that's not the point. There's something mesmerising about a striptease. I never understood that until working here. It seemed too predictable and trite to really be compelling. I couldn't imagine anyone would *pay* for it. But now —well, I have a healthy bank balance convincing me otherwise.

The therapist in me tries to understand it, placing it squarely in the realm of physiology. Something to do with executive functioning. The primitive brain takes over; men hand over ridiculous amounts of money. *My* executive functioning worries about whether they can afford it—do they have wives or children? Do they regret it the next day? But in the moment, nothing beats it: the money, the rush.

Being someone else for a while.

I tug gently at the thin strip of black lace covering my genitalia, revealing small glimpses of bare labia for his perusal. I find this part arousing. I know some girls rub olive oil over themselves to give the illusion of wetness, readiness; I don't need to. I'd fuck someone senseless here if I could, I'm so good at this. Mostly it's the rush I get from the power, the groaning desire I can hear but not see behind me. I can imagine they are anyone; this is anything. They are completely under my spell. Their desire is urgent, primal...and restrained.

When I started, my heart crashed against my ribs the entire shift. I was sure every client could see the panic in my eyes, my thudding heart. But the work was so easy, and the freedom was titillating. I was surprised at how amorous it made me. It was a lot of food for thought.

I still wonder if I could do it in real life, if I was in a serious relationship. Pretending and anonymity is one thing. If I *liked* the man...

The tightness I feel is like being snapped to by a rubber band. Snapped toward myself—allergic to the vulnerable or exposed. I shake myself imperceptibly; these thoughts do *not* belong here. I get back to the job at hand. Touching myself lightly, exposing my wetness, spreading my legs farther apart, and raising my ass ever so slightly. I hear Chad thump back against his seat, make a strangled sound. "I'm sorry. You're gorgeous," he says roughly and stands, his huge hands on my hips. The shock of it is electrifying against my excitement. So unexpected and illicit. A bolt of desire shoots through me. I know he's not trying a fast one—he's too nervous, and besides, security will be here in about three seconds. Touching is strictly not allowed.

But it only lasts a second, and then he is gone.

I stand up awkwardly, the move to upright not meant to be so sudden and unplanned. I focus on his retreating back in the gloomy light, his shoulders massive, loping away, the crowds parting to accommodate him. By the stairs, he throws a glance over his shoulder. His eyes are flashing, conflicted, crashing against my own. Then he vanishes.

———

THE NEXT DAY, I sleep late, earplugs blocking out the morning traffic and blackout blinds blocking out the day.

When I finally wake, it's close to midday and I stretch luxuriously in my smooth Egyptian cotton sheets, my first gift to myself when I started stripping. Or, more to the point, got the hang of stripping and started making money at it.

My apartment is my favourite space. Littered with books, flowers, and baking treasures, I love nothing better than a lazy weekend at home by myself, reading new releases and cooking myself treats.

Not today though. I have my other job to get to.

I pile my hair into a high bun and linger under a hot shower, washing away the night before, the girl who works there.

Back to reality.

Dry and snug in a white bathrobe, I switch on the kettle and count my earnings. My best night yet: two thousand dollars. It seems obscene against the backdrop of my real profession, but I don't think about that at present.

Instead, I remember Chad, my tummy flipping and my insides clenching deliciously at the memory.

Pushing the wads of cash aside, I shrug off the bathrobe, slide my index and middle fingers under the elastic of my sensible cotton panties. I imagine security too slow, the booth too secluded. His hands on my hips, fingers digging possessively into the soft skin around my waist, dominant, urgent. Thrusting inside me, grunting. No conversation, no foreplay. I've come by his fourth thrust.

Satisfied, I get ready for work.

———

MY FIRST CLIENT for the day is Kate: tall, lean, with sharp grey eyes and an even sharper wit. And a ten-year history of problems with food.

"I've decided to run every time I want to vomit," she says.

Her knees hurt, she goes on to tell me, but she responds well to success or failure dichotomies. Success is something she understands. If she frames abstaining from purging as success, and purging as failure, she thinks she might succeed.

She's allergic to failure.

Two afternoons a week, I rent a room from a friend for my private psychotherapy practice. I usually work late, the hours convenient—both for me and for my clients.

"Running is like punishing myself," Kate continues. "It might work in place of purging. Maybe it will ease the anxiety that precedes throwing up, of not coping. Maybe I will just feel too damn tired and sorry for my body to have the energy left to vomit. But I am stopping this right now. Today." She looks at me expectantly.

"Running's not as convenient," she adds. "But I've joined a 24-hour gym."

I love my job. I'm endlessly curious about our internal worlds and how they're shaped. The stories that we tell ourselves.

Yet, I can't give up my other job.

At the time, I told myself it was just to get me through a gruelling psychotherapy degree—the most I could earn for as little time invested as possible. While all my friends waited tables or worked night shifts in refuges, I worked a night or two a week dancing and marvelled that everyone wasn't doing it.

Yet, I could earn a living from my practice now, if I extended my hours and accepted more referrals. For a while I kidded myself about my reasoning.

The money is so good. Just till I get a bit of savings behind me.

Just till I'm confident the private practice will keep attracting clients.

I knew I was lying to myself, but in an impressive feat of doublethinking, I avoided confronting myself about it for quite some time.

Half the truth? I just like being someone else sometimes.

Someone fun and confident and a little bit wild.

Someone lustful and able to articulate it.

Someone without secrets, without ties.

Another half-truth? Unsavoury, confronting:

I just like the not-quite sex.

2

LUCAS

THE FIRST FEW nights that I watched her, I didn't ask for a dance.

It's easy to lurk in a strip club. It's so dark, so busy. Girls rolled over me like waves, one after the other, gorgeous and eager and syrupy. Occasionally I took a dance, so I didn't stand out, cause talk, invite lingering glances.

Who knows how much these girls gossip about the men in the room.

The one time she started toward me, I hastily grabbed the nearest girl and disappeared with her into a booth for a dance. A quick one.

But in general, I could stare at her in her skimpy lingerie and look like any other guy there.

Younger.

Soberer.

But leering at a semi-naked girl? I blended right in.

She wasn't what I was expecting. Some of it, sure. All long crazy hair, big smiles, flashing white teeth.

Teasing, flirting. Popular.

Sultry as all hell on the pole.

All of that I expected.

But I didn't expect her to be *quite* so tantalising.

It wasn't just her appearance. Legs that invited lingering eyes to travel up, up, up. And loiter on her perfect ass for a while. So perfect that my hands ached with the effort involved in resisting grabbing it. Squeezing it. Using handfuls of it to yank her crotch against me.

A waist with contours so enticing that for a while I forgot why I was there.

I'd never wanted to touch a curve so badly in my life.

That was unexpected.

But it was also something *in* her.

At first glance, she was just like all the others. Perfect, cheerful, sexy. Accommodating. But there was something else there as well. If you watched for as long as I did.

And I watched for quite some time.

It would pass across her face every now and then, as she moved between clients or exited the podium. When she headed back to the change rooms. Fleeting, rolling across her face, her eyes momentarily deeper, full of something.

Something darker.

3

CLARA

"So, any clients want to share their life stories with you this week?"

Beth and I are sipping sauv blanc in her therapy room, finished for the day. The last rays of sunlight settle on her blinds, the room warm and cosy. A bunch of fresh gerberas blaze a deep maroon between us.

Also a psychotherapist, Beth is my closest friend and the only person who knows about my other job. Everyone else thinks I'm at the practice more than I am and would be mortified, angry, or upset if they knew any different.

Sex sells, but not to your family.

"Nope. I've learnt my lesson. I try not to talk," I wink at her, mock confidential, topping off our glasses from the bar fridge in her office.

She's referring to my dancing clients, the odd way in which somehow my therapist aura seems to permeate even that scene, if I let it. At the start, I found it extraordinarily hard to keep the two roles separate. Hard to believe, given one is set in a quiet room with the cliché couch and box of tissues, and the other requires sky-high stilettos and a couple of pieces of lace passed off as underwear. Yet somehow the conversations seemed to gravitate in the same direction.

Much to Beth's amusement, initially I tried to operate in a strip club like one might anywhere. In probably the most ridiculous place that I could have possibly sought it, I conversed on the expectation that I would be valued and esteemed for what I thought and said. I pursued intellectual conversations. I forgot I was there to make money. Hours would tick by, just talking.

Semi-naked.

That worked just fine for those incongruous outcomes. I was told that I was radiant, exquisite, exceptional. I was told all sorts of things. I was handed countless business cards, my number asked for again and again. Weekends to Sydney offered, dinner dates proposed. Overseas "business companion" trips offered like a toy to a child by someone who desperately wants to be liked. Or, you know. Like a bribe to a girl twenty years your junior whom you desperately want to want to shag you.

But I wasn't making any money.

Cue some new rules. No talking except for smut. Even smut expires now at three minutes if a dance isn't secured. I talk dirty, and I dance on laps.

"So, give me the details. Hit me up." Beth looks at me expectantly. She's insatiable. She loves to try to wrap her head around the absurd stuff that goes on in a strip club. It's become a bit of a post-work ritual—her poring over my anecdotes in fascination. A kind of dirty version of a parental check-in (*What was the best part of your day? The hardest part? The part you would change if you could?*). In a strip club, it's more like—the weirdest part, the funniest thing, the sexiest dance moves. The hottest guy.

"Ass-talking. Hands down winner last night."

Beth bolts upright in her cosy recliner. "What? WHAT? What the fuck is ass-talking?"

"Well, a chick talks to the men using her butt cheeks. True story," I nod at Beth. "Weird, but true."

"What does her ass say?"

"Oh, you know," I wave my hand around in a vague gesture. "Asks them who wants to see her tits, who wants a dance, that kind of thing."

Beth stares at me for quite some time. "'That kind of thing,'" she imitates me. "Oh, I *see*."

Then: "Actually, I really don't. I don't see at all. I cannot imagine. But moving on. What else?"

"Well, it's not so weird, it's more stupid. So, two girls did a girl-on-girl show, and you know, they pretend to go down on each other under all their hair, and of course they aren't *really*. But the guys go wild. And I just think—surely they know it's fake? Can they really be so dumb? It's *so dumb*. So *that's* weird."

"Huh." Beth ponders this for a minute. But it obviously doesn't capture her imagination. She's back to the ass-talking.

"Can you...uh...demonstrate?"

I throw a cushion at her.

"What about the practice? Still planning on just sticking to two days? You know I have a vacancy coming up on a Wednesday in your room if you want to pick up another shift."

"Hmmm. I love it here...but I'm not sure. I like doing half and half," I tell her. "The club is easier than this, to be honest."

Except that that's not entirely honest.

If I was really honest, I'd tell her that I'm hooked on the dancing. There's something about it that makes me feel alive. Invincible.

Hot.

But there's also something about it that makes me feel secure. Like it's a safe place to relegate that girl to—the girl that I have been, that I sometimes am. Who makes bad choices. Who does bad things.

In a strip club, she can't do any real damage.

She can be let loose to spread her wings.

And between the two, there's a strange niggling sensation that

I haven't learnt my lesson yet. Exactly what that lesson is escapes me. But I feel like I'm close to learning something big. Maybe not something *healthy*. But still.

I trust my gut.

But I'm not sure how to frame all this to Beth, so I keep quiet. "Hiding things" being another secret talent of mine.

Beth ponders me for a minute. She's the girl you go out clubbing with till 6 a.m, but also the girl who asks the hard questions. She looks like she's about to say something, then changes her mind.

We move on to plans for a night out the following week. Then we kiss cheeks and both head home to bed.

———

BACK AT HOME, I think back over my conversation with Beth.

Idly, I open my bedside drawer, peruse its contents.

Dancing clients, for the most part, think I'm 22. Even this week, when I'd tried to age myself a year, testing out the sound of 23, a client had laughed at me and insisted I couldn't be a day over 19.

I find this hilarious. I'm actually 27.

I have a stash of men's business cards and phone numbers in this drawer.

I keep them, not because I will ever use them, but to remember that what people see is not necessarily what they get.

Along with the cards, I have a plethora of adjectives like "luminous" and "extraordinary" tucked away for my consideration. Phrases like "you don't belong here" to comfort and enrage me, to take home at 5 a.m.

Like a man in a strip club might know where I belong.

4

AARON

*Nine months **earlier***
12th April 2016

Dear Clara,

When you said I couldn't see you, I decided my efforts to be respectful were wasted.

I'd thought about you so often—that hair, good God—but every time I thought about how it would feel clenched in my fist, all bloody two feet of it, I resolutely turned away from the thought, the fantasy dying before it had even begun.

I didn't want to demean you in the way my fantasies were wont to demean the subject of them sometimes. The object, perhaps.

I'd wanted us to be different.

Pure. Good.

Helpful.

But then you said no, and I have to admit the first thing I felt was anger.

Why the fuck not? I didn't want to see anyone else. I wanted you.

Yeah, yeah, we'd only met a handful of times. So what? I didn't care. I still knew. It was you or no one.

It wasn't even how you looked. Your hair. Your legs. God, they went on forever. All the way to your perfect butt. I wanted to run my fingers along the line where they met. Perfect legs met the perfect butt. It was primal, yes. But mostly it was how kind you seemed. You looked at me as though you actually could see me. You spoke to me like a person, not a walking ATM. I wanted more of that.

But you were firm. Kind, but not budging. Not even entertaining the idea.

So I went home that night and clenched my cock hard, imagining that scene with another ending.

You, saying you couldn't see me; me, grabbing fistfuls of that gorgeous hair and yanking your head back, forcing you to your knees. Forcing my cock into your mouth.

Telling you how sweet and wet and hot your mouth felt.

It went downhill from there.

I had you over your desk, against the wall, in the toilets, in alleyways. You were always trying to get away from me, but always loving it in the end. My cock.

Me.

They weren't angry fantasies, mind you. I wasn't punishing you. And it's not what I ACTUALLY want. It feels important to write that down. In case someone ever finds all these pages. I'm not a psycho. I don't actually want to rape anyone. I don't find anything sexy about REAL pain. Mine or anyone else's.

It's just I found them hot. We all fantasise about weird shit sometimes, right? Stepsisters? Real sisters? The taboo? I don't know. But after you said no, I let my mind wander the way it does in fantasies. Instead of stopping it. Reining it back in.

I always felt dirty and wrong afterwards. They're stupid fantasies, I know. Ugly. Dangerous, even. You can probably infer all sorts of things from them. About who I am, where my insecurities lie. My flaws, my imperfections.

I would have told you them upfront. I could have catalogued them for you in alphabetical order, with helpful footnotes. I'm not even *ashamed of them. Curious, perhaps. Which would fall under D for "Detached" or maybe "Dissociative."*

I've thought about them all so much we could have covered them impassively, counting them off, A to Z. Curious together.

A would be for "Anger." And I don't need a therapist to work that one out for me. Anger is what you feel when you don't want to feel pain. So much easier to be angry than to be sad. Anger feels powerful. Anger might dominate something. Sadness. Fuck. Sadness is wimpy and floaty and gets nothing done.

I'm not saying it's HEALTHY. Just that I get it.

We could have talked about all of that.

All you had to do was ask.

5

CLARA

BACK AT THE CLUB, I put the finishing touches on my makeup.

Black liner around my silver eyes. Grey and silver eyeshadow making them look smoky and sultry and huge.

A dash of shiny pink gloss highlights my full pink lips. It's the perfect combination of girl-next-door and sultry temptress. Long, glossy hair. Girly pink lips. Men see me and think about how young I look. They see my lips and imagine me sucking their cock, I have no doubt. And if there is any doubt at all, the slow, textbook tongue run along my top lip gets them there.

So easy, men.

I play the hell out of that.

I've tried all sorts of looks, but this is my most successful. I look available and untouchable all at once.

Forbidden.

They don't know it, but they really want to see me with my ass in the air; to feel, however briefly, that they could have me. Control me. See me submit.

Or maybe they want to see which look wins out over the course of a striptease: innocent girl or alluring adulteress. Maybe the incongruence drives them wild. It drives me a little bit wild, too.

The makeup is actually not that critical though—the light is deliberately low and warm. No one wants bright lights shining too much reality on the goings-on in the dark corners of a strip club. Imperfections and all manner of things can be hidden under a dim enough light.

I'm wearing my favourite outfit: a black and red racy lingerie set with a see-through four-inch excuse for a skirt over the g-string. It covers nothing, but has proved invaluably alluring; a grin thrown over my shoulder, inviting a peek up my skirt a favourite among clients. They almost always follow.

Like I said. So easy, men.

It's nine o'clock and I'm up on the podium in fifteen minutes. Girls grumble about it (wasted time!), but I don't mind it. Showing off on the pole never fails to get me a little bit excited. Wondering who's watching. Wanting me.

The whole thing is a little off, I know. Narcissistic and dangerous. But somehow I always feel safe. I befriended the security staff, keen early on to know how they work. I've seen the camera room, someone always watching every corner of the building, every dancer. Burly men in large numbers. I have seen them move fast.

If I asked, they would always walk me to my car at the end of a shift.

But the excitement? Even I don't know how to classify that. Or maybe I do know, but don't like what it says about me. The hit I get from being desired, without having to truly reciprocate. Without having to risk anything. What it might say about how I measure my self-worth. That I need to get a self-esteem hit from men in a seedy club? Certain men, to be sure. The young, cocky, cute ones. But still. It doesn't seem like a healthy way for a therapist to ratchet up some "feel goods" in the slightest.

None of it seems very healthy, actually.

Nevertheless, I just bury my doubts and use it to my advantage. Tease and flirt freely. Everybody seems to know the drill. If it's sex clients want, there are plenty of places within easy reach. Probably it'd cost them less than the pleasure of just looking. I always wonder why they're here and not just at a brothel. Perhaps they frequent both sorts of establishments. Who knows. I don't ask.

Sexy, trashy pop music fills the crowded space. On the podium, I focus on the slower beat. Unhurried movements, trailing my fingers right down and up my legs, letting my hair curl and crash down my body. Sensual touching, teasing, taking my hand away right before I reach my g-string.

Clients need to pay for that shit.

I pepper my routine with turns and flips on the pole, but frankly they're tiring on a long night on your feet, and I don't find the use of them any more likely to get a potential client's attention. So I sway and touch and titillate, saving my energy, surveying the crowd from under my hair, looking for interested parties.

Meeting the eyes of a suitable candidate, I smile and saunter over.

"I'm Zefi," I introduce myself, lying, pushing my lips up close to his ear, nibbling his earlobe a little, breasts pressing against his pecs. "I want to get to know your cock." Turning around, I press my butt against said cock, rubbing just a little. "Come with me. I'll have you hard in seconds."

Cock talk and cock touch. My stripping allies. It's terribly crass—but I *want* to shut down their thinking.

I really do just want them to think with their dicks.

He looks bemused and very relaxed. The opposite of Chad. Similar frame, just how I like it. Huge shoulders, well-defined biceps. And nice, big hands.

"Sold," he laughs, following me to my favourite booth. It has both a seat opposite his and a wall I can lean against.

"I'm Lucas," he adds, handing me a fifty without waiting to be asked. As I reach for it, he captures my fingers in his, his touch jolting me into a closer awareness of him. It's strangely intimate. Almost like a question, but one I can't decipher. Usually, the thoughts behind a client's eyes might as well be branded on their forehead:

I like you (shy and unsure where to look—ridiculous, given they've just given me cash to look at me naked).

Nice tits (ogling me hungrily, wanting to get their money's worth).

I'd fuck your brains out; you want to? (Leering, shameless, thinking—incorrectly, I hope—that this is a game of numbers. If you ask enough strippers, one will say yes eventually).

Lucas's eyes are dark and wanting something else. Not to ogle, not to buy me dinner. He'd like to fuck me, sure, but that's not what his eyes are asking me right now. He's searching my eyes like he might find something there.

I try to take the fifty-dollar note, but his grip tightens. I have the peculiar sense that he's trying to catch my thoughts, not my hand. My heart is beating faster in my chest. Partly because he's so good-looking. When a guy this hot takes your hand, of course your body lurches in response. I can see his arm muscles flexed under his T-shirt, holding my hand, unyielding. The shape of his stomach is enticing.

Without thinking I reach out my other hand and hook it under his T-shirt, run one finger along the top of his jeans. Touch his flesh there. Feel the faintest trace of him shiver.

I snap my eyes back up to his.

He's gone even stiller, watching me. His fingers loosen on mine. And I realise it's not just his physical attributes making my heart leap—it's also partly something else. A hint of danger. A hint of the unknown.

It's not often that I can't fathom someone's motives in this place.

I tug my hand way, confused and aroused. His fingers release mine without protest and he relaxes, smiles warmly at me, looks like any other hot guy again. Here for the show. But my body is on high alert.

It didn't imagine that exchange.

Slowly, my thoughts and body muddled, I start my routine. The routine for hot guys. Though the clients are not allowed to touch me, I can touch them if I want to. And, hell, I want to.

Pushing my disquiet aside I straddle him, my barely covered crotch pushing into his cock, riding it slightly as though we were fucking. I can already feel it twitching beneath my weight. I'm taking shallow little breaths that suggest arousal, contained desire. It's usually an act, but not tonight. Lucas is hot. Those hips. That stomach. I haven't had sex in a very long time. I want to fuck him. Or maybe I just want to *pretend* to want to. The line is blurry, even to me.

Pulling back from his crotch, I push my breasts together and push them into his face, one nipple tracing his lips through the sheer fabric of my bra. Then I abruptly turn around and bend over, my ass centimetres from his face. Straight back, ass out, I run my hands down my legs to my ankles, then snap my head down and—ignoring my own rules—look up through my legs at him, hair cascading in great, dark waves to the floor. His lips are slightly parted, but he shifts his gaze and meets my eyes. He still looks slightly bemused and fiendishly hot. We both know that he doesn't need to pay for this. Why he's at the club is anyone's guess.

Slowly I straighten my back again, running one hand up to my g-string, tugging it aside, revealing myself fully. Two fingers slightly part my labia, showing him how wet I am. I slide a finger right down the length of myself. I'm distracted, so horny I can barely remember my routine, forgetting to tease him, so eager I am to touch myself. He leans forward, and I can feel his breath on my ass. I have an urge to push myself back onto his mouth, to feel his tongue against me. Even from this angle I can smell him. I know nothing about him. He could be anyone. It's electrifying.

"That was definitely seconds," he drawls, unashamed of his straining erection. I push back onto him, my back against his torso, rub myself against the length of his cock, let out an involuntary groan. Remembering the security cameras, I reluctantly disengage and turn to face him, but have left a wet patch on his pants, right against his cock. He laughs ruefully, then looks up at me, hungry and intense.

The rest of my routine I must be on automatic pilot, because I can barely function through my lust. Somewhere along the way, riding him again, almost climaxing, his breath in my ear, he makes the usual offers. Dinners, trips. He gives me his card as he leaves, winking self-assuredly. He's utterly divine and a *maybe* flashes through my mind. But I got what I wanted. Desire, contact, a soaring self-esteem hit. The real thing opens up a whole other world of problems that I'm not interested in just now.

The rest of the night passes in a blur of delayed satisfaction. I have fantasies crowding my brain about what happens next, none of them bearing any resemblance to reality. I can't wait to get home to play them in slow motion and touch myself.

I can't believe I get paid for this shit.

———

BACK IN MY apartment the next day, I am satiated and spent.

As much as I love the rush of a hot dance and the sexual fantasy wonderland it leaves me with, the reality of stripping is more often seedy—the men older, sweatier, leerier. Lucas is the exception, not the norm.

I love to leave at the end of each shift.

Beth pops in at lunchtime and flops on my couch, raising her eyebrows at my bathrobe. Jasper takes the opportunity to ingratiate himself. A huge, fluffy grey Persian, he manages to look perpetually cranky while purring at megawatts and draping himself over anyone who sits still for more than a minute. Beth strokes him absentmindedly.

"Late night?" she asks.

"It's always late," I reply.

Her raised eyebrows inviting more information, I fumble around for a name.

"Shit, I've forgotten. But he was electric." Grinning, I toss her his card.

"Lucas Evans. No profession on here?"

I shrug.

"Seems a lot easier to get laid with a boyfriend on hand than waiting for hot encounters at, frankly, a place more likely to be full of sleazebags," she comments, knowing full well my preference for avoiding the real thing.

Beth has recently moved in with her partner, but her curiosity about my lack of interest in "meeting someone" is less rooting for the nuclear family or pushing stereotypes and more curiosity about my decision-making processes. The façade of sexy, independent temptress who shirks traditional romance could fool anyone but her. Such are the ups and downs of having a therapist best friend.

It's not that I'm for or against romance or relationships. If I'm very honest, it comes down to self-protection. Raunch is easy. And fake. And I'm *very* good at faking things. It's my superpower.

Or maybe it's my super curse.

But love? Love is...real. And that is terrifying. I haven't even dipped a toe in those murky waters, and I have no intention of starting now.

But one has to do something with a healthy sex-drive.

I chuck a spatula at Beth and invite her to make cherry chocolate biscuits with me. I don't feel like wading into my vulnerabilities and fears today. I know the allure of a good biscuit batch will focus her attention somewhere else.

———

UP EARLY THE NEXT DAY, I pull on my running gear and head out for a run along Merri Creek. The first ten minutes suck, as they always do, and I think I've made a grave mistake; that I could be baking muffins in my pyjamas and sipping tea while reading my book instead. But then I find my stride, feel the rush of endorphins start to lift my mood toward ecstatic, and remember why I love it.

I can hear the constant drone of traffic in the background, but amongst some greenery down the small valley of the creek, you can almost feel that you're away from the city. It's not the hills, but it's all right.

I have a quick shower at home then put in a long day at the practice. After my last client has left and my notes are finished, I slip into the small bathroom, rinse my face, and pull out my change of clothes.

Beth and I are meeting some of her friends for a drink and a dance. It's been forever since I've been out and I feel like dressing up. I slip on a strappy black fitted dress with silver heels and refresh my makeup, leaving my long hair bundled into a high bun. With my glasses on I look kind of sexy librarian, or maybe stern headmistress, and I consider letting my hair loose. But it's long and unruly and tends to get me a lot of attention. Stripper hair. I check my pins and leave it up.

Beth pops her head out of her door as I walk out. She's already in her dancing gear and shoots me a grin. "Ready?"

"Yep."

We take a taxi to the city and treat ourselves to a cocktail at Lui Bar, high above the city. The sunset is long gone, but the twinkling lights across the bay are satisfying enough in themselves. We sigh contentedly and settle into our seats.

"I had an interesting client today," Beth tells me, peering over her glass at me cheekily. "A stripper." She watches me expectantly.

"No way! How weird," I reply. Myself aside, therapy is not something I associate with stripping.

"Mmm-hmmm," she goes on, eyes twinkling. "Bit like you, in fact."

I roll my eyes. "Unlikely," I reply, both of us aware that a one-session comparison is probably overstating it. But given the amused look in her eyes, I wait patiently for a punch line.

"Very reflective, introspective. Wanting to explore her thoughts about love."

I raise my eyebrows. "What conclusions has she come to so far?"

"She's afraid of getting hurt. So she avoids love. Very normal. Run of the mill. But she's keen to change that."

"Really? Why?"

"Wants kids."

"Good lord. What a strange first session. Not what I would expect. So love is a hurdle to tackle before kids. Have you—" But I'm interrupted by the waiter gliding over to us; his tone is subdued, respectful.

"Excuse me, ladies. From the gentleman in the far corner." He presents us with two beautiful cocktails, dark and luscious. We glance at each other, then try to peer discreetly at the purchaser while sniffing the contents of the drinks.

"Blue curacao," I declare. "Haven't had it in years." Taking a sip, I can't place what else is in there, but it is definitely delicious. We can't see who our suitor is through the crowd, but we raise our glasses as thanks in the general direction and promptly forget him.

Distracted, I move on to when and where we're meeting Kath

and Rebecca. I prefer having Beth all to myself, to be honest. Intimate conversations covering all manner of topics are more my thing than casual banter, but I'm up for a dance and am looking forward to the giggles that the others usually show up with.

Beth is not letting me off the hook just yet though. "Made me think about you, that's all. I worry if it's just fear that's stopping you. I know you like to give the impression that you're blazing your own trail, needing no one. But I know you want kids. I just don't want to see fear get in the way of you getting something that's important to you."

I ponder this for a moment.

I know that all it comes down to is insecurity. Why let someone near your heart when they may take it out, inspect it, and throw it in the dirt? What could possibly be worth that? How does anyone manage to risk it and not self-combust? Because what if that person gets to know you better and decides that they don't want you? What if you're not deemed loveable enough?

I know the flaws in this line of thinking inside out. As a therapist, I can articulate them just fine. But what I think bears no resemblance whatsoever to what I *feel*. Which is, quite frankly, terror.

I open my mouth to try to articulate this to Beth, but the words don't make it out. Our conversation is cut short by the gentleman who bought our blue drinks.

It's not that he actually interrupts us. Or even, in fact, that I know that he definitely sent the drinks. But he casually lopes past, staring at me unashamedly, grinning with an expression somewhere between glee and mischief. Inadvertently, my jaw drops.

I have never before run into a client from the club in my real life. It's a jarring collision of embarrassment, arousal, and confusion. A fleeting impulse to be *her* is quickly replaced by rational thought (I'm in the real world) but leaves me feeling unsteady—neither ballsy Zefi nor my normal, contained self.

So I basically just stare.

He disappears into the bathroom, my neck craning to follow him the entire way, my thoughts scattered too quickly to herd them effectively back under my usual air of thoughtful contemplation. Beth prods me back to reality.

"Jesus, Clara, what just happened?" She's staring at me in amazement, like she just saw an intriguing flash of some rare creature nearing extinction.

"Lucas," I mutter, unable to keep the curl of my lips from her. He is too closely remembered, too sexy. Larger than life in my fantasy world, Lucas's intrusion into the real world makes me feel wobbly, giggly, and about fourteen. It's too weird, and I snap my attention back to Beth. "Let's get the fuck out of here. I feel all exposed or something." Already moving to uncurl my legs and put my drink away, Beth puts out a hand to stop me.

"Nuh-uh-uh," she says, eyes glinting. "No way. I want to see what happens next. And actually, I want to see a bit more of whatever that was that just passed across your face," she says, also now wearing an expression a bit too close to glee.

Beth has commented before that she actually can't imagine how I present myself at the club. She can't reconcile the Clara she knows to the Zefi I tell her about—there is no way she can marry them in her mind.

That's probably the point, I have told her dryly in the past. *That's how it works. I compartmentalise her and me; and they're so far apart that it's easy to get on with the two roles.*

But it's definitely not possible to be the wrong one in the real world.

Lucas is sauntering back, eyes fixed on me, radiating something that makes my heart thump against my ribs in such a haphazard fashion that he surely must see my ribcage lurching erratically in response. He towers above most other people in the bar, black eyes boring holes into me, those perfect arms exposed in a svelte black T-shirt against perfect-fitting jeans. He looks somehow both casual and worth a million bucks. Effortless. Edible. My chest feels tight with the effort to breathe normally.

He passes without a word but doesn't take his eyes off me. I get the sense that there is more to come. That he's just waiting for the right moment to strike.

My desire to flee, however, is wrestling against my desire to throw him against a wall and press my body all over him.

Shaking myself crossly, I refocus on Beth. "Christ, what's wrong with me?" I mutter. "I've gone all stripper airhead with exposure."

Beth is smirking over her blue drink. "I've never seen you look so flustered, darling," she says. Then: "I'm kind of enjoying it."

I make to flick her with my handbag strap, amusement winning out over discomfort. "Well, I've basically had dry sex with him in public. It's a dirty little secret that is supposed to stay nicely contained in the dimly lit corners of a strip club, not smack me in the face with my smuttiness in a fancy bar."

"He didn't look perturbed by the intrusion. He looked kind of like he might hunt you down, actually," she says, mirroring my own thoughts. She is still grinning, the dissonance between the conversation immediately prior to spotting him and my teenage flushing after not lost on either of us.

"So. Love, huh?" she says, rising to go to the bathroom, raising her eyebrows at me. Acutely aware of Lucas's new position, sitting directly facing us. Acutely aware of seizing the moment and making a space.

————

OF COURSE HE COMES OVER. As Beth knew he would. Minx.

"So," he says.

"So," I say.

"I hoped I'd see you again. You make quite an impression... Zefi." He knows it's not my name, invites me to talk as the real me, not her. The acknowledgement of this now being a different, other world mellows me somewhat. Inside, that is.

On the outside I remain icy and stiff.

"That's the job, I'm afraid," I reply tartly.

Nice invitation, but this reeks of the type of messiness that I have no intention of muddling up my life with.

Also, I'm having difficulty breathing again. The man has featured quite predominantly in my imagination of late. His tongue has done all sorts of exciting things. Those hands....*good God.*

But fantasy is one thing. No relationship grows wings from a dry hump in a strip club, in my opinion. In my case, no relationship grows wings, full stop. And if casual sex is what he's after...well, I get close enough at the club without the extra hassle.

But he catches my roving eyes lingering on his arms. He shrugs, spreads his hands in a hapless, knowing, give-it-a-go type of gesture, his grin boyish and irreverent. His complete lack of self-consciousness is infuriating. I've never been so blasé about being attracted to someone in my real life. Imagine having that much confidence. To just walk up and give it a shot.

It makes me cross and self-conscious.

"Look, thanks for the drinks—I assume that was you? But I don't talk to clients outside the club. I like to keep my two worlds separate." Even to me, I sound prim and prissy. And in all likelihood, anyone could probably spot the gaping chasm between my words and my body: the rapid breathing, my inability to refrain from looking appreciatively, objectifyingly at his hands, his arms, the way his T-shirt hugs his stomach.

"Have a drink with me. I'd really like that." He's looking at me sincerely; the mischievous look replaced with something darker. Desire, perhaps.

Where the hell is Beth, I wonder.

"Look, no." I lick my lips nervously. "I appreciate the offer. It's just a bit too weird for me. That's a different world, a different girl. I just prefer to keep them separate."

He nods, gets up. His face becomes a mask. I suspect he doesn't get a lot of no's from women.

"If you change your mind, you have my card." With that, he is off, my eyes drawn to his departing hips, the way his T-shirt falls, the way his jeans hug his butt. I grind down on my teeth, hard. The man is magnificent. I wonder if I've made a mistake. I want so badly to touch those arms. To have them encircle me. Capture me. But my sensible brain kicks in, as always. Too hard, too complicated, any man who goes to a strip club...etcetera etcetera.

Beth comes back; we move on to the dancing joint.

There's a lingering irritation fluttering over me, obscure, unsettling. I know it was the right choice, but I spend the night with the elusive sense of something being not quite right.

Something missed.

6

AARON

26TH APRIL 2016

I watched a family at the local food court today.

It would be difficult to find a more depressing expression of the modern family than what one finds at the food court in the lower-socioeconomic suburbs.

I just wanted to get a script filled. But I got assaulted with humanity instead.

The noise was terrible. An open space with a hundred hot bodies. Kids shouting, adults shouting. The smell of vinegar and chips so thick in the air I could almost taste them. I tried to barely look. Just glanced enough to pick my way between tables as a shortcut to the pharmacy. But as I threaded my way along, I passed right by this table.

The mum and dad were hidden under layers of baggy cheap clothes. Half-eaten chips and chicken nuggets were spread over the double table. Mum was on her phone, scrolling. Dad was staring vacantly at the bodies nearby. They were young, maybe early twenties. They looked unhealthy. Pallid skin, oily hair. Pimples rashing across their cheeks and necks.

And then there was the baby. I couldn't see him that well. He was in his stroller, the hood partly lowered, his tiny form mostly covered by blankets. But I could hear him. He was crying the most god-awful cry. He was raising his little arms up, fists bunched, his little face screwed up. Trying to get their attention.

And they both just kept doing what they were doing.

His cries were breaking my heart, and they didn't even look at him.

I wanted to scoop him up and cuddle him, assure him that everything would be okay. That people would love him. That there'd be food, and warmth, and hugs, and laughs. But maybe there wouldn't be. Maybe that's what was breaking my heart.

Oh, I know what people say: you can't judge parents in a snapshot. Maybe for the other 23 hours in the day they are attentive and doting, lit up by his toothy grins, unable to keep their hands off his chubby limbs. I don't know the full story. I just saw a glimpse.

But those cries, they pressed on me in ways hard to describe. I felt them in my skin, in my stomach, in my soul. They hurt me in the past and the present and the future.

Because there is nothing worse than not being seen. Being vulnerable and hurting and asking for help. And still being invisible.

I don't care if people LIKE me. I just want them to see who I am.

7

CLARA

THE MORNING AFTER LUI BAR, roaming around my apartment, I ponder my encounter with Lucas some more.

As a therapist, none of it is new to me. I've visited it all before, in great and agonising depth.

It's embarrassingly run of the mill, this fear of love.

The therapist in me says, *ah, yes—but we are driven to connect with other people. And for connection to happen, we need to allow ourselves to be really seen. And to allow ourselves to be really seen, we have to believe that we are worthy of love.*

I do believe I am worthy of love, I retort haughtily to myself.

Yet the knee-jerk reaction away from it hasn't shifted, I counter. Not in years.

Tell me about *that,* Therapist Clara asks.

Therapist Clara can be a right pain in the arse at times.

It's incongruous with the intimacy and ease of my relationships with women, yet somehow I just can't seem to make that leap with men. I am terrified of pain, uncertainty, and being hurt.

At the same time, I know all too well that being vulnerable is a risk we have to take if we want to experience love and connection.

Professionally, I can champion this with great conviction and aplomb.

Personally, I just can't seem to actually sit in that space.

———

LATER THAT NIGHT, I wrap up my shift at the club and slip into a worn singlet and skirt, tying my hair up loosely and fishing my keys and glasses from my bag. It's just past midnight and outside, the Melbourne summer night hits me like an old friend. Balmy, breezy, enveloping me with a feeling of general good will.

Lucas is sitting out the front in a topless sleek black sports car. I'm not a car girl; I've no idea what it is. But it reeks of money and entitlement.

"Ok, now you're just getting creepy," I snap, eyes flashing. I glance toward my car, so close I didn't bother with security tonight, and I start toward it, anger flaring along with a niggling little sense of fear. The streets are empty. The warm enveloping homeliness of my city takes on a distinctly sharper, less friendly edge. Isolation springs to mind.

"I know, it's totally creepy, right? I know. Would you believe I was in the area and I just thought I'd try my luck?"

"Um. No. And in any case, if you were just hanging out in the dodgy area of town at this hour, you lose all points anyway. Nice men don't loiter around here," I say over my shoulder, striding toward my car.

"I'm sorry. I'm scaring you." He hangs back by his car, apparently self-aware enough to realise following me now, all 6-plus feet of him, might incite terror. "Please. One drink. Take your own car. I can meet you at Red's. It's very public and will still be busy this time on a Saturday. If you think I'm a jerk after that, I promise you'll never see me again."

"Sunday," I correct him, my back against my car, hand on the door handle, feeling calmer with the empty distance between us. "It's Sunday now," I repeat, in response to his confused expression.

"Right. Yes." He is watching me expectantly, lounging against his stupidly sexy car in his stupidly sexy jeans.

"So. Will you come?"

My resolve falters. He looks earnest and sincere.

Probably how all serial killers fool their victims, I think to myself crossly.

However, I'm also suddenly all over the idea of lust. Previously, I had scoffed at it. Sure, I looked at people and could see they were *hot,* or *sexy,* or *desirable.* But it had all been in my head—it wasn't a feeling in my body. It wasn't a force of nature, taking my breath away. It wasn't something that made me wonder if I could actually keep my body in check, keep it from hurling itself against someone, primal and hungry and out of control.

Right on cue, words come out of my mouth without my better judgement consenting to them.

"Sure. One drink. See you there in fifteen."

Once driving, I am full of doubts again. Sometimes even I am not entirely sure how I make decisions. A lengthy process of weighing pros and cons, weeks of agonising deliberation about some things—then wham, instant decision based on nothing substantial whatsoever about others. A cute butt, apparently, is motivation enough in this case.

With the decision made, however, I start justifying it to myself.

I can always leave.

It's worth finding out if he can hold a decent conversation.

God, even if he sucks at conversation, it's probably worth it just to kiss him instead, run my fingertips up and down those arms.

Stop it, I tell myself sharply.

That's what the club is for. Real men, in the real world, are not my thing.

He's right—the bar is still lively, mellow music in the background, cosy dim red lighting, posh couches and expensive-looking lamps. A low buzz of conversation. I choose a couch not too far from other couples. And not too far from the door.

Lucas comes in a few minutes later. He glances around the room with a slight edge to his laid back, world-at-my-feet demeanour. It passes as soon as he sees me, his shoulders relaxing, his grin broad.

"I wasn't sure if you'd come," he says.

"I wasn't sure either," I reply.

We look at each other for a few moments. He's wearing a pale blue shirt, open at the collar, perfectly cut to highlight the shape of him, the lines of his muscles, his narrow hips. His jaw is perfection, the first hint of emerging stubble lending him an aura of casual masculinity. Effortless appeal. His eyes are intense. I'm suddenly conscious of my dry sweat from dancing, my shabby singlet and sandals—the contrast to the glitzy girl he saw the last couple of times.

I wonder what he's seeing, what the big deal is. Why he's here. This is not a lack of confidence; I know I scrub up pretty well. But he's virtually a god. I doubt he has any trouble getting women, ever. So why is he bothering to chase me instead of just sizing up the next girl, who'd probably be more receptive? Is it just that I said no, I wonder? Does he like the chase?

"A drink? I'd like a sauv blanc. Something from New Zealand, please." I'm buggered if I'm going to go get it; safely tucked into a comfortable couch, I'd much prefer to watch him than vice versa.

"Of course,..?" He waits for me to fill the gap.

"Clara," I tell him.

"Clara." He says my name slowly, watching me closely. Then he nods to the bar staff.

Of course, it's table service. No one need go anywhere. No

break from the strange intensity in his eyes to collect my thoughts.

While we wait, he says nothing. He stares at me piercingly. A thousand thoughts flash behind his eyes, but I can't decipher any of them. I'm usually better at this. Reading people is part of my job. But I have no idea what he's thinking. It doesn't seem to just be something lustful.

"So....what's a guy like you doing at a strip club?" I ask when he's ordered us a drink and when I can't bear his silent scrutiny any longer. I'm slightly irritated that he is not leading the conversation, given the circumstances.

To my alarm, the waiter returns with a whole bottle. Lucas waves away the taste offered and indicates to pour us both a glass.

"Friend's bachelor party. It's still the most popular thing to do," he shrugs.

It's a mildly depressing thought. Of all the things one could do to celebrate a life milestone—particularly one so specifically related to forming a close and loving bond with a woman—going to stare at other semi-naked women jumping around on a pole does not spring to mind for me. I profit nicely from it, but nevertheless, my shoulders sag a little.

"What else do you do? For work? For fun?"

"Well. I run a security company. And I train showjumpers. That's what I do for work. And play....well, I travel for work a lot. I incorporate some play into that. I play on the stock market. I like nice restaurants." He looks at me intently, the corners of his mouth starting to curl. "I like nice girls."

"You don't know if I'm nice or not," I retort, trying to sound sharp, to challenge him, to point out that he doesn't know me at all. But somehow it comes out sounding suggestive. Like an invitation to find out, almost. I bite my lip. He grins.

"I wasn't talking about personality," he counters, his eyes travelling appreciatively down my top, lingering on the swell of my breasts, before rising again to meet my eyes, smiling lazily. My breath quickens despite myself. I can almost feel the languid path of his eyes against my skin, my breasts jumping against an imagined touch. My stomach tightens involuntarily, a pulse starting between my legs. Outside the club—inside the club frankly doesn't count—I don't think I've ever been so blatantly hit on before; it so clearly yet classily conveyed that someone wants to have sex with me. I'm used to more crass attempts at seduction. I'm surprised by how immediately arousing it is. Is it him, in all his glory, I wonder, or is it more primal? Attitude more than appearance? Like he's staking a claim on me and it turns me on.

"So you like casual sex? What a surprise." I feel irritated, like I've been misled somehow, by both him and my body's traitorous response. As though his determined tracking of me meant something more than finishing off our heated encounter in the club and moving on. If it was just sex he wanted, surely he could just click his fingers and a hundred women would come running. Why did he bother chasing after me?

This is closely followed by irritation with myself for being so naïve. What exactly did I expect him to be responding to, based on that dance? An appreciation of my insight, wit, and intellect?

Exactly why I avoid this type of shit. My body might be leaping against my better judgement like a caged animal, hungry to touch him, but my better judgement will fucking well win.

I think.

"Who said anything about casual?" He moves closer to me on the couch, watching me closely, like a stealthy cat creeping up on its prey. I'm alarmed to find myself so overwhelmed by lust that I can barely speak. This is not how I play it with men, twitching with desire, nearly jumping out of my skin. *I* pull the strings; *I* elicit desire. *I* walk away when I'm satisfied. Usually, that is what turns me on.

But Lucas...I'm completely overwhelmed by his presence. I want him on top of me, inside me, right here on the couch. His fingers rest on his knee, tapping almost imperceptibly, barely an inch from mine, and my body is screaming for them to bridge that space. To stroke me, or grab me, possess me. Anything involving his touch, really. I've never felt anything like it. It's absurd.

Scrabbling away from him, desperate to claw back some control, I scoot into the corner of the couch, as far as I can go without getting up.

"What, so personality doesn't count; you choose a monogamous sexual partner based on hotness alone?" I'm aiming for a steely, sarcastic edge, to throw a wall up between whatever is happening between my body and his, but it comes out more like an indignant teenage squeak. He basically just has to touch me and I'd throw it all out the window, do whatever he wanted. I wonder, through my mental fog, if this is how women usually respond to him and if he knows it all too well.

Most men I meet in my day-to-day life would see a woman scurrying away from them on a couch as a stop sign, a rejection. They wouldn't dare to follow it up with a touch, another try. But then again, they know it would be a trespass. Judging by his amused grin, Lucas knows I would collapse into his touch like my life depended on it, throw my legs wide to him, panting, desperate. The dissonance is acute, unbearable. I have no explanation; we've barely spoken. There's nothing to it but the sheer pull of his physical being.

The bar is full of people but somehow Lucas seems bigger than all of them together; he takes up so much space. Electricity is humming off him, crackling. *How is everyone else in here managing to keep talking?* I wonder. *Why aren't they all staring at him too?*

My body is on high alert, acutely aware of every move he makes, every breath going into his lungs, every twitch of his fingers. My brain, on the other hand, seems to be shutting down —much like I orchestrate all the men's to do in the club. Later, this might be interesting for me to contemplate, to be on the other end of that. Right now, I'm too overwhelmed.

But, no doubt, millions of other women's bodies want him too. *Get a grip, Clara. You'd be his plaything for a night and be left feeling like shit when he doesn't choose you.*

Or would I, I wonder. This much electricity might make casual sex worth it.

I try to focus on the sexual hangover. Not being called the next day, or the next. How that would feel to me.

But on the other hand, restraining myself seems like it might make me self-combust.

As though he can read my thoughts, he reaches across, puts his enormous hands firmly around my waist, half-lifts, half pulls me effortlessly back closer to him, the length of our torsos now pressed together, my breast pressing into his bicep. My brain is exploding, my clit throbbing, my breath escaping in shallow pants. I feel completely exposed and out of control.

"Desire is just the catalyst to get us here," he murmurs, his hands feeling like they're everywhere and nowhere near touching enough of me all at once. "Where we go after that is where it gets interesting."

I don't even know what he means by that. Maybe he means it might go further. Maybe he means dating. Marriage. Children. Or maybe he means he has three more women and a seriously built dude waiting for his call and things are going to get very interesting for the both of us. But I don't even care. I want more of his hands. On my skin. In my hair. Right now, I'll take any version of interesting he likes if it means he keeps his hands on me.

Reading my mind again: "I want you," he whispers in my ear. "Come home with me."

———

OUTSIDE, giddy and non-functional with my need for him, he pulls me into a dark doorway, one hand gripping my ass, pulling me against him. I can feel his hard-on straining against my crotch, and the promise of him entering me is almost more than I can bear. I'm wet, beside myself, as he lowers his mouth onto mine, finally. His kisses are firm, possessive, perfect. Running his tongue along my lip, dancing with my tongue. As his kisses deepen, become more urgent, I feel like he is opening up all of me, not just my mouth. Cracking something in me wide open. Exploring me, owning me. His hands dance across my back and waist, a perfect salsa of touch, making my legs feel weak and making me want more, more, *more*.

God, he's good at this.

Even as I think that, with perfect rhythm his kisses start rippling outwards—my earlobes, my neck, my collarbone falling prey to his explorations. Nibbling, teasing, driving me toward recklessness. His hands mirror this investigation, the pressure and urgency increasing. I am moaning, oblivious to pedestrians walking by, completely lost in him, both of us aware that I am his to do with as he pleases. I have lost all self-control.

I grind my crotch against his cock, my need so great I'd take him right there in the doorway if he wanted it.

His fingers slide up my skirt and under my panties, running along the length of my wet, slick lips, considered and controlled, teasing me. Slipping back around to my ass, he pulls me against him.

I'm rubbing myself against his cock, unable to help myself, the friction exquisite. I can't wait, and I can't stop.

"Ah! Ahhhhhh," I gasp, panting, thrusting against him.

In contrast, Lucas remains in complete control of himself, his attentions almost clinical—assessing what I like, giving it to me. Thrilled or self-satisfied by my response.

It is so freaking hot my orgasm explodes over me embarrassingly quickly, great shudders wracking my body, and I collapse into him, still rubbing against him, whimpering. Common sense vanquished from my being, I cling to him, shuddering, shaken, shattered. Waves of ecstasy throb through me for what seems like forever.

As reality starts to seep back in, however, there's an element of embarrassment. That I've just come all over him in a doorway in a public space.

But more than this, I'm dismayed he's not inside me. It's impossible, but I want more.

I reach for his belt, urgent, desperate, but he gently pulls my hands away. "Not here," he whispers. "Come home with me."

8

LUCAS

Clara sleeps extravagantly.

I don't know how else to describe it.

She's stretched out diagonally across my bed, her arms flung wide, her hair flung wider. A crazy nest of shiny opulence. Her skin is flawless. She looks peaceful, adorable.

She looks incredibly young and impossibly sweet.

I'm sitting in a chair by the window, watching her, a whiskey on ice in hand. Thinking.

Remembering.

Wishing that I wouldn't.

I'm at home with my mother.

Her partner, Leonie, is doing dishes at the sink. She's scowling away in that way that she has, her mouth a puckered little prune, her eyes squinty. She looks a lot older than my mother.

I'm nine, maybe ten, and Mum is waving a rolled-up newspaper at me, swatting at me, threatening me.

"Help your mother!" she instructs, though she's my mother, and

Leonie is just another girlfriend—angry and resentful like all the others. Resentful at sharing my mother with me or just resentful in general, I'm not sure. Usually these girlfriends don't stay around long enough for me to find out.

I have homework to do and a long list of chores after that— mowing, weeding, vacuuming, mopping. It's Saturday morning and our neighbour had dropped by earlier to invite me to play soccer at the park.

"I can't," I said. "I have to do chores."

He shrugged, his interest elsewhere already.

Now, I can see him with some other kids kicking a ball in the sunshine, running, laughing. Parents with picnics scattered around the edges of the field. Relaxed. Attentive. Smiling.

A million miles from my reality.

I hurry over to Leonie and offer to take over. She grunts, like I should have offered earlier, like I'm a burden and a pest. The water's lukewarm, full of brown flotsam. I put my hands in gingerly.

Mum and Leonie go out. I do the chores and my homework, wait for them. When they get home, it's dark. They smell of beer and fish and chips, but they shout at me anyway for not having dinner ready. For being too loud or too sullen. It really doesn't matter which.

I go to bed, stare at the ceiling. I dread going to sleep, dread waking up. Dread having to endure another day.

9

CLARA

I HAVE STRANGE DREAMS.

I am sitting on a lounge room floor in my black cotton underwear. It's quarter past two and I am writing in my little blue book. I am writing by moonlight, overlooking a swimming pool, sinking into the carpet, feeling luxurious and sensual. Luxurious because I can feel this carpet: so thick, so soft. Sensual because I am sitting in my underwear with moonlight glowing on my shoulders and breasts. Everything is beautiful by moonlight. The roundness of my belly, which usually offends me—I sit and pat it, because it's so soft, and pale, and, well, naked. I feel detached from my body, like I am seeing it for the first time. But it's just because it's so beautiful in this light. In the morning it will just be what it always is, and my belly will offend me and I'll skip dinner so it offends me less, or to punish it for offending me at all.

I couldn't sleep. I'm in this strange house, with this strange man, playing this strange game, and I'm exhausted but still I can't sleep. I'm anxious about how the game is going. So I'm sitting, and I'm writing. We've been out, and it was kind of fun, and now I just want to be naked and write, with his parents asleep down the hallway and him asleep upstairs.

I feel beautiful; I feel adventurous. I feel a long, long way from anyone's reality, so it's okay to be like this: naked and wandering around a stranger's house. Looking at their photos. Running my fingers along their mantelpiece.

Everything feels cool and smooth.

I explore it all.

He comes and sits behind me. He starts drawing figures on my back. I tell him to go back to bed. He asks me why, and I have to state the obvious. Because I need to write, and I can't concentrate with him watching me; and I *certainly* can't concentrate with him watching me write in my underwear.

He doesn't move. I tell him to take off his T-shirt. He pulls it over his head, and I pick it up and pull it over mine. I continue to write, but all I'm writing is empty now. My thoughts have disappeared. There is no room in my head for them *and* for this strange game I'm playing. It takes all of my concentration.

I write meaningless scrawl.

I wait for him to leave.

Everything stays blue and cool and smooth, except for his orange T-shirt. It is the only bright thing in the room, the only thing with any colour at all.

I pay no attention to him. I let myself get lost inside my head somewhere.

I think he leaves.

I struggle to find my way out of this. There are ropes as thick as I am, everywhere. There is no light.

––––––––

WHEN I FINALLY WAKE UP, I'm disoriented. Bright sunshine is crashing across the room. I'm in a huge four-poster, with beautiful white sheets and beautiful views across the bay. An enormous painting of a naked woman towers above me, her huge breasts thrust skyward, her head thrown back recklessly, carelessly.

Daring anyone to judge her.

I try to piece together the events of the night before. It takes me a while to separate my dreams from reality; the sense of confusion and foreboding is pervasive. There's no pool, there's no guest bed. But the sense of being trapped...that remains.

I roll over. Lucas isn't there, but I can smell him. I start to panic. Why can't I remember anything? Where's my car? Where's Lucas?

There's a thick white bathrobe lying across a recliner opposite me and a folded note sitting on top of it. I reach for it gingerly, observing that I'm still in my old singlet and skirt.

Had to go in to work to sort something out. Hope you slept well. I longed to undress you, but I promise I didn't.

I had someone bring your car up—it's in the basement, keys on the kitchen bench. I'd love you to stay till I'm finished. Let me take you out for lunch?

Lucas x

I wrap the bathrobe around me and curl into the chair. I can see the bay being lit up by golden strands of morning light, joggers making colourful lines along the beach, dogs on leashes, a rush of early morning traffic. Kite boarders on the surf.

An endless pale blue sky.

I remember kissing in Lucas's car, him gently disengaging and starting the engine, looking at me like a prize exhibit, something tender about the way he checked my seatbelt. My hand on his leg, desire fiery in my lungs, my lips, my crotch.

Then nothing.

It occurred to me that perhaps he'd drugged me, though I dismissed the thought immediately. I was hardly resisting his advances. I had to conclude that it was actually plausible that after eight hours of dancing till the early hours, followed by wine and then frantically making out and climaxing in a doorway, in a way I hadn't in years—perhaps not ever—the car ride had nodded me off to sleep.

Searching for my car keys, I wander out to the kitchen, where I find orange juice and fresh croissants.

———

BACK IN MY OWN APARTMENT, Beth gets my text and comes over immediately.

It's Sunday morning—bright, clear, perfect. We're sitting on my deck soaking up the flawlessness, the promise of the day. At odds with the strangeness of my night.

Miss Try-Love-It's-Wonderful has done an about turn and is suspicious and worried.

"What the actual fuck?" she's saying, though her suspicions don't stop her from spreading thick butter on a croissant I nabbed from Lucas's on my way out.

"It's not that," I say. Worry is not why I need her here. "I don't think I'm in danger. I just don't understand what's going on. I need to talk it out."

She nods vigorously and waits, croissant crumbs on her lip, her attention divided between some kind of croissant bliss (they *are* mouthwateringly good) and serious-attentive-friend-here-to-talk-about-solemn-stuff conscientiousness.

The croissant is winning. Her attention wanders back to the butter, spreading a bit more, eyeing her next mouthful while trying to appear attentive. I roll my eyes.

"So—first thing. Why has he picked me? The guy is hot, obviously has money, is independent, and must be smart; he runs his own business. Why is he chasing a stripper for a date? I mean, obviously I'm a super hot, super talented catch," I grin at her. "But he doesn't know that. All he's seen is Zefi, who's kind of a tramp, and let's face it, there are a million hot women out there. Why is he going so far out of his way for this one?"

We both ponder this for a while, thoughtful.

"Well, perhaps there's something we don't know yet that is unattractive about the man. Perhaps he can't get a date once women see this part of him?" Beth lists off a few flaws that might plague him. "Poor conversationalist? Alt-right inclinations? Peculiar sexual kinks? Violent? Lies, cheats?"

"But that still doesn't explain why he's going to all this effort to pursue me. On the surface, he's a catch, and he could pick up pretty easily, I'm sure of it. You saw the guy. He's sex on a stick."

I'm not underselling myself—I think I *am* a catch. But this feels surreal, not based on anything. Not based on anything inherent to me, I suppose. If I long for anything romance-wise, it's to be seen—as I truly am, in all my madness, and loved anyway. Lucas has seen nothing. Just the mask I wear to work. For anyone not close, not trusted.

His desire for that girl seems so farfetched that I am suspicious, untrusting. She's pretty, but she hides in the shadows, makes herself forgettable. Never stands out. Watches until she feels safe enough to fully emerge.

No one climbs castle walls for that girl. No one would even know that she was there.

"Here's a thought," Beth says, leaning in, croissants momentarily forgotten. "Let's take you. Sensible, calm, thoughtful, no-nonsense you. Having dry sex in public *twice*. Completely losing the fucking sexual plot over this guy, right? Your physical response is just so strong. You've never experienced anything like it before. So maybe—*maybe*—he's experiencing the same thing. Irrational, overwhelming, unstoppable lust, for you, my foxy friend." Beth grins at me, satisfied, reaching for another croissant.

"This is my problem," I mutter. "This is why I can't get involved in this shit. It makes no fucking *sense*. Where's the rational, logical explanation I can relate to? Where's the signature on the dotted line? Where's the guarantee? Just say that madness suddenly runs out, and it's too late, I've fallen for him? *Then where will I be?*"

Beth grins at me affectionately.

"I fucking hope you don't say shit like that to your therapy clients," she says.

10

LUCAS

AT THE OFFICE, I trawl through video footage from Tasker Brothers, muttering to myself.

They were broken into early this morning and somehow we have absolutely no footage of the vehicles involved. And given what was taken, there was a vehicle somewhere close.

Understandably, the manager was on the phone screaming at my terrified on-call guy about how the hell this could possibly have happened. With their hundred-thousand-dollar security system recently installed by us, it was a fair point.

An hour drifts by, then two. The two cameras covering the front gates show cars approaching for a good kilometre. Two, four, six cars pass harmlessly along the road. It's industrial; it's never completely quiet, even at 5 a.m. on a Sunday morning.

The other cameras log four professional thieves, gloved and masked, methodically working through the building. Removing hardware on trolleys, for God's sake. *So where is the vehicle through all of this?*

It makes no sense; we test everything meticulously. There's no way the cameras missed a car driving in, parking close enough to load all this shit. Then finally I see it: the barest start of a bumper bar. Not even a second's worth that vanishes instead of drives into view.

The recording has looped back. An earlier section has been spliced over the real section. Someone has accessed their system. Someone who knows what they are doing. Someone, I would guess, who has a password.

On the phone to Bruce, the manager, I hand over the details that I have. An admin user logged in at 4:59 a.m. Three of the cameras have a splice from the previous hour replayed over the critical time when the vehicle entered, parked, and left. It seems like an insider was involved. I'm leaving my best guy working on seeing if he can pull any partial backups from the cloud before they were interfered with.

Then I fly out the door. Back toward Clara.

Which is curious, because last night was supposed to be an assignment, not a bloody date.

———

WHEN I GET BACK to my apartment, I am strangely anxious, my heart thudding through the floor. Clara is gone.

I kick myself for taking the call that morning, going in to clean up the mess, not outsourcing it. Work always comes first. I haven't gotten to where I am by letting anything get past me. I deal with everything. People trust me, rely on me. I always get everything done right.

This is the first time I've cared so little if something had stuffed up. I wish I'd left the call to voicemail. My team would have worked it out. Maybe not as quickly as me. Maybe not as charismatically with Bruce. But sufficiently. Eventually.

I move around the apartment methodically, looking for signs of her. The bed is neatly made, the bathrobe folded where I left it. Croissants gone, crumbs wiped away. Shower not used.

Spotless, luxuriant, understated quality in every fitting. Always calming, always reassuring; but for the first time that I can remember, it feels empty.

Missing something.

11

AARON

4ᵀᴴ May 2016

Dear Clara,

It helps me to write this as if to you. Otherwise, it feels stupid and juvenile. Who the fuck keeps a journal at 23? I feel like a lovesick schoolgirl. Writing about how I feel, what I think.

What a fucking wank. Yet here I am.

Because: you. You told me that journaling might help. That I should try it. So of course I did. I am.

I wonder what you are doing right now. Working? Dancing? Dating? Sleeping?

I can see your soft silver eyes, your long black hair, the curve of your breasts. Those legs. What I wouldn't give to touch those legs. Kiss those soft lips. You're all woman. So soft in my imagination. So accommodating. It makes me long for things that I didn't know were possible to long for.

I had been so sure no one had anything to offer me. No one would ever touch me beyond that layer of dead skin cells on the surface—that was as much as they would get, as much as they deserved.

A few flaky dead skin cells of my time and attention.

Then there was you.
And I'm pretty sure I'd have given you a kidney if you'd asked me.

12

LUCAS

ALONE IN MY suddenly-cavernous feeling apartment, memories stir and bubble.

Things that I haven't thought about in years.

Is it the disappointment? I wonder. *Is it finding loneliness instead of Clara?*

I don't want to think about this shit. But the memory is already there anyway.

I'm fifteen, another day, another girlfriend in our house.

Mum has aged, her short grey hair unkempt, her teeth yellowed. My father's fault; I never hear the end of it. Left her with nothing. A son to raise on her own. Nothing but a burden. No money. So hard.

"Men are useless," Mum rasps, pushing me aside and wiping the table again herself. It's not that I did a bad job; it's her narrative now, she clings to it. It offers consolation, explanation, hope. Men are shit, and that's why my dad left. Men are shit, so she has a stab at happiness with women.

Men are shit—it's not her fault.

Sharon is sitting on the worn, shredded couch watching daytime TV with a plate of hotdogs on her enormous lap. Sauce drips onto her faded white T-shirt, joins the stains already there.

As far as I can tell, Sharon is also shit. Mum works, Sharon bludges. Mum cooks, Sharon eats. They both shout at me about how shit I am, how shit men are, bonding over their common bitterness.

I try to imagine them cuddling, having tender moments, sharing something. It's inconceivable.

———

AT SCHOOL, *the counselor is watching me quietly.*

I've been called here for reasons unclear to me. Though a million different thoughts crowd my head, I've no language to articulate the erosion, the emptiness. The self-doubt.

"We don't always get the parents we deserve," she says eventually. My heart strains, crashes, opens. Slams shut.

I don't respond or engage.

But it was the single most useful sentence uttered to me in high school.

———

I FIND the note I'd left Clara, now on my pillow.

It doesn't say anything. But there's her name and a mobile number scribbled underneath my words.

13

CLARA

WHEN LUCAS FINALLY CALLS, Beth has long gone and I'm warm from a long, slow bath and some gentle yoga. Trying to still the restless pacing in my mind, still wrestling with the meaning of all this. His attention, my response.

"I missed you when I got home," he says.

I've thought about my next question all afternoon. Whether it's crazy. Whether it's crazy to *not*.

My conclusion: just to go with my gut.

"Are you free now? You could come over for dinner." A pause. "I'm not going to sleep with you. Just to, you know, have a try at a normal date."

Despite myself, I dress carefully. Super sexy but casual: dark figure-hugging jeans, my favourite grey cashmere jumper. Light makeup. Silver shoes.

Glossy, near-black hair tumbling in unruly waves down to my waist.

He arrives an hour later and pulls up a barstool while I chop and sauté in the kitchen. Chicken, mushrooms, wine. I'm not a great cook, but I have a few impressive dishes up my sleeve.

"I'm sorry I didn't wait," I begin. "I just needed some thinking space."

"Of course—I'm sorry I left. I should have handed the issue over to someone else to sort out. I get a little perfectionistic about work."

We're both careful, kind, trying to please one another. But it all is still escaping me—the *why*.

"Why are you making such an effort over me?" I blurt it out without thinking, it tripping from my confused head and out of my mouth before I can stop myself.

He looks surprised. "I like you," he says. "Obviously, I find you very attractive," he adds, deliberately leaning over the counter and appraising my ass, laughing. Then serious. "But it's not just that." He seems to be searching for the right words, or deciding whether to say something or not. I stir halfheartedly, watching him.

When he seems to have lapsed into silence, I push a bit more.

"Look, I'm sure you get pretty nice offers from attractive women all the time. I just need to understand why me, and why so suddenly?" I blush a little, then add: "I'm not usually so attracted to someone. I'm not really comfortable with it, and I need to understand it more."

It's awkward being so honest, though the therapist in me can see what a small crack it is I've opened. It's hardly forthright self-disclosure. Admitting that you find someone attractive. Jeez. But it's new territory for me and I'm fumbling, uncertain.

The kitchen island is between us and I'm grateful for the distance. Even over my Parmesan sauce, I can smell him. Or maybe I'm imagining it. There's something so magnetic about him, I need to keep my distance if I'm to have any hope of having a sensible conversation at all. Something about him slows my brain down, my thoughts drawn out, stuck half-formed in honey or treacle, useless and sluggish and virtually in a foreign language.

He looks amused. "I don't think I've met anyone who wants to talk about it," he comments.

"What do they normally want to do?"

"Act on it," he smirks. He moves to come around the bench and help me, or maybe waylay me, but I wave him off forcefully.

"No, chance, mister. You stay right over there. We are going to eat and talk."

I dish up two plates of creamy pasta and carry them over to the table, feeling his eyes on my ass the whole way.

"Stop leering and get us a bottle of wine," I call over my shoulder. "Glasses above the bench, and there's a white in the fridge."

Sitting opposite him, spooning the dripping pasta into my mouth, I watch him carefully. He's as delectable as ever, languid, charming, unperturbed by my directives. But I still have no more answers.

"Why are you set on there being a 'why'?" he counters eventually, shrugging under my determined stare. "You're kind of killing the romance, don't you think?"

"I'm more a fan of dotted i's and crossed t's," I respond tartly. "I'm all for being swept away when I know the sweeper has been spellchecked and copyedited."

"Ah, you want certainty and guarantees." He's smiling at me, affectionate, amused. "No falling till you've checked the safety net, the parachute, and the safety harness?" he teases.

"What's wrong with that?" I say defensively. "Seems like a sensible approach if you ask me."

"But what about that space in the middle where you don't know someone yet, and it's exciting, and the possibilities are endless, but you've really got to just jump in feet first if you want to truly give it a shot and experience the magic?"

"Well, excitement for one person might just feel awful and exposing for another," I counter. I sound calm and nonchalant, a tone I've fine-tuned over the years. But deep down, my tummy is doing cartwheels and backflips. I hate the uncertainty you're stuck with in the midst of emotion. It's so uncomfortable that it feels like I might die.

What if I jump in and you decide you don't like me anymore? is what I'm thinking, watching him.

In my head, I know that this is about risk. How mountainous exposing my true self and risking rejection appears to me. It's not that I feel unworthy or unlovable. It's just that love seems so capricious to me. So unstable. Like it might just float away.

So much easier to flee from these kind of encounters than to sit with the uncertainty, the discomfort. Let alone talk about it.

Lucas is watching me closely. Again, I can't quite decipher his expression.

"Have you been hurt?" he asks softly. "Being hurt can make a person wary."

His eyes have taken on that almost black intensity. It's unsettling. And I don't know how to answer that. Hurt has certainly been involved. But have I been hurt by love?

That's a complicated subject.

An image comes to mind. A hand on a door handle. Pulling the door quietly shut behind him. Walking away. The sickness I felt. The despair.

"Not really," I deflect him. And steer the conversation away. To a second glass of wine, less confronting topics.

He tells me how he got his start in business, the perks of his job, the places he's lived.

"What about family?" I ask. "Do you have siblings in Melbourne, or your parents?"

A dark cloud passes imperceptibly across his face. "No siblings, no parents," he responds, in a way that advises that the topic is closed. I open my mouth to enquire further but think better of it.

"What about you? How did you get into stripping, anyway? It doesn't seem like something smart young women aspire to."

I shrug, trot out my well-rehearsed line. Not that many people have heard it, but I like to be prepared.

"I was studying; it paid so much better than anything else. I know there are darker elements to it, but I like it. The power, the money. I can flirt like mad and go home feeling like a million bucks."

"Do you ever go home with clients?" he asks, staring at me intently.

"What? No! I don't need any more than what I get right there."

"Really?" A raised eyebrow, a knowing grin. "I could have sworn you actually enjoyed a bit more."

I blush furiously. "That's not my norm. I don't know what came over me," I mutter.

His grin widens, and my heart starts thumping. "Maybe you just like me," he murmurs, leaning toward me, his eyes glinting with pleasure. "Maybe you should just jump right in."

———

Leaving, he pulls me close to him, kisses me gently. He tastes like garlic and cream and seems familiar and comfortable. Safe, even.

Pulling away, he keeps hold of my waist, stares right into my eyes. "When can I see you again?" he says.

"I'll call you," I reply. Run my fingers up his forearms tentatively. Lean in to kiss him some more. Snuggle into his chest for a moment. Think about what it would be like if he stayed.

But as agreed, he doesn't stay. Kisses me one more time. Grins at me with something between a hope and a promise.

I close the door firmly behind him, lean against it, heart tripping over itself. Wondering.

The next few days pass in a blur of activity. A couple of days at the practice and shifts at the club, I keep focused on work and studiously avoid thinking about Lucas. Or thinking in any depth about where to next. He pops into my head over and over, unbidden, and I push him right back out.

But I'm distracted and off my game, the club irritating me, the work not arousing me. For the first time in a very long time, getting ready for dancing feels like a giant chore.

In darker moments, I think he'll only stick around till I sleep with him or something shinier catches his attention, and I'm left wrestling with self-doubt and uncertainty. Wrestling with the bigger notions of vulnerability and connection and relationships. Love, even.

I don't call, not because I don't want to see him, but because I do.

14

AARON

17TH MAY 2016

I have this memory of my mother. Not my father; I have no memories of him at all. Apparently I lived with him for a while when I was four. Mum dumped me there and took off. But I can't remember anything about him. He dumped me right back not long after.

Fabulous to feel wanted, I expect.

But Mum—I have lots of memories of her.

Are you interested in this? It seems like you would be. Why I might feel like this, think like this, write the things I write to you. It's the best explanation I can come up with for my failure to thrive, emotionally speaking.

That is, my mother stunted me.

So...this memory.

We're sitting on the edge of the local pool. My brother is swimming laps. It's the first time I've seen him in a long time—he was supposed to take me swimming, but somehow Mum ended up there too, ruining what might have been something good.

He's manly, with broad shoulders and shaggy hair. Girls watch him in his swim shorts and giggle hopelessly behind their fingers.

Mum glances at me, a sly sidelong glance that I know well enough not to trust, to brace myself against the inevitable barb to follow.

"He's so handsome. So strong. The girls are always going to choose him," she says.

I'm nearly fourteen, gangly and awkward. There's a rash of pimples across my neck and my chest and I'm huddled inside a baggy T-shirt, partly to protect my pale skin from the harsh Aussie sun, partly to protect my scrawny physique from the imagined appraisal of the bubbly girls sprawling on the grass in every direction. Their long limbs and lean, girlish hips are desperately tantalising and so far out of my reach I don't even bother, half-formed hopes dying on the plane of my imagination before they even get started.

She has this innocent look on her face, like she means they'll choose him over the other guys in his office, like she's not meaning over me. But I've lived with her long enough to know that she means her words to cut me.

It's ludicrous, because he's finished high school. He's working. He's all man, all cocky show, his good looks opening all sorts of doors for him for as long as I can remember. So her reminding me is almost funny. As if I don't know. As if there's any competition, any fair comparison.

Except she's not reminding me of his physical superiority.

She's reminding me she doesn't love me.

That's her punch line.

That's where she finds her joy.

15

LUCAS

I'M LATE.

I never go in to work late. Zara, my PA, is hovering anxiously. "You have a meeting in five with the buyers from Abu Dhabi," she scolds softly, fussing around me, straightening my tie. "Their portfolio is on your desk. Do you need anything else?"

"No," I answer tersely. Zara ought to know by now that she doesn't have to fuss or scold. I always get the job done, pitch perfect.

She smiles meekly. "Sorry," she says, reading my mind. "I'll leave it with you."

In my office, I throw my briefcase onto my desk and loosen my tie. The buyers don't care about my goddamn tie. They care about bloodlines, training history, my percentage of winners. They care about getting on the ground and seeing the horses work. They care about vet checks and straight cannon bones.

This visit today, it's just a formality. I had them the minute they clapped eyes on Starlander.

Of course, they'd already seen his flawless round at the Nationals. Not to mention all the vet checks already completed, x-rays analysed and sent. They were really just coming to pump my hand and chatter idly. Build relationships.

With a few minutes to spare, I open my laptop and wait for it to load.

Clara hasn't called.

I thrum my fingers on the table, thinking.

I haven't got any answers. I haven't even come close.

But that's not what's bothering me.

What's bothering me is what the fuck I'm actually doing. The whole thing is starting to seem pretty stupid. Obsessed. Unhinged.

Is it okay, to be a bit unhinged after someone dies?

Eight months after they die?

It seems like if you're going to lose the plot, that's the time. At least, that's the time people might be forgiving. Or after eight months, is the grace period of understanding over?

Because the worst of it has passed. The choking feeling. The sensation—semi-permanent, for a while there—that I couldn't get enough air. My limbs so heavy, like I'd never be able to move them again. A strange intensity of feelings I didn't even know existed, let alone existed inside me.

But then they shifted. Morphed into something else. Anger. White-hot rage.

My laptop whirs.

I don't actually have a plan. I'm just being methodical. I'm good at crossing my t's and dotting my i's. Not in Clara's romance world, but in my work. I got to where I am in business because of my attentiveness to those little minor brushstrokes that Clara likes so much.

So I tell myself I'm just gathering information.

Clara Black. Aka Zefi. Psychotherapist. Beautiful. Well-educated. Good reputation. Working part-time as a stripper.

That.

That there.

That just doesn't work. There must be some story there. You don't study for four years (Psychoanalytic Psychotherapy Training with the Victorian Association of Psychoanalytic Psychotherapists—yes, I checked, all legitimate), launch your own practice, and then decide actually, your stop-gap job is quite the treat. Job prospects galore in a strip club! Stay a bit longer for the perks! No. It doesn't make sense.

Especially not after you've spoken to the woman. Had those eyes settle on you, with everything ticking away behind them. Clocking everything.

So I go back to Google, with more patience this time.

I'd checked social media previously; it gave me nothing. Her privacy settings were very private, and I wasn't going to try to friend her. She wasn't on Twitter.

But my methodical browsing today doesn't show up much else. The abstract for one published paper—on early family experiences contributing to eating disorders in teenage girls. But other than that, nothing. She doesn't leave much of a footprint on the web. Not like the other women I've dated, with their Snapchat and their Instagram and their Twitter and their whole damn showy lives and bodies on display.

Frustrated, I close my laptop and wait for the buyers to arrive.

I don't even know why I care that much. Even the anger is dissipating. And I have better things to do than stalk strippers online.

Yet here I am. What the fuck?

But even as I think this, I know I'll delve further. Find other avenues.

The best one, obviously—seeing her. Getting to know her better.

I know I'm kidding myself—that it's not strictly necessary. That something else is motivating me here.

But I choose not to think any further about that.

———

AFTER THE PAPERS ARE SIGNED, I tell Zara to help the buyers arrange international transport for the horse and head out to my acreage.

An hour or so out of the city, I have thirty acres sitting on the edge of state forest. It's divided into orderly paddocks, the neat white rail fencing comforting and quaint-looking—although it's actually plastic and flexible and costs a fucking bomb.

Just another example of how looks can be deceiving, I think to myself. And even I'm not sure if I'm thinking about myself or Clara.

On the side of one of the rolling hills, a state of the art indoor training arena has been cut, with twenty stables at the front and two separate arenas at the back. Mirrors line two of the four walls.

My heart hitches every time I drive down the driveway, plain trees lining my passage, their growth slow but steady. It's not just the trees or view of the hills and the valleys stretching out in front of me. It's the freedom that speaks to me. Me, my horses, the capacity to be alone for a while. The calmness that that engenders.

Bree scurries out of one of the stables when she sees me. She's my newest junior trainer, all gangly limbs and nervous energy. I grin at her, noting the slow blush that creeps up her neck.

"How's the colt?" I ask her, my newest acquisition only arriving this week. I have high hopes for him as a competition horse as well as a stallion at stud.

"Gorgeous," she breathes. "He's so sweet. A bit nervous, but settling in well."

"Great. We'll start the groundwork tomorrow. You can help me if you like."

"Oh, I'd love that, so much, please," she mutters, brushing wispy strands of hair out of her eyes, glancing up at me through her lashes, then hurriedly glancing away.

I smile absently at her.

Usually, flirting with the juniors is a favourite pastime of mine. They're all so eager to please me, to learn from me, so charming and adoring. But my heart isn't in it today.

"I'm going to take Rocky for a ride in the forest. I'll be back in an hour if anyone needs me," I tell her, slipping into his stable and running my hand along his silky, toned neck. He whickers softly, shoving his nose into my hand, looking for treats. I lean my forehead against him, breathing in his smell. Suddenly feeling tired and empty.

I think about my dinner with Clara. Her soft, big silver eyes. Her wariness. The curve of her breasts under her cashmere jumper. I've never wanted to touch anything so much in my life.

What is it about this damn woman?

She's gorgeous and interesting and skittish as hell. And there's something else behind those fiery eyes. I don't know what it is. But I kind of want to lean against her like I'm leaning against Rocky. Breathe in her smell. Stroke the skittishness out of her. Rest a little bit.

I pull myself upright, shaking my head as though to shake her out of it. I probably just need to screw her. Screw her, get some answers to some questions, then move on. Get back to normal. Fun, flirty Lucas who doesn't dwell on all of this shit.

But I managed to not ask her any of the questions. The opportunity was there, plain as day. Why did I hesitate? Why did I flirt and kiss her instead? Why am I checking my phone, hoping that she's been in touch?

She's right to hesitate, of course. I can't be trusted. But most women would lap up the attention. Play it for a wedding ring. God knows enough have tried.

Yet here I am, fretting.

I *want* her to call me. I *want* to see her again. And I can't quite figure out why.

16

CLARA

IT'S ANOTHER TUESDAY NIGHT, another bottle of wine, my long legs swung casually over Beth's lap. Dusk plus wine plus balcony.

"I've been derailed," I complain, frowning, moody. "It was all going along just fine. And now it's all not quite good enough."

"Was it, though? Really fine?" Beth asks. The space stretches between us, comfortable, thoughtful. "Perhaps these are just the questions that you need to address. If not now, sometime. Eventually."

Brooding and silent, lost in my own internal world, I'm eventually pulled back to the present by Beth asking what it is that scares me.

I have pondered this a lot. The irrational terror of it. The knee-jerk response which I feel like I can't undo, can't short-circuit.

A long silence.

It's something to do with value, and I find it hard to put it into words. A weightless, unfurling, disconnected sensation floats across me. I can't pin anything down, can't make sense of it. I feel like I might float away.

"If someone appears to value me..." I start, stop, searching for the words. "Well, I don't know what to do with that. Where does it come from? What is it based on? I feel like he can't possibly understand me at all or have any concept of who I am. It's not like you valuing me. You know me. You see me. But Lucas...I haven't shown him anything of me. So I distrust what it is he is valuing. It seems so...flimsy. And then—well. The run of the mill part, I suppose. I don't want to value something and then lose it. I feel overwhelmed by it. It seems too hard. I just don't want to bother."

Beth raises an eyebrow at me and I shake my head, irritated.

"I'm scared and I'm telling myself I can't be bothered," I correct myself, rolling my eyes. "I don't think I can cope with the fallout when it all turns to shit."

What would you say to a client?" Thoughtful therapist, as always.

"Of course I understand that," I say tetchily. "I understand it completely. *In theory.* I just can't shift it into practice. The horror of it. The horror of valuing something, and then losing it. Of not being valued myself. I turn away from it. I want to stay. But I can't. I flee."

"Tell me then," she says, serious. "Humour me."

I sigh. "I would explore what's underneath that. You know, what experiences have led to feeling scared, of opening up to other people. How that response was self-protective, adaptive at some point. But how perhaps now it's not serving me so well. I'm missing out on being close to a partner. Explore whether I really don't want a partner or whether I'm just scared. Talk about selectively numbing emotions. Blah blah blah."

Beth raises her eyebrows at me. Maddeningly, she doesn't offer anything, waits for me to continue.

I sigh again. "You know all this. I've told you. It's just the unknown context. The uncertainty. It took so long to find my own value, and believe in it, and hold onto it. And for some reason it just doesn't seem sturdy enough to weather a failed relationship. I'm scared I might crumble. I'm scared I might lose myself. I'm scared I might hand my value over to someone who discards me and then I'll doubt my value too. It feels too hard, too soon. That's all."

I have snapshots of memories, isolated, out of context. I wonder if they are actually real memories, or the memory of the memory of the memory, altered in each remembering by the interpretations, the perceptions I overlay them with. Moving subtly each time, like the course of a river over centuries, a millennium.

My mother, intruding on me naked, pushing against the boundary of privacy not so much through some perversion but more through a desire to acquire my slender waist, stake some claim on it.

"I never had a figure like that." Admiration. Envy. A belief conveyed like truth that being thin was the most important thing.

Me dressed hopelessly in a tiny bright pink dress, trying desperately to shout to the world that I didn't care what anyone thought of me, whether anyone accepted me, but already not eating. Revelling in my hunger as though it were my strength, my supremacy.

Pushing the boundaries of what people would accept, over and over. Seeing where they drew the line with their loving. Do you still love me now? What about now? Or now? Or now? *Desperate— ugly, clawing, out-of-control desperation—to see proof of love. Again and again.*

I was just a child. Then a teenager.

But still I can't quite love her.

Beth is watching me quietly. She does indeed know most of this, but previously it has all been theoretical. Previously, no one has pushed gently against that boundary and created tension.

No one has made me want to stay.

———

WHEN I FINALLY CALL LUCAS, he's interstate and seems cold and distant. He's not sure when he'll be back. He'll call me. The anticlimax is unbearable. I've spent so long hesitating and wondering and starting to anticipate this being *something* that the shock of the letdown is like a physical pain, lodging somewhere between my throat and my stomach. Choking me.

Feeling foolish, I imagine I left it too long—that he's already met someone else, someone more responsive to his advances—and resolve to put the whole embarrassingly juvenile incident aside and get on with things.

At the very least, I have a lot of material to percolate on.

Like how a therapist who counsels other people about relationships, intimacy, and worthiness can be so terrified of relationships, intimacy, and worthiness herself.

Or how my "no relationships" policy can be thrown out the window at the first sign that someone might be interested. The reality that "no love" might in fact translate into "no interesting offers and I'm determined not to care and I didn't want love *anyway. So there.*"

Funny how much I love stories when they're other people's stories. My narrative? Really not enjoying it so much right now.

Half kicking myself for waiting so long that he disappeared, half wondering why I care about losing someone I know nothing about, I shake my head repeatedly, trying to clear it. Clear him.

Someone I know nothing about...except the way he touched me, kissed me.

Looked at me.

I know about that.

The yearning that I'm left with.

My body's wild response.

17

LUCAS

ANOTHER MEMORY.

They're coming thick and fast and I'm unable to shut them out the way I usually do. Dull them with girls and laughs and toys and winning. They're slinking into my psyche, creeping and crawling, finding all the cracks in that carefree existence. Busting them wide open.

I'm five, maybe six, and Mum is pushing me under the shower. It's too hot, and I yelp, and she pulls me out and cranks up the cold in hard, angry jerks. She doesn't say anything. Just pushes me back in. I'm crying; it's so cold now. But that's not why I'm crying.

She doesn't care about me; she doesn't love me. Her rough hands, pushing, shoving, furious about things I can't conceive, can't fix for her. Oblivious to my distress.

Satisfied by my distress, perhaps.

Somehow, everything that my life affords me is not satisfying me at present. The appeal of it—easy encounters with beautiful women who I can be casual, superficial with—is exactly what it now seems to lack.

Being quiet with somebody.

Being liked for who I am—not who I pretend to be, or what I can offer.

Being visible. Being still.

Being close, even.

The memories swirl and delve and skulk around and wind me.

And they're all now rendered sharper, crueller, closer because of Aaron.

———

CLARA CALLS, amidst my reverie.

I can't talk to her with these thoughts about my mother in my head.

The hollowness, the physical pain of it is suffocating me.

The furious desire to punish someone. Anyone.

Feel satisfied as they slink away.

I'm sitting high up in the Shangri-La Blu Bar, hand gripping my Glenfiddich glass tightly, knuckles white.

I think about all the things I didn't tell Clara about my family.

Staring vacantly out over the Harbour, I ponder how it all panned out. In many ways I suppose I could thank my mother. She inspired in me an unshakeable determination to leave that life. And I might be smoothing the fabric of a custom-made merino suit, sipping a crazy-expensive luxurious drink, but it wasn't always sexy. It wasn't always like this.

Leaving school, working three shit-kicker jobs. Avoiding my mother but needing her house. Her needling, her mocking. Her endless put-downs.

The idea for the business. The months and months spent canvassing for clients on foot after working nights. The dogged, miserable first few years. Till the business took off and I could get out. Get away from my damn mother.

She calls me now, every week on Sunday, like clockwork. Ingratiating at some times, entitled at others.

"I always said it would be the most important thing I ever did, raising Lukey," she tells her friends, the proud, successful single mother. "You know he bought me this apartment," she adds, swollen with misplaced self-importance. The grateful son rewarding her for her love, her sacrifices.

I can't bear it, but I can't bear seeing her even more. The successful son providing financial security can get away with being otherwise elusive, I have found.

Paying her bills is a lot less painful than seeing her for dinner.

———

I THROW my glass down on the table as the waitress comes out. She's young, with long black hair and big eyes. She reminds me of Clara.

I stand up and smile at her, stretching my arms above me, my shirt riding up, showing off my tight stomach. I watch her eyes widen as they travel appreciatively down toward my crotch.

"What time do you finish?" I ask her.

Then, not waiting for an answer: "Visit my room. 5400. I'll get us a nice bottle and wait up for you."

She knows I'm good for it; the Glenfiddich 30 year old set me back $150 a glass. But even as the words leave my mouth, I know this way of trying to feel good isn't going to work for me this time.

18

CLARA

Life falls back into its regular routine.

The practice absorbs my attention. Kate returns from a holiday, tanned and sombre.

"The fantasy of sun, sand, and being kind to myself didn't quite work out as planned," she says.

"Maybe I should have been born in a third-world country and have had to concentrate on finding food and water. Surviving. Then I wouldn't bloody throw it up! All this misery is so self-indulgent by comparison. Sometimes, I am not only swamped by despair, but also self-disgust."

Later: "I can lie on a beach and not do my hair or put on makeup for ten days and not think twice about it. I wish I could let go of such obsessions when it comes to my weight. The reality is, I want to weigh three or four kilos less than my "equilibrium" weight. I will not become obese—I will just put on those few kilos and my body will be at its natural resting place. The effort involved in keeping those extra pathetic few kilos off is consuming my entire life."

I ponder her for a moment, deciding which path to take.

"You know, it can be helpful to think about this both as an

internal and an external force. And externally, it's useful to critically assess the society we live in. We don't exist in a vacuum. We have images fed to us from a very early age about how we're supposed to look as women to be valuable. It's impossible to avoid those messages. And when we're young, trying to fit in and find our place in the world, we're particularly vulnerable."

"I know. I know that," Kate interrupts me, irritated. "There's a multibillion-dollar industry that benefits from me being dissatisfied with how I look. Although, to be fair, I don't buy beauty products. I buy ice cream. And then I throw it up." She glares at me.

"The message we internalise is the same. The helpfulness of the response or the coping mechanism varies," I counter.

She pauses for a moment, then carries on: "I read this line in a book, something about the Western beauty ideal being impossible for most women to achieve without an eating disorder. It was a revelation. But somehow, it feels even worse to intellectually understand this, yet still be unable to do better. To respond differently. It makes me even angrier with myself. It makes me want to punish myself more. Because how fucking long do you give yourself? If it took me this long to learn to ski, or learn a language, or scuba-dive, I'd have given up a while ago. Fifteen fucking years later I still haven't managed to convert this knowledge into any form of emotional intelligence whatsoever. And my stupidity and slowness in embracing self-care infuriates me."

"Yes. But you're trying to unlearn fifteen years of conditioning. You haven't had that to contend with, with skiing or language-learning. And on top of the external bombardment, you're contending with the internal stressors that have brought you to this place. What you experienced as a child. Your response is a perfectly understandable way for a child or adolescent to try to manage their feelings. And sure, it's not helpful, but it's understandable. Children don't have the resources to choose better ways to cope. So that young girl? She did her best to keep you safe. And now we need to gently untangle those habits—but they've been there a long time. Of course it takes a long time to undo them. Especially when in your mind you equate them with safety, being in control, being able to do that projected value well."

Kate frowns.

I frown, too.

My insights move and churn around me, troubling and dank. What I said is true. But the young me? The me that made mistakes? She isn't given quite so much leeway.

Something struggles to unfurl deep in my tummy. I push it back down into the soggy damp swamp.

———

THE CLUB ABSORBS LESS ATTENTION. Something has shifted, somewhere. Something subtle and troubling, for my bank balance at least. The promise—illusion?—of sexual satisfaction is less enticing. The men greyer, more grating. My performance equally lacklustre.

"What are they contributing to?" Beth asked me once, when I first started. I had shrugged, countering with the obvious: *What was I contributing to?* But the question starts to hang over me, heavy and clammy. Love—so long avoided—is looming large.

———

A FEW DAYS LATER, I hear from Lucas.

He's upbeat and warm. Charming, even.

"Can I come over?" he asks, after updating me on his work trip, the food, the contracts won.

I'm baffled and self-protective. *Where's the consistency?* I mutter to myself, crossly. But in light of my introspective evening with Beth, I give my fears the finger and carry on.

He arrives an hour or so later, a bottle of Moët under his arm and a shock of red roses against his white shirt.

"Cliché, I know," he grins, handing them to me. "But they are stunners. Just like you," he adds, laughing, acknowledging the cheesiness, the double whammy of cliché.

We settle in to easy banter, my terror, as always, well-disguised. Besides, watching him, his huge paw wrapped around my dainty crystal champagne flute, his laughing eyes, I am wondering what the big deal is. Shouldn't I just sleep with him? I could call it research into the realms of love if I had to justify it to myself. What, really, was I waiting for?

Apparently catching something pass across my face, Lucas puts down his drink, leans forward, and grabs my hand. He pulls me easily over to him, not taking his eyes off mine for a second.

He kisses me slowly, lingeringly, his eyes still fixed on mine, his arm wrapped tightly around my waist. With the other hand he reaches up and cups my face, his thumb stroking my neck, my cheek. His controlled movements and certainty are polar opposites to my muddled mind and undercurrent of fears. They're magnetic, reassuring, like I don't have to decide anything because he has decided everything already, and it's magnificent. I fold into his body with the relief of the recklessly subservient.

Manly, decisive, dominating: the way he moves my body is delicious to me. Every move, every action conveys his desire to fuck me, to possess me. Without asking, without pausing and barely without breaking eye contact he unzips my shirt, pulls loose a bra strap, freeing a breast that he starts to stroke, in control, despite the desire written all over his face. Hoisting one leg across his lap, he pulls me in closer, staring at me intently before lowering his mouth to my nipple. Despite myself, I'm arching my back and moaning already, as he slowly sucks and nibbles, all the while his thumb stroking the underside of my breast and his other arm encircling my waist and holding me fast against him. I couldn't move, even if I wanted to.

Which I don't.

I have often wondered about this feeling. It's not a Dominant/submissive dichotomy. It comes from knowing in equal measure that if I said to stop, he would, but nevertheless every move, every breath he takes, every look and every gesture, says *I am going to fuck you now. I want you so badly. You are mine.* It is being possessed while knowing I fully consent. Half arrogance, because he hasn't asked—but knowing my body, my response, even after three short encounters. Knowing I want him just as much. How hot it is, that confidence, how primal my response.

I run my hands up and down his arms in wonder at the feel of him, the strength of him—his hard biceps, his forearms. His control of this, of us. His shoulders and back muscles ripple underneath my fingers as he moves. I can feel his abs, hard and flexed beneath me, his arms holding me in place. All against the flash of his dark, piercing eyes.

I feel like I can just leave it all in his hands, and it will be spectacular.

I can feel his erection underneath me, maddeningly dulled by various layers of clothes. I want to feel the skin of his cock sliding along the length of me, and move my hands down to find his jeans button, but he pulls me tighter to him, blocking access.

"Not yet," he growls, still circling my nipple with his tongue. Gripping me firmly, his other hand slips down the back of my jeans, squeezing my butt cheek then sliding swiftly along the crack of my ass. I gasp and he grips me tighter, standing up with my legs around his waist, and carries me in quick, long strides into my bedroom. Laying me down, I go to sit up on my elbows and he gently but firmly pushes me back.

"I want to unwrap you," he whispers, slowly unbuttoning my jeans and sliding his hands under my hips to free them down to my knees. He's kneeling between my legs, resting one heel on his thigh, carefully unbuckling it, removing it, kissing my instep. For the first time he lets out a groan.

Suddenly, he's moving faster, the other shoe off, my jeans tugged over my ankles, his face suddenly buried in my crotch, his breath hot and jagged against the cloth of my g-string. Pulling it aside with some urgency, he runs his tongue from the base of my slit to the top in one long, wet, hot stroke. For a second, he places his mouth over the whole of me, sucking urgently, and I arch into him, one breast still bouncing free. Catching sight of me, he pulls back, breathing heavily.

"Christ, you're divine," he mutters, slowly standing, leaning over me and gesturing for me to roll over. After I do so, he unhooks my bra and pushes the straps over my shoulders. He runs his hands down to my buttocks, squeezing them gently, then taking my hips in his hands and gently pulling my ass up a foot off the bed. He crouches behind me and pulls my g-string aside again and starts licking me, slowly and rhythmically, his tongue pushing thickly between my folds, moving to circle my clit then ascending again. I'm moaning and gasping, pushing back against him, hopeless with desire, wanting his cock inside me but desperately not wanting him to stop licking me either. I can't decide whether coming now will be brilliant or waste everything else that might follow.

Then, when I'm almost climaxing already, he slows down, pulls my g-string further over and places his thumb firmly against my butt hole, pressing in gently, while sliding two fingers inside me. The suddenness and shock of it is too much. As desperately as I wanted to wait for him to be inside me, I can't. I'm rocking against him, the muscles inside me gripping his fingers urgently, the orgasm washing over me in brilliant, clenching, satisfying waves.

This doesn't last long though. I sink onto the bed sheets, my face buried, feeling shy and exposed and terrified. He keeps stroking my buttocks, kissing them, running one hand along my thigh.

Rolling over to look at him, trying to be my bravest self, I smile languidly and advise him that my fantasies did not do him justice at all.

He grins widely, wiping me off his mouth with the back of his hand. "So how many fantasies?" he wants to know, falling down beside me, kissing me deeply. I can taste myself on him, smell myself, still feel his erection through his jeans against my bare leg. "What was I doing in them?"

"Oh, you know, just one or two, amongst the other guys," I say nonchalantly, waving my hand around vaguely to indicate the plethora of men, of fantasies that I indulge in around him. Then breaking slowly into a smile, rubbing the back of my hand along the length of his cock, the other hand exploring tentatively under his shirt.

"What do you like?" I whisper, starting to unbutton his shirt, but he catches my hands, staring at me intently, leaning in to kiss me slowly, hungrily.

"Pleasing you," he says, pulling back, one hand meandering down to a breast, followed shortly afterwards by his mouth to the other. His licking and stroking is reverent, fully enjoying my breasts for himself, but at the same time teasing, flicking gently over my nipples, arousing me again already. Hearing my breathing thicken, he looks up from my breast, slowly smiling with the satisfaction of a man who knows what he is good at and is getting the reaction he expected, but nevertheless is delighted to see it.

"I can wait till you're ready again," he murmurs, resuming his sucking, licking, teasing.

"Well, you could hurry that along by taking all your clothes off," I say, lifting up onto my elbows, cocking my head to the side and raising an inviting eyebrow.

He rocks back and stands up, taking me up on my invitation, slowly unbuttoning his shirt and moving from side to side to give me all the best views; rotating his hips mock-seductively as he undoes his jeans. We both laugh at the gesture, but I am watching him hungrily, the way the muscles move on his arms as they attend to various items, his flexing pecs, the delicious V leading down to the bulge in his underpants, his cock finally springing free. My breathing betrays me; I'm hopelessly overexcited again already.

"Fuck me," I whisper, spreading my legs slowly in front of him, pulling my thong aside, showing him the whole of me. He leans forward and grabs my ankles, scooting me down to the edge of the bed, then slowly peeling my g-string off me, not taking his eyes off me, even as he reaches for his jeans and rolls a condom on, his hands expertly caressing his long, hard cock.

Keeping my eyes fixed on his too, I turn around, watching him over my shoulder, lifting my ass up in front of him, spreading my legs slowly. I want him to fuck me like an animal, dominate me, thrust so hard that he propels me up the bed. But I also want the option to avoid eye contact, tone down the intensity, which is overwhelming me.

He groans, grabs my hips, pushes into me with one hard thrust, and I cry out with the pleasure, the force of it. Groaning, he pulls out slowly and thrusts in hard, again. Then again. His controlled thrusts at odds with the noises he is making: the primal grunts of someone *out*-of-control. The combination is electrifying. Moaning with each thrust, I come in moments, followed shortly afterwards by Lucas, the pulsing of his cock huge inside me, my insides gripping him like my life depended on it. He's squeezing me against him, holding my hips hard, his fingers biting into the soft flesh, like he wants more of me, to be further inside me, to merge into me. His breath is hot between my shoulder blades, murmurs and groans escaping his lips.

Finally, our breathing returning to normal, his cock softening, he pulls out of me and pulls me into an embrace on the bed beside him. Kissing my hair, my face, his eyes closed, a faint smile hovering around his lips. He looks like a god, and already I'm wondering how many times I can fuck him before he has to go.

———

SLEEPING RESTLESSLY, unused to having anyone in my bed, I find myself awake at 3 a.m. Lucas's arms are around me firmly, possessively. He's snuggled around me, his breath warm and rhythmic on the back of my neck.

I can hear traffic on the road outside, even at this hour. But even with the noise, the light of street lamps clearly delineating items in my room, the "nightness" of the moment opens up doors to my terror.

I'm terrified that already I want more of this. I'm terrified of what will become of me when it's gone.

———

IN THE MORNING, Lucas is up and showered early, nuking any lustful thoughts I have upon awakening.

I wander to the kitchen in my nightgown, watching him collect his things, have a glass of water.

"When can I fuck you again?" I ask him, teasing, all sexy confidence. Hiding. Faking things.

He grabs me, grinning, kissing me deeply. My legs can barely hold me up.

"Whenever you like, you gorgeous thing," he tells me, but glances at his watch, frowns. "I'm sorry—early meetings. I have to run. I'll call you tonight." He blows me another kiss at the door and then vanishes.

I wander around my flat aimlessly.

Eventually, frustrated with myself and my worries, I pull on my gym gear and head out for a run.

———

THE DAY CARRIES ON, uneventful and slow.

The beauty of my profession means I can talk to myself with some authority about my fears.

The downside is that sometimes knowing is not enough. You have to feel it. Believe it. Knowing, by itself, might be even more frustrating when you keep falling short of applying it in your life. At least if you're as much of a perfectionist as I am.

Connection is why we're here. It gives purpose and meaning to our lives, I tell myself, argument against the unsettled feeling enveloping me, the desire to flee. Because I still haven't showed him anything of myself. If I fled now, I could still claim it didn't matter. He can't reject me if he hasn't seen who I am.

Seeing who I am and *then* rejecting me? That's the precipice I can't afford to fall off. That's the one that might shatter me.

But...

In order for connection to happen, we need to allow ourselves to be really seen.

Which means staying. Opening up. Seeing what happens.

If nothing else, it's an experience to study, I tell myself...and stop short, recognising the familiar, unhelpful nature of this coping mechanism. Disconnection, not connection. Dissociating almost. So I can tell myself that lie: that it doesn't really matter. But it does. It does.

It does.

19

LUCAS

"WHAT ARE YOU DOING TODAY? I have a plan."

It's two days after our perfect, mind-blowing sex and I can't believe how badly I want to see her again.

Clara mutters something incomprehensible into the phone.

"Hello? Did I wake you?"

"Yes," she says. More muffled sounds.

"I'm coming to get you. We have an excursion."

"I'm asleep," she says. "Call back in three hours."

"Wait, wait! It will be worth it. Look outside. It's frigging glorious. Please."

She grumbles some more and I hold my breath. I feel like a little kid wanting to show off my new toys. But really I just want to see her. Come up with things that might be exciting for her. See her joyful smile—be the cause of it.

"It involves ponies," I say, singsongy, never yet having met a woman who doesn't like horses. It's like a silver brumby fantasy leftover from childhood. Horses are romantic. And well-built men controlling seven-hundred-odd kilos of stallion? That is sexy, by all accounts. I have a decade of pulling women in my jodhpurs to convince me of it.

"Ponies are for children," says Clara dismissively, putting paid to that fantasy. But then: "Fine. I'll be ready in an hour. I need a shower. See you soon."

"Wear something casual. With boots," I tell her.

There's something in her voice that makes my heart leap. Some kind of amusement or excitement, despite what she says about ponies. I grin into the dial tone like a fool.

———

WHEN I PICK CLARA UP, she looks positively glowing. Her hair is tousled and shiny, pulled around in a loose ponytail over one shoulder. She's wearing pale blue jeans and black boots with a baggy black jumper. She makes casual wear look divine.

The breeze is fresh, but the sun is shining, and there isn't a cloud in the sky. There's something in the air that holds the promise of joy. It's like the first day of summer holidays. When you have six weeks of uninterrupted play ahead of you, running amuck in the glorious Aussie sun.

Well, you did if you were most kids. I remember the promise of it; the actuality never quite lived up to the dream.

We head out of town, the top of my Porsche down, even the edges of childhood memories not able to dampen my mood. I turn up some Billy Joel and grin at Clara. She looks adorable. All soft curves and pale skin and huge, expressive eyes. But it's not that. It's something about the way she looks at me, those soft silver eyes. Usually, women look at me with lust, and that's nice too. But Clara looks at me like she's curious about me. Like she might like to know more than where we might go for dinner or where I might fly her for the weekend. Her eyes have a kind of... oldness...to them. Like she's seen all the things and knows all the pain. Like she's weathered everything and still come out smiling. I can't explain it. It's just like she might know me. She might look at me and see who I am and be able to weather that too. And it's like I didn't even know I wanted to let someone see me until she looked at me as though she could.

———

Pulling into the driveway, meandering down it toward the gigantic building in the hill, the outdoor arena sporting two of my young showjumpers, it's hard not to feel a swell of pride. Sure, the security business made me my money. But the horses are where my heart is. And they make a pretty nice return, too.

"So. 'Ponies' seems to be kind of an understatement," Clara drawls, watching Latte and Flash popping over fences to our left as we cruise down the driveway. They make it look deceptively easy, unhurried and effortless, soaring over jumps that are easily Clara's shoulder height, their legs neatly tucked underneath them. They're powerhouses, glorious in the morning sun.

I park in front of the stables.

"Yeah. You want to meet them?"

"Sure," Clara says, uncurling her long legs and stepping out of the car. I beckon Zoe over, and she brings Latte to a halt in front of us. Clara smiles at him. Despite her earlier grumblings, I can tell she's a little awestruck. Towering over her at nearly seventeen hands, he's a magnificent sight, all rippling muscles and glossy coat. She holds her hand out and he blows softly on it, then nuzzles her for treats.

"His nose is so soft," she exclaims, looking at me in wonder.

"You've never ridden?" I ask her, and she shakes her head.

"I used to always watch the eventing in the Olympics though," she smiles shyly at Zoe, stroking Latte's neck. "Such beautiful animals. So powerful but so gentle."

I smile watching her. She moves with confidence, seeming to know where to rub, devoid of fear. Latte nudges her gently.

"How's he doing?" I ask Zoe and she nods, moody. I haven't brought any women here before.

"Perfect. Settled, attentive. Hasn't put a foot wrong so far."

"Great. We might watch for a while."

I lead Clara over to the spectator seating. It's cooler here than in the city, a good few hundred metres higher. I pull her close to me as we watch Zoe and Latte take off, Latte popping into canter, his easy stride misleading; he covers the ground at a great rate.

I thread my fingers through Clara's, enjoying the sunshine on our backs, the quiet of the countryside.

"How long have you had this place?"

"About eight years," I tell her. "I added all the horse facilities. It's perfect for all-weather training, and there's thousands of acres of forest over there," I point to the rolling hills, covered completely in native forest. "There's tracks all through it. It's really peaceful to ride through. I'll take you out sometime."

Clara smiles at me. "You better have a beginner's horse. Those things are big."

"Don't worry. I have my old boy. He's retired from competition now and as quiet as they come. In fact, let's go meet him and I'll show you around."

We spend the morning wandering through the indoor facilities, patting horses and watching them being schooled. I show Clara plans for a new house and where I hope to build it. The view across the valley is spectacular.

"What will you do with the old house?" she asks.

"Keep it. Some of the staff live there. It would be good to extend it so we can have more horses in training, but for now this size works well. But I'd like a private home for myself when I'm here. Me and my woman friends," I tease, thinking of her. Only her.

"Hmmm. You'll need plenty of bedrooms then, I'm guessing." She's smiling slightly, teasing too. Then: "So do you ride these horses as well?"

"Yep. And I compete them. The staff are all under my training, and I supervise the work they do. But the security business keeps me in Melbourne and travelling a lot. So I need staff I can trust to keep them in training when I'm busy or away. They also compete in the lower grades for the experience. It can be quite nerve-wracking when you start, and the horses pick up on your nerves. So it's good to get on the competition circuit early and get used to it."

"So do I get to see you ride? Those jodhpurs always looked so much hotter on the women than the men," she muses. "But still... I'd like to see you ride." She smiles at me wickedly. "Very...*snug*, aren't they?"

"I have it on good authority that they look equally hot on me," I smirk at her. "But no, not today. I want to take you out to lunch."

I take her further out of the city to a local winery, the sun bouncing off the lake the decking overlooks. Vineyards stretch out across the hill. The place is peaceful, too early for the lunch rush. We order a couple of pizzas and a cool-climate chardonnay.

I watch her for a few minutes, thinking about my next question. She's staring off into the distance, peaceful, enjoying the view. But I plunge in anyway.

"Why do you really strip?" I ask her.

The question catches her off guard. I can see something pass across her face. Indecision, I think.

"I told you," she says, tense.

I watch her carefully. She seems uncomfortable. Her easy smile has disappeared. She seems, in fact, to be quite masterful at shutting a conversation down. She might as well have thrown a sturdy brick wall between us, her intention is so clear.

I wait for a few minutes, just watching her. The sun makes her hair look so black, so glossy. Her eyes are hidden behind huge sunglasses and I lean forward and push them down her nose with one finger, looking into her eyes.

"That's it?" I ask her.

"Uh-huh," she replies, and points out a wedge-tailed eagle, floating effortlessly on the currents high above us.

We sit, sipping our wine, watching him soar. He's beautiful and untouchable. All alone up there. The kind of perfection that makes my heart hurt a little bit. I don't know why. Is it how free he is, how graceful, how self-sufficient?

Or is it how alone he is up there?

20

AARON

23RD MAY 2016

23RD MAY 2016

> *You know what I have realised, Dr. Black?*
> *I have finally realised that there is no meaning to life.*
> *There is just nothing there.*

> *All we do is run around filling our lives with irrelevant, inconsequential, and largely meaningless crap; then we realise that it is in fact all a waste of time, and despair. So we run around frantically to hide this minor little fact from ourselves. But basically we're just filling in time until we die.*

> *Which raises the question, is there any point to life?*

> *I think not. Unless you're a totally self-sufficient entity, it's just a series of disappointments, because once you let people into your life they invariably let you down or hurt you or fuck you up in some other obscure and probably unintentional way.*

> *What would this fall under, I wonder? F for Feeling? Because perhaps it's just that everything hurts so much. I saw some concept of the infinity of feeling and pain I was capable of and I rejected it. But now I see an infinity of emptiness, and no one has any importance attached to them, and I am alone, alone for infinity, eternity, forever.*

> *Perhaps L for Lonely is more appropriate. Because I've built the*

walls so high and so impenetrable that I really can't reach anybody and they can't reach me. It's like I was so easily hurt and so miserable that to escape I had to go to the other extreme. But how long can I survive with no one's arms to curl up in? How can I reject all notions of love and intimacy when it leaves me so alone and so cold and so goddamn sad? Where did this irrational fear of intimacy come from? I feel like someone's hit the pause button and I'm frozen in the middle of my life, and it's a failure. I've achieved exactly what I intended to achieve—I've avoided pain. But it's a failure nonetheless—because I'll end up alone and I won't want loneliness anymore.

21

CLARA

AFTER LUCAS DROPS ME HOME—ANOTHER pleasant and death-defying date achieved, *tick!*—I sit on my couch, trying to savour the experience.

Nice dates, *tick!*

Hot sex, *tick!*

Sharing important things in his life with me, like horses, *tick!* —Which are, frankly, pretty sexy, whatever I might have said to Lucas in jest.

Maybe, *maybe* this feeling—this hopeful, jittery, swoony feeling—is that elusive connection with a man that I have so long been terrified of?

But however hard I try to feel joyful, I manage to only feel restless and uneasy. My mind shoots all over the place, a wild hunted rabbit trying any bolthole it can find. Thoughtless, panicked.

Straight down into a snake's nest of unhelpful thoughts and feelings.

For God's sake, I think to myself. *How did I get my therapy degree, again?*

I'm trying to sell myself on the virtues of trust and vulnerability, but they sit so uncomfortably with me—on a personal level, at any rate—that I'm relieved to hear the phone ring.

It's Jo, the manager of another strip club that I've done a few shifts at now and then, though I prefer my regular.

They're light on this afternoon, she tells me. Am I interested in coming in, even for a few hours? They'll waive the dancer fee...

Irritated with my ruminating, I agree and throw my prep case into the car. Within half an hour, I'm in the dressing room doing my makeup and hair, happily distracted.

I ponder the irony of this, my inability to do exactly what I would ask a therapy client to do: sit with the discomfort. Stay with it. Talk about it.

Feel it.

Beth will have a goddamn field day.

———

READY TO START MY SHIFT, I shake off all thoughts of love and vulnerability and focus on sexiness instead.

Idly, I wonder how sexual satisfaction might mess with my profit margin. Despite my terror, I feel like I have something else, something better. The edge and urgency has gone out of my hunting on the dance floor.

Nevertheless, I set myself a target of $1000 for four hours. I have twenty minutes before my first podium session—long enough for a dance or two—and start looking for a likely target. There are several—Jo was right, there aren't enough girls in here to service all the men.

I'm just making my way to an eager-looking middle-aged man in a corner when I see him, off to my left. I stop, bewildered, my brain trying to make the leaps to catch up.

Lucas, gorgeous, seated at a table in a gloomy corner with a dancer perched on each thigh, one arm around each of them, stroking their abs just beneath their breasts, with a raging erection. They're giggling, sipping cocktails, tossing shiny hair and whispering in his ears. He looks completely at ease, like they're his girlfriends, like this is his home ground. Like he's never been anywhere else.

I feel gutted, shattered, like I'm going to be sick.

I should be getting the fuck out of there, but I'm rooted to the spot, just staring. Staring and shattering.

Finally he glances my way, and half jumps up in shock, a guilty look flashing across his face, girls tumbling sideways. Our eyes meeting breaks my stupor and I turn and rush back the way I came, into the change room, already tearing up, willing myself to *breathe, don't sob, breathe, don't sob.*

Jo catches my elbow on my way past, concerned.

"Love, what is it?"

Her warm brown eyes undo me, and I can't help it; I sob. But I don't have any words that make any sense. *The guy I just started seeing three days ago is betraying me here with other girls?* Even to me it sounds ludicrous. We haven't even spoken about anything remotely serious.

Being exclusive.

My dancing.

It's just in my head that the leap to caring, or thinking it might be worth *trying* to care, trying to *let* myself care, has been so huge, so momentous.

The pain I feel is not just that he's here fondling other girls, though there's a healthy dose of that. But it's also rage against myself—an "I told you so!" whipped up into an instantaneous, tsunami-sized frenzy against love, against vulnerability.

A few weeks ago—no love, no vulnerability, and everything was just fucking fine.

Today—not so much.

————

BACK IN MY APARTMENT—HALF-COHERENT mumblings about my need to depart immediately accepted by Jo graciously—I sit in the bath, quiet and still.

My phone rings intermittently in the living area. I suppose it is Lucas. I hope it is Lucas, then loathe the thought. Fantasies, hopes, and dreams are crashing and burning all around me.

Logically, I try to tell myself it's not that bad. I make quite a good living off ordinary men going to strip clubs. Many of them are married or have partners. Some partners don't know what their mate is getting up to, but many do. Relationships survive.

I tell myself all this, but I know in my heart what it means to me, what it says to me. That I'm not enough. Not good enough. Not desirable enough.

Not *loveable* enough.

All my worst fears and deepest insecurities.

As it turns out, I've fallen off that precipice anyway. Even without showing him anything of me it does, apparently, matter.

Crap.

Is that the problem with getting close to someone?

It's a deadly arrow flying straight into my sense of value. Forget Cupid and my stupid heart. Leaning toward Lucas and being rejected isn't about *him*. It's about all love, everywhere. It's about hope and connection and meaning. It's about *me*. My worthiness.

If a guy wants you and wants you and wants you but then needs to go feel up a stripper three hours after your last date, there's no connection. Is there?

No hope.

That's what I sit with in the bath.

I LOSE TRACK OF TIME. Minutes or hours pass. It feels like days.

More memories, unbidden, float before my eyes.

Walking around and around the local park, obsessed. After every meal, walking for an hour, cute little short shorts exposing my long, lean legs. Beautiful summer sun, crisp breezes. Picture-perfect, apart from my motivations.

No calories surviving the process through my digestive system. Or at least, simple mathematics spurring me on: what goes in must be worked out.

On days of weakness, pausing by the public toilets to throw up whatever hapless morsels had found their way into my stomach against my better judgement.

Already working as a counsellor, effortlessly moving from clear personal dysfunction to supporting young people with mental health issues. The irony not lost on me but not attended to, either.

I was already lean, naturally—one of those annoying people who can eat whatever they like and not put on weight. But I walked for an hour after every meal just to be sure. And on the days I felt very bad, there was always purging.

I tried to explain this to my sister once, after one too many glasses of wine. Purging as a way to manage anxiety rather than manage weight. These boundaries sometimes crossed, of course. But largely, purging was something concrete to focus on when I could no longer tolerate my misery.

It was also an attempt at smallness. Being invisible. How terrible it felt to be visible, to take up space. But that was another story—one I didn't share with her that day, or any other.

"You've just got to stop it!" Agitated, alarmed. Gripping my arm, her eyes wide, shocked. The complexities escaped her.

I didn't try explaining it to anyone again for a very long time.

Sitting in the bath, confused and hurt, I'm needled by these memories. They come clear and close, linked so closely with the idea of value that they're crowding the bathroom with me, inflating anxiety, feeling familiar and dangerous.

So many memories.

I remember hunger being my friend.

I remember a continual vague sense of vertigo—some sort of mild high (*that would be the electrolyte fluctuations*, Therapist Clara interjects, nodding sagely).

I remember being distracted—this took up so much space. I never had the energy to look at anything much else at all. I wonder sometimes where I might be now if I hadn't invested fifteen-odd years of my life preoccupied with food.

But that was the point, I suppose. There were things that I didn't want to look at. Things that I still don't want to look at. Our minds are clever like that. Hiding things. Hiding away the things we don't want to see.

I remember the bruising around my eyes—burst blood vessels from purging. No one ever mentioned them. Did they not notice, or did they not know what it meant? I guess until I started throwing up it would never have occurred to me that that might happen.

I remember the exhaustion. The secrecy. The midnight trips to Coles to find suitable food to consume in order to have something to throw up.

I remember when I started trying to stop—my body carried on without me. A glass of wine, feeling full—I couldn't *not* throw up, at some point.

The panic, the absent sense of self. Focusing on food feeling like the only thing that stopped me from floating away completely.

These are the things the helplessness of lost connection—lost worthiness—throws up in my mind's eye.

Cunty fucker.

—————

EVENTUALLY, dragging myself away from the dark tug of dysfunctional coping, I clamber out of the bath.

Despite myself, I check my phone. Five missed calls, all from Lucas. But he didn't leave any messages.

I shuffle through the rest of the evening listening to mopey music: the playlist I compiled for just such occasions.

Not that catching a new lover with other strippers was something that I had ever anticipated. But still. David Gray, Mad Season, Ben Lee. Jeff Buckley. Song after song compiled deliberately to encourage sitting in that painful space. That I prefer to flee from.

Right on cue, Beth pops around and we sit on the couch, holding hands.

"So, here we are," she says, watching me with quiet concern. "The exact space you wanted to avoid."

"Not really. Just the edges of it," I correct her.

It's hardly the heartbreak of great love.

At least, I don't feel like anyone will understand how big it feels to me.

But Beth does, of course.

"That's not how it feels to you, though, is it?" she asks gently, and I look away, tears pricking at my eyes.

I wonder how people navigate this stuff without therapy, professional experience, or therapist friends at their disposal. It feels impossible to me even with all three to draw on.

"So tell me how it feels," Beth says softly, and despite my reluctance to cry in front of anyone, I lose the fight to keep my mouth straight, controlled. I clutch a cushion to my stomach and sob helplessly, mouth agape, snotty and messy and uncontained.

All the things I never am.

"Like I'm not good enough," I sob. "I know it's only been a few dates. I know it's not serious yet and it's how I met him, for God's sake. I don't know why I'm so surprised. I just thought there was something about him. Something different. And it made me start thinking about being close to someone. And now I feel unraveled. And stupid. Why aren't I enough? Just me?"

The problem with pain is that you can't go over it, under it, around it—you just have to go through it. We both know this. And so Beth sits with me. Partly to comfort me and convey that I am not alone, but probably also partly because she knows that otherwise I might shelve it and flee.

And the problem with fleeing is that you always go too.

———

NEVERTHELESS, even with the best friend in the world, I wake up with renewed vigour and the illusion that what I need is a distraction.

So, like the clichéd plumber with his leaking pipes, I do what the therapist with unresolved intimacy issues does—and start looking for a distraction.

If intimacy is going to fuck with me, I will fuck with it first—faster, harder, louder, and more successfully, I assert. *In the knee-jerk way that dysfunctional people do*, Therapist Clara interjects, but I ignore her.

I give notice at the club, the myth of it meeting my sexual needs thoroughly exploded. After poring over Google searches for a couple of days, I decide that a sugar daddy will fill the financial and sexual void nicely, and hurtle head first down another steep and treacherous path to wrestle with value and intimacy and do my very best to avoid pain.

Therapist Clara holds her hands up crossly, her gesture a "you're on your own, buddy" kind of dismissal. But all in all she looks kind of resigned to this new course of action. She's not surprised, at any rate. I don't think I've ever managed to surprise her.

Action has always made me feel better, and I move at an alarming pace.

I put up my profile and start searching men.

Older men. Men with a lot of money.

Within days, I have my first meeting.

Beth raises her eyebrows, but says nothing.

22

AARON

31ST MAY 2016

I have decided that I am not a human being.

I do not feel.

This is a prerequisite for humanity, and I do not pass the test.

I am not sure how long this will last, but I must experience all life has to offer while emotions and feelings absent themselves from me. When they return, life might injure me; I might be filled with fear, and life might torture me.

I had decided that I must either feel everything—every tiny little nuance of feeling that everyone around me experiences, that I must be sensitive to every single one of them—or I must feel nothing at all.

And the former was too much—it overwhelmed me. There was either too much joy or too much pain. Not even that. The joy could not be worth the pain, is what I am trying to say. The despair would negate it in the end. Whatever joy there is at any one time will be hunted out and squashed by misery, because the misery is stronger, bigger, better. What's more, it's liquid, and it can get into every corner, every crevice. Joy comes in these useless bloody chunks that don't fit into anywhere comfortably and are generally just fucking useless.

I thought this would be better, this absence of feeling. Safer, calmer, stronger. I chose it. I groomed it. I watered it and nurtured it. And oh, how it bloomed and blossomed.

But it turns out feeling nothing is just as bad. It's safer, and you can survive like this for a while. But not forever.

23

LUCAS

I'M SITTING in the bar of another expensive hotel with another ludicrously expensive whiskey.

Drumming my fingers on the glass, agitated and dissatisfied.

What was Clara doing at Peaches, anyway? That's not where she works!

I catch myself with this line of thinking, though. What was *I* doing there, perhaps was the more pertinent question.

I think about Clara, her fiery eyes, her defiant chin. The softness of her skin. Her shy smile and womanly aura. The way her hair looked across a pillow.

I don't know why she keeps invading my thoughts. She's nothing like the girls I usually sleep with, with their brittle smiles and life goals and financial expectations of their men. Their clamouring to please me.

There's something strange and vulnerable about her. And somehow it makes me want to know things. It feels like a gift, this need to know. A gift to myself, more than anything. Curiosity about someone's thoughts. What makes her tick? What are those troubled thoughts that pass across her face? Are they dark enough to withstand mine? Could we let them out, together? Sort through them and let them float away?

Perhaps it's just about me. All these dark thoughts and memories. My mother. Perhaps I just want someone warm and soft to endure them with me. Perhaps I'm just a coward, too frightened to be alone with them. So perhaps it's not her at all. Perhaps it's just all in the timing. She's the one who's appeared, at this time. A different month, a different year, and maybe I would barely even notice her.

It doesn't feel like that. But how do you know? How do you work out what drives you toward someone?

It feels like an opening. Like for so long I have looked forward, travelling along a tunnel. Counting off my successes. Heading somewhere.

But while I was busy succeeding, I didn't even notice how small my world was getting.

Somehow, looking at Clara, I can see something bigger. It feels like a yearning, but I don't even know what for. It feels like my chest is unfurling, stretching, being big enough to take in the sky and the stars and the sunlight. Like I could look up and around and take things in and *be still*. Be still with myself. Like I might be enough, sitting still.

I can't explain it any better. I just feel like there's the possibility of something more.

So of course I go and bloody ruin it. It felt so precious, so fragile, so unsettling that paying to see some other women naked seemed like the fastest route back to normalcy. Where everything was back within my control. Where anything potentially painful was kept the fuck away from me.

But it's all wrong, anyway. I may have fucked up at Peaches, but I fucked up even more before that. I might feel bigger, but anything that happens with Clara will be sullied by how we met.

I thought she'd allay my guilt in one way. An ugly way. A

selfish way. Now I feel like she might help me in some other way. A softer way.

But it's still selfish nonetheless.

It's still me wanting her to make me feel better.

24

CLARA

FLYING BUSINESS CLASS TO SYDNEY, courtesy of my date, I sip a glass of Bollinger and stretch luxuriously in my seat.

I have some papers to go over about recent research into attachment theory and eating disorders, but I feel like I'm playing truant, not just from my profession but also from my whole life. The papers remain in my carry-on and I stare vacantly out the window at the vast blue sky.

Sydney is a balmy 28 degrees and I step confidently out to the taxi rank, my trusty silver heels glinting in the sunshine.

Gary is 52 with short silver hair and an athletic, tanned physique. He's the third sugar daddy I've met in the last couple of weeks, and I feel at ease with him immediately.

"So, you're new to the scene then?" he asks, amusement flickering in his eyes. He has a relaxed smile and is unperturbed about what still seems pretty awkward to me.

"Yep. I tried dating for romance this year and it wasn't for me, I'm afraid."

He raises his eyebrows in a question mark, a gesture that reminds me so completely of Beth that I feel a shot of probably unwarranted warmth toward him.

"Intimacy issues," I smile self-deprecatingly. "This works much better for me. All cards on the table, no surprises, thank you very much."

"Ah, well, let's get to that then." He leans back in his chair, watching me kindly but with some amusement. "What are your terms?"

I am still getting used to this. It's so transactional, so acceptable just to advise what you want, negotiate, and agree on official terms.

We're sitting in the bar of the Park Hyatt, drinking strong, rich coffee and eating macaroons. It's so civilised, and the whole encounter already reeks of class and money. Gary has paid for my room, where I have already checked in and had a good scout around, sighing with joy at the massive flowers on the table and the luxurious towels on the bed. I have three days here so that Gary and I can get to know one another and decide whether to set up an arrangement.

We've chatted on the phone a couple of times and I'm basically here to see if there's any chemistry and if we can enjoy each other's company. If so we will firm up the terms of our arrangement.

"So, I'm after a pretty, young date for social functions," he starts, and now I raise my eyebrows. "Young*er*," I correct him, aware that in sugar-baby terms, I'm almost over the hill.

He smiles. "Young*er*," he agrees.

He's already told me this over the phone. There was no point coming up to meet if his terms didn't appeal to me. I suspect he's reiterating them to put me at ease for stating mine. I'm grateful for his thoughtfulness, and am starting to think this whole arrangement business could work very well indeed.

"Yes, thank you, you were very open with me on the phone. I feel clear about what you would like." His desires stretch to some time together every month for dinners, shopping, and theatre. He likes to spoil his dates.

Then the big one—he'd like to progress to a sexual relationship when and if we both feel comfortable. He would fly me to Sydney for all these things, a planned weekend once a month, and other commitments as they arise. Or on a whim, if it suits both of us, he might come to Melbourne.

I smile at him coolly, then we both laugh.

"I'd like an allowance of $5000 a month in advance for an exclusive arrangement," I deadpan, though I think it's ludicrous, unlikely, and to be honest, somewhat greedy. Niggling doubts about the ethics of the arrangement and my own worth bubble away under my cool exterior, too. But Gary doesn't blink. He doesn't look in the slightest bit fazed by my terms.

"That sounds fine," he says. "Let's call this weekend the start and review things in a couple of months."

That easy. It seems too good to be true, and though it won't cover my monthly income from dancing, it is minus the long hours, constant personal maintenance, and income uncertainty.

It sounds, frankly, quite all right.

———

THE WEEKEND CARRIES on in an entirely pleasant manner.

After leaving me to relax in the hotel for the day, Gary comes back in the afternoon to take me shopping for some clothes to suit his tastes (elegant, feminine dresses and discreetly sexy shoes) and some jewellery to match. He is unashamedly directive about what he would like to see me in.

"I have business functions to attend. I need a classy date," he shrugs. "When we know each other better I'll probably trust your judgement, but for now, I'll need you to show up in something that I've bought you."

For my part, I am surprisingly unfazed by his dictating my wardrobe. There's something kind of sexy about a man knowing exactly what he wants and ensuring that he gets it, without apology.

I get the sense that Gary often gets what he wants, but his laid-back demeanour and air of slight amusement give off a sense of warmth and security. And to be honest, the certainty of the situation has it's own allure.

No wondering, no what-ifs—the man wants to pay me for my attention, and the terms are very clear.

Therapist Clara is raising her hand, ready with an opinion she'd like to share, but I pointedly ignore her.

For the Clara on the more dysfunctional end of the spectrum, this arrangement sounds like it will work very well indeed.

———

GARY HAS tickets to the ballet for the evening (I've never been before; it's captivating) and afterwards takes me to an upmarket restaurant overlooking the Opera House and Sydney Harbour Bridge. The view is utterly enchanting. A Melbourne girl all my life, I have always thought of Sydney as the somewhat snooty "other sister," but her charms have won me over already. I'm not going to mind visiting Sydney regularly at all.

Gary attends to the wine list and selects a bottle without consultation, but thankfully leaves ordering food to me. I opt for a sashimi entrée and duck main, the dishes arriving beautifully presented and stunningly tasty. It's the type of dinner Beth and I might celebrate a big event with, but on rare occasions and with a certain amount of horror at the price tag. I relax into the abundance of it, my enjoyment so profound that thoughts of love, Lucas, and vulnerability seem like a bad and distant dream.

"So, what line of work are you in that has proven so lucrative?" I ask, gesturing at the table and the view. He gestures toward me, his elegant hands moving up and down an approximation of my length, and he smiles amusedly, adding me into the things his profitable career has achieved. Half of me winces internally at the objectifying nature of it, but the other half of me swells with pride: my worthiness, my desirability (recently so wounded) confirmed once more.

Confirmed with a price tag that says *Very Fucking Worthy Indeed*.

Therapist Clara rolls her eyes. She has a whole lot to say about this, but I still don't give her any airtime.

Plus, the food is excellent, the wine even more so, and I like Gary much more than I had expected to.

"I'm in the stock market," is all he offers, before steering the conversation toward me. He's attentive and interested, but keeps a certain distance between us, which is fine with me. I, too, am careful about what I say.

"When were you last in a relationship?" he wants to know, and I am cagey in my answer.

"Well, I was kind of seeing someone a while ago, but it was brief and not serious," I offer. A while ago being quite an understatement. I haven't had a boyfriend since I was in high school. And even that would be a stretch to call a relationship.

I think about my regulars at the club. All the men there when I first started, telling me about their divorces, their cheating spouses, their pain. The beautiful, young guy who visited every Thursday for a while, the sorrowful depths of his eyes. Eventually I was so concerned for him I gave him some numbers of therapists I recommended.

At least, that's part of the story.

I think about my hopeless desire to connect on some level, however superficial, however masked. Always searching for that connection. Even in a strip club. Before I learnt better.

Ashamed of my bad choices, I don't elaborate.

How do you explain to a stranger that a date with a lap-dance client was as close as you've come to a romantic connection in the last decade?

Even I know that girl sounds like a bloody desperate lunatic.

———

WE MOVE ON; psychotherapy in particular fascinates Gary.

"But how does it work? How is it different from counselling?" He tells me he has never seen a therapist of any sort, though he knows his daughter saw a counsellor once for some anxiety.

"She had ten sessions," he tells me. "It seemed to help."

"That was most likely Cognitive Behavioural Therapy with a psychologist or social worker. It's more focused on fixing the problem rather than exploring where the problem came from. A toolkit for life, if you like."

"And psychotherapy?" he asks.

"It's relational—the relationship between the therapist and client is critical. Because of the intensity of the therapy—sometimes twice a week, sometimes spanning years—what the client brings to their other relationships will eventually be brought into the therapeutic relationship. It's very exploratory. There is a lot of wondering about why and how a person has come to this place in their lives. I've heard it described as re-parenting, you know, with a parent with unconditional positive regard for you. I don't know that I'd go that far. And it doesn't mean that your parents were necessarily bad parents. It's just that our families leave us with stuff. It's universal. Even parents doing their absolute best might get things wrong. Or the way a child perceives things might be really a long way from the truth, but still damaging. We're complicated creatures," I smile at him. "We're really very interesting."

Nevertheless, as I talk, I squirm uncomfortably in my chair. The incongruity between my profession and my currently seeking this arrangement is suddenly painfully obvious to me, but probably—hopefully—completely obscure to Gary.

"Fascinating! What made you pursue that as a career? It sounds pretty intense."

I ponder that question thoughtfully, sipping my wine. *There's an opportunity here*, I think to myself. Self-disclosure in a sort of safe space—safe in as much as I am not invested in this relationship. It seems like a chance to try out vulnerability with a man without being too heavily invested in the outcome. *But does that defeat the point?* I wonder to myself. *Isn't that just like self-disclosure within a friendship?* I can do that. It's the romantic space that terrifies me.

Still, keen to get my money's worth (*his money's worth?!*), I try out showing a little of myself.

"I had poor mental health when I was younger," I offer, slowly. "Depression, eating disorders. It made me curious about mental health and how to address that, I suppose. I saw a psychotherapist for a long time. It was the thing that made the difference. I'd seen counsellors before, but none of them helped in the long term. They felt like Band-Aids. Psychotherapy helped me integrate a sense of self."

Gary raises his eyebrows. Somehow this gesture is soothing, lighthearted. "Sorry, psycho-babble! I didn't really know who I was or why I made the choices that I made. It helped. I needed that space to really find myself."

"That's very honest of you, I appreciate it." Gary looks thoughtful too, gazing over my shoulder and slowly chewing on a bite of his succulent-looking lamb. His eyes wander back to me and he smiles, but looks serious. "I wasn't expecting such an...*intimate*...answer."

I chuckle slightly, feeling a little caught out. "Yeah. I'm trying to be more open about myself."

"Is that why you've come to Seeking Arrangement? To practice for the real thing?"

"Gosh, no. I mean, not consciously. And in my line of work we do consider the unconscious quite a bit, so maybe I'll think about that! But, ah…I just wanted to explore something, companionship maybe, without the uncertainty of dating. At least that's what I told myself." I smile self-consciously, aware that I am in fact occupying an interestingly vulnerable space.

"I could take this back to my therapist!" I joke, and Gary smiles, but he looks wary and I can feel him withdraw a little bit. I wonder if he's having second thoughts about taking me on dates to business functions, like I might disintegrate in front him or embarrass him in front of his colleagues.

"It's all in the past, if that's worrying you—my stability now," I offer, watching him carefully. He relaxes a little, saying, "Yes. Sorry. It did occur to me that some unstable people do come to the site. You have to be a bit careful. But you do seem quite mentally well," he smiles at me. He really is quite charming when he smiles.

Still, I can feel a certain unease has settled over him.

So my foray into self-disclosure with a man didn't get off to a good start. And it occurs to me that this may not be the safer space I had imagined after all.

So I remind myself to stick to the assigned role and I stay there for the rest of the evening. Which all in all, seems to go very well. We make plans for our next date, then Gary kisses me goodnight, with just the right balance of respect and sexiness.

BACK IN THE HOTEL ROOM, I make myself a strong cup of tea and send Beth a brief text to check in that I'm alive and well, then I settle into bed with my Kindle.

My mind keeps skipping to my self-disclosure with Gary, and doubts about whether I said too much, let him see a little too much of the real me. The crossover with my fears in real relationships is particularly striking.

But I've started now. There's no turning back. For the time being, at any rate. I've quit stripping and I need the cash. And though I'm agitated and uncertain, it's nowhere near on a Lucas scale. So I buckle in and sit back for the ride.

25

LUCAS

I swan into the office on Monday morning, replete from a weekend of food, wine, and women. My heart neatly boxed back up, packed away for some other day. Though it's getting harder and harder to keep it there.

Zara has a stack of paperwork awaiting my attention. She gives me a run down of who I need to get in touch with today and which things need to be achieved, smiles at me suggestively, and then sashays out of the office, her modest pencil skirt probably covering much less modest underwear.

We've had sex in almost every room on the floor, which is no small achievement in a bustling office with twenty-odd staff members coming and going. My favourite was the women's toilets, her bent over the bowl, ass out, her tits bouncing gloriously with each thrust of my cock. Trying to be quiet while other women come and go. It was so hot. My dick is getting hard just thinking about it.

I pick up the phone to her office. "Zara. My office," I command her, and she sashays back in, flicking the blinds to closed on her way, smiling demurely. She sits on my desk in front of me, parting her legs ever so slightly, watching me knowingly. God, the woman knows me well.

"Suck me," I say, hoarse, my voice thick with my need, and she drops to her knees obediently, unbuttoning her shirt a couple of buttons and exposing a pink lace bra, finely embroidered. It looks expensive and classy—all part of her role here. Taking care of my calendar. Managing relationships. Greeting guests. Keeping records. Sucking my cock while looking pretty.

Momentarily, the depravity of it causes me to wince. I'm pretty sure Zara is waiting for our clandestine encounters to blossom into a relationship, despite my warnings that they would not. Not that she's not a great catch—smart, sexy, motivated. It's just that she's part of my façade. She sees what everyone sees. What I want them to see. Lucas Evans—smart, successful, confident. Always good for a laugh. Always funny.

Not a worry in the world.

She doesn't see this hollow in my chest, my body yearning toward something different, something my mind will not consent to. Something Clara has stirred up. Something that snakes uncomfortably around my mother, my brother, my memories. Something I have shunned and shirked and never experienced: closeness.

No one sees anything like that.

But I don't think about that right now.

She's swirling her tongue around the head of my cock, looking up at me through her long, dark eyelashes, her pretty pink lips stretched wide. Grunting, I come in her throat almost immediately and she swallows, staring straight in my eyes the whole time. She then daintily wipes her mouth with a tissue and leaves the room.

And it strikes me—again—that I'm being kind of an entitled pig.

26

CLARA

THE NEXT MONTH passes without incident as I settle into my new routine.

Without dancing, my calendar has freed up significantly, so I take Beth up on her offer of another day at the practice. The additional space means some new clients, which is always intense but invigorating. Of particular interest to me is Sophie, who's twenty-five, bright, and bubbly. It's hard to grasp what she is coming to therapy for initially, in fact.

The usual opening question—"So what brings you here today?"—yields very little.

"There's just some stuff that's bothering me about my relationships," she says. It's not exactly evasive, but she doesn't follow up with any more details either. Instead, she rambles from one topic to another, cheerful and funny.

She works in retail. She's already in a management role. She's doing well and the staff like her. She plays basketball and likes to keep active and challenge herself to new things. Recently she's started roller derby just to spice things up in her life a little, push her boundaries.

She's self-deprecating and smart and interesting and I like her immensely. I think, as I sometimes do, that we'd probably be great friends if we had met under other circumstances.

Our fifty minutes is almost up when she abruptly changes tack, coming back to the question she has avoided numerous times throughout the session.

"I mess up my relationships," she says, looking at me with her chin out, eyes blazing with something that looks oddly like defiance. "I can see it coming a mile off, but I can't seem to stop it."

"Well, we can talk about that," I say and smile at her. "Though our time is almost up today. You hesitated about telling me that till right at the end." I leave the comment there, not a question or a judgement. Just an observation.

"Yes," she smiles back. "Look at that! Time's up! I guess we'll have to talk about it next time." Sparkling with amusement, she confirms our next appointment and sweeps out of the room.

————

I PONDER THIS PROBLEM LATER, with wine and Beth.

"I just read *The Course of Love* by Alain de Botton," I tell her.

He's hardly professional research, his speciality being in philosophy rather than psychotherapy, but I found his book very compelling.

"He says that we will marry the wrong person, that everyone will. That human nature guarantees that we'll infuriate and disappoint each other, without exception. And that doesn't *actually* mean you've married the wrong person; it's more a case of trying to decide what sort of madness you choose in your relationship, rather than being able to avoid it. Because we're all stark raving mad. But we already knew that." I smile at Beth affectionately, this point particularly close to our hearts, our friendship forged on our own respective nuttiness.

I remember the first time that I saw her. She was sitting alone in a coffee shop, reading a book and stirring a coffee. She had long black hair back then, with shocking red stripes in it.

I kept glancing at her, not because she looked different (though she did) and not because she was beautiful (though she was). I kept glancing at her because I was listening to a couple near us arguing and I was watching the expressions cross her face as their argument progressed. By the end, she was muttering comments under her breath, rolling her eyes, getting agitated.

I couldn't hear every word of the argument, but the gist of it was that the girl wanted to be exclusive and the boy was trying to convince her that she should be faithful, but that he had needs she couldn't meet and that he wanted to be able to keep sleeping with other women.

"But I'll only love you," he said, at one point.

And she mouthed that exact sentence at that exact moment and then looked up at me. And our eyes met and we both laughed.

It wasn't funny; the boy was much older than the girl, and you could see her twisting herself in knots, convincing herself that maybe it wasn't fair of her to demand exclusivity. You could see her getting ready to accept whatever he offered. It was heartbreaking, not funny. But it *was* funny that this girl with her crazy hair had heard that same old shit so many times that she had it pegged. It sounds so unlikely. But we both knew it was so common that she could say it in real time with him. We didn't have to talk about it. We locked eyes and laughed and knew we were on the same page.

When they left, still arguing, she slid her coffee over toward me.

And that was that.

"I've read it," Beth says, pulling me back to de Botton. "I liked the way he explores what we bring from childhood to adult relationships. It's accessible for people who've never even heard of psychotherapy."

"Yes! It's the book I would have written if I could collect my thoughts about the subject. And, you know, not be a walking advertisement for my own incompetence in the area," I grin at her.

She doesn't smile; she looks serious. She seems to perpetually be about to say something, then not, these days.

I could probably say it for her and save her the internal struggle with just how much a good friend should push. But I'm settling right into denial and say nothing.

We part ways, things unspoken between us a new and worrying aspect to our friendship.

It's not like Beth to not say it. It's not like me to hide.

Not from her, at any rate. Because if you can't be honest with your best friend, who can you be honest with?

Yourself, I suppose.

Otherwise, there'd be no end to the loneliness.

But then, even saying that to myself is not entirely honest.

The truth is, Beth doesn't know everything about me.

For instance, she doesn't know what happened to my last best friend.

And if I'm not entirely honest with myself or with Beth, what does that say about my loneliness?

I have a niggling worry that it could make it infinite.

An eternity of being alone.

———

TOWARD THE END of the month, Gary flies me back to Sydney for a company dinner. He doesn't have time to meet up beforehand, so he organises a taxi to pick me up from the hotel at 7 p.m.

I arrive in the early afternoon and take my time, ordering some nibbles from room service and relaxing in a full, hot bath. I'm tempted by a glass of champagne but don't want to risk being tired or tipsy for our first public date, so I stick with mineral water and lounge around the room, relaxing and feeling pampered.

Idly, I flick through Kate's journaling homework. Usually journals are a private tool for clients to explore their internal worlds, but she wanted me to read hers: "Easier than saying it out loud," she had grumbled last session.

The gravity of it is at odds with the opulence of the setting, the high-calorie finger food I'm munching on, the purpose of my being here. I pause, a fetta-stuffed olive halfway to my mouth.

HOMEWORK – *Therapy Holiday Journal*
<u>Day One</u>

I am now waiting to depart. And it is so weird. I really cannot comprehend the next 10 days. I can't comprehend what one does on a holiday. I can't actually get a grasp of what it might look like to not have anything to do but enjoy oneself. It's kind of a big, blurry, empty space. It seems so stupid, but I am realising just how much food and exercise dictates my life. And I don't know what I will be eating tomorrow, and am damn sure I won't be exercising—and it's like they are the things that define my existence, and without those boundaries or structures or whatever they are, I'm like a half-witted rabbit teetering on the edge of a big empty hole, which is not so much scary right now, as it is baffling. Beyond comprehension. I think I will be surprised if I actually continue to exist through such uncertainty.

I am aware how mad I am, by the way! But I can't explain this feeling any other way. It's like stepping into a completely different world—one where I can't control and define myself with food.

It is also, I might add, stepping out of what I do to cope—marking time by inconsequential things. Filling it in, in fact, with pathetic crap. So I can think, I've filled in two hours! That's two hours closer to dinner (which is important, cause I'm so fucking hungry all the time)! Or two hours closer to bed! And even if I know that that two hours was wasted on something that I might as well have not done—like going to the shops to buy something that could just as easily have been left for my next shop online. But if time has passed, then whatever the activity—it seems a success.

This is not life, I fear. This is a test of endurance—and the point of it escapes me.

Usually there is a point to enduring something unpleasant??

A reward?? A pleasure??

Hmm. Well. It is liberating, in a way, this travel business. I am curious to see if I will in fact die. Not in a suicidal way, before you pounce on your phone! I guess by the time you read this I'll be well home, anyway. But I mean in an existential kind of way. What will I do without my rigid self-imposed rules to get through the days? Will I in fact either self-combust or turn to smoke? Or float away? Cause it feels like there is nothing beneath me. Without this, what will I stand on?

In a way I suppose it is liberating just to see how stuck I am. How unrelenting.

What does it say about one's life if one seriously considers rejecting a holiday because you can't go to the gym?

What do you say about that, Dr. Black?

DAY TWO

I wonder if I can take a leaf out of Bridget Jones' book and rate my days. On the important stuff. Just like Bridget. Ha ha ha.

The thought amuses me immensely, and I worry that that is not quite right...

Nevertheless:

Day Two

Purges: 3

Panicky feelings when spoken to by other human beings: 2 (more significant than it looks....as I only spoke to two people today....)

I feel guilty, disappointed, embarrassed...all those things. I feel like *how can I be trusted to do anything when I can't even manage my own anxiety? And while I know that like in an addiction model, relapses are normal, they flag something and should be paid attention, nevertheless I just feel hopeless and like there's no point to any of this.*

———

I PUT my laptop down abruptly. The incongruence between my two paid roles is niggling away at me, and Kate's journal sounds a little too familiar, a little too close to my heart. Somehow, it puts me off-kilter. I can't quite sit with the subterfuge—I feel like an imposter in both roles. I might be an elegant—*healthy*—therapist with all the skills and tools to support Kate with this particular problem...yet here I am, escaping my own problems with intimacy and worthiness in a highly suspect and peculiar manner.

For a while, I stare vacantly out the window, vaguely uneasy. There is something almost unethical about it. If my clients knew I coped like this, would they trust me with their stories, their truths?

Nevertheless, there's not much to be done now. At 6:30 p.m. I slip into a dark grey cocktail dress and stylish black heels—Gary's purchases. Applying understated makeup in the bathroom mirror, I admire my long dark hair, but decide to tie it up. I still manage to look terribly young with it down. A great advantage in a strip club, but it makes me feel uncomfortable for a business dinner with an older man.

I add Gary's discreet row of delicate pearls and step back to observe the effect. It's not a dress I would have chosen. I wouldn't have even tried it on. But I look classy and sensual. I hope Gary approves, and then ponder that. Is my desire for approval about success (*I did it right and better than anyone else*) or worthiness (*I am desirable and loveable*)? And what would disapproval mean, I wonder.

Not for my bank balance, but for my self-esteem.

In the taxi on the way, the driver tries to make chitchat, but my mind is darting around anxiously. In theory, it all seemed so easy. In reality, uneasiness straddles all aspects of this role.

I wonder whom I will be talking to and if I will fit in, hold my own.

I wonder if Gary will desire me.

And I wonder what the hell I am actually doing.

———

I NEED NOT HAVE WORRIED, at least about the first of my concerns.

In a room full of older men and attractive women, my safe subjects provide more than enough conversational punch. Psychotherapy can always be relied on to spark people's curiosity. I trot out the same explanations to numerous interested parties. Two get the profession confused with hypnotherapy and another two feign mock alarm that I will see into their souls and extract all of their secrets. I laugh politely but don't get bogged down in details. Light, charming, and friendly—not my natural state—I am exhausted by the time Gary drops me back at the hotel. He too looks tired, and we make no further plans for the weekend.

He thanks me for my time, his warmth and smiles assuring me that I did just fine. Then he pecks me on the cheek and drives off.

Relieved, I head straight to bed.

Within minutes, I drift into an exhausted and dreamless sleep.

27

AARON

4TH JUNE 2016

I wrote a letter to my brother last year.

I remember how I was aching, how I was overwhelmed with sadness over the ability of people to disappoint me. I remember concluding that human beings were the most singularly uninspiring creatures I had ever come across. I decided that I didn't want them in my life—that I would do so much better without them.

Someone or other had let me down. I think my expectations were too high.

I wrote: "All I want is to curl up in someone's arms and cry. And it's a pretty lonely thought when you realise there's no one in the world who will let you do that. There's just me, and my computer, and my own insanity. And I can write, and I can play guitar, and I can spin myself out with how many thoughts and revelations I can find in the world, but really all I want is for someone to hold me and tell me that they'll never let me go. Maybe that is what love is. Maybe having someone's arms around you is enough."

He never wrote back.

Then I felt even more alone.

And now? I'm sitting at home on a Saturday night, by myself, sober and miserable. The rest of the world is out experiencing life and having fun. Me—I think I'm forgetting how to even talk. My language is deteriorating, my vocabulary shrinking; I am trying to write this, and sometimes it takes me a trip to the thesaurus to remember a simple word like deteriorate. *Not because I care so much to get the word right for you—because sorry, I don't. I just hate it when I can't remember. I hate that I can't even get that small thing right. In my life full of wrongs, not being able to find the right word embodies so much more. So I spend the time finding the right word.*

Hell, it's not like I've got shitloads else to do.

I just sit here and write the same old shit in the same old pages— using the right words, mind you! God. It would bore any reader senseless. How much I sit and wallow and think about these problems and seem to be monumentally ineffective in solving them.

Why wouldn't you help me, Dr. Black?

Why wouldn't you see me just one more time?

28

CLARA

THE NEXT WEEK, Sophie is like a different client. As often happens, once she decided that I was whatever it was she needed —trustworthy, professional, kind?—her story came out in a garbled rush.

I let her talk, making some notes, some thoughtful comments. But mostly I listened.

"It's this goddamn ridiculous cycle. I go round and round and round. I meet someone that I like—or who seems to like me. It doesn't even matter which. And then I try to make it work. I assess what they want and give it to them. I'm so attuned to the needs of others that I bend myself into all sorts of insane positions to try to fit that. I contort myself. I get lost. And it becomes a personal challenge. Not to connect and relate like adult human beings—oh no! Nothing civilised and grown up like that. No. The challenge is to be liked, to be respected. No matter who I have to become for them in order to achieve that. And I actually lose sight of whether I even want to invest in this relationship. It's about my self-worth being propped up by someone else, someone who doesn't even matter! Who doesn't even know me. Worse than that, actually. I think maybe I'm setting myself up to fail? Because if I can't be authentic in a relationship—if I'm just a people-pleaser—of *course* it's not going to work. It's not built on truth. It's not built on someone seeing me and choosing me. So it seems like I just keep going round in the same circles where someone can confirm to me that I'm not worth being loved. But then I do it again! And then I think, 'See? There's just no fucking point to this...' But it's me. It's me who sets it up to fail! It's me who's not authentic and doesn't try to truly connect, just as I am. I don't give anyone a chance to know me. So how can anyone ever choose me?"

I ponder her for a while, watching her struggle not to cry. Some clients cry from the start, unafraid to show emotion or unable to contain it. Others need to control their feelings, themselves. They strive to do so as though their lives depend on it.

"What do you think would happen if you were your authentic self with these partners?" I ask.

"Some of them wouldn't like me! And I'd actually have a chance to sort through the rubble. I'd stop wasting time." She stops, glaring at me. She's seething with rage.

Then her shoulders slump, and she sags into her chair. "Or maybe none of them would like the real me," she says in a small voice. "And I'd be alone forever."

———

THAT'S THE PROBLEM, *isn't it?* Therapist Clara mulls over our session that evening, another glass of wine in hand.

We need courage to show people who we truly are—courage to be our messy, imperfect selves.

Why is this so difficult for some of us? After Sophie left, writing my case notes and noting areas to explore further, I felt like I was almost writing a road map for myself.

First we need to know ourselves; then we need to value ourselves.

Then we need to show up as our true selves with no guarantees about the outcome.

And that's the problem, for both Sophie and me. With our masks off—truly showing ourselves to others—we risk rejection and disapproval. Which perhaps is not about self-esteem at all. Perhaps it's just that it simply *hurts*.

But not everyone will like us, and that's okay. So why did being visible to Lucas feel so dangerous to me? Why does he keep seeping into my thoughts, a remembered touch making me jump as though he was physically right here? Why does his rejection feel so intolerable to me?

I think about another client, whose take on this problem so closely mirrored my own: "It's a risk, right? I don't want to let someone matter so much and risk losing them. It's not like my friends. We can choose as many friends as we like. With your partner, they have to just choose you. Out of all the people in the whole world, they have to choose *just you*. And keep choosing you. Every day. Forever. It just seems so unlikely. To find it and keep it. You know?"

Oh, yes. I know. I so know.

29

CLARA

THE NEXT NIGHT, Gary takes me out to dinner in the city.

He suggested a visit to Melbourne for Easter and, true to form, I embrace the distraction with open arms.

He wants to start at Lui Bar and alarm unfurls deep in my belly, remembering Lucas there. His T-shirt. His ass.

Just the mention of it brings to the forefront dark feelings that I can't reconcile, can't even attend to. Vulnerability and authenticity and fear and value.

I steer Gary in another direction, waving it off vaguely as being a venue more for the youngsters.

And push down that niggling dissatisfaction in my soul.

———

AFTER A COCKTAIL AT GIN PALACE, cosy and intimate and bustling with life, we head to some fancy restaurant, where somehow Gary has managed to secure us a table at late notice. I've never eaten at such an expensive place before and I feel out of place, fraudulent somehow just by virtue of being there. But then I cross my legs, catching a glimpse of my spectacular new shoes, their suggestive red soles, courtesy of Gary. And I remember that I'm playing a role—sugar baby, living the life—and it seems easier to relax and enjoy it.

Playing a role is something that I've been doing my whole life. My mind meanders back to where that started.

When I look at my childhood from the outside, it has a shiny veneer that is almost blinding it was so damn privileged. Loving parents—though they divorced when I was eight. A committed mother who nurtured my gymnastics talents, driving me all around the country to train, to compete. To be better. To be the best.

A funny father who was always physically there, always pleased to see me, though never truly present. Who would never think to call me. I experimented once. Stopped calling him, to measure how long it would take him to make that effort. To think of me and reach out. After seven months, I called it a day and started calling him again. He was pleased to hear from me, as always. He didn't seem to have noticed that seven months had passed since we last spoke.

My bossy, loving, successful older sister.

Then there were all the awards, the accolades. Academic, sporting, artistic. They followed me wherever I went. They practically dripped off me.

Yet somehow, even before my father left, I knew my mother needed something very specific from me—and my father needed something else. It didn't matter *what* they needed. Just that I made sure I gave it to them.

Somehow, even way back then, there were the eating problems. The perfectionism. The need to be *just right*.

And after that, when mum remarried, there were other problems altogether.

I don't talk to people about that. Not even Beth. Because the problems pre-dated Darren. But people will think he was my problem. But he wasn't. He was just another problem. He added to things, sure. But he wasn't the start of everything that went wrong.

The waiter arrives, pulling my attention back to the table. Gary is watching me thoughtfully.

We order the matching wines to go with the tasting menu, and I'm conscious that this means I am probably going to end up very drunk.

"I'll make sure you get home safely," Gary says in a low voice, noticing my uncertainty. Something about his tone makes me look up sharply. In the dim light against the black walls, his eyes are dark and sexy...and slightly predatory.

Good lord. *He's thinking about sex.*

He is watching me intently and I lick my lips, suddenly nervous. Suddenly feeling his desire reflected right between my legs.

Confused, I press my knees together and take a slug of my champagne—a starter that is certainly not going to help me keep my wits about me. But I feel suddenly reckless and like, what does it matter? If I can't manage love, sex might be all I get, right? Gary is kind and thoughtful and sexy. Maybe that might be enough?

Therapist Clara is sitting beside me though, and she gently places the champagne flute back on the crisp white tablecloth.

It DOES matter, she's telling me softly. *It ALL matters. YOU matter.*

She's like a kind, thoughtful parent who sees me, truly sees me, and loves me anyway. My flailing, reactive, destructive self is witnessed and accepted. She will patiently wait for me to work it out and come back to my senses.

She's quite all right, sometimes, Therapist Clara.

I remember why I'm so good at my job, despite these recent imperfections with my coping. I take a deep breath, looking Gary back in the eye.

If I'm going to sleep with him, it needs to be because I want to

—not because he's paying me a wage, and not because I feel hurt and confused and am lashing out at the world and, in particular, at Lucas.

I smile at Gary and vow to go easy on the wines.

———

LATER, we stroll along St Kilda pier, a fresh breeze off the ocean pleasing against the warm autumn dusk. Gary is holding my hand, his thumb gently stroking my palm. He's been especially attentive all night and I'm pretty sure he's geared up to explore that sexual angle of our relationship.

"Soooo...you're being quite the charmer this evening," I venture, keen to bring into the open the rising tension between us. But possibly it's just in my imagination. I tend to overthink things. My intimacy danger radar is like a meerkat on speed.

Once again, I pause to marvel at just how grown up and composed I can be when my heart isn't on the line. How brave, how articulate. I file that away under "Things to be attended to" with all the other things currently lurking under the carpet, not so much swept there as kick-boxed the fuck out of my sight.

"I like to think I'm always quite the charmer," Gary replies, the twinkle not exactly missing from his eyes, but shrouded in something else. An awareness of his own desire, perhaps.

He continues to run his thumb over my palm, the rhythm of it somehow seductive and slightly hypnotic.

"I get the feeling now might be a good time to talk about expectations," I say, breathless, his thumb more distracting than anticipated. I feel a confused mess of desire—so familiar in the club, and so easily diverted into harmless friction—and uncertainty. Of course I expected this moment to arrive, but nevertheless, what I want or feel is not immediately clear. All I know is that sleeping with Gary does not feel right, despite my libido springing into action. I feel validated by his desire but confused about what sex with him constitutes. Is it prostitution if I want it too?

"Shhhh," he says, and continues rhythmically stroking my hand. My mind skittles all over the place, other places he might stroke to such satisfying effect. But at the same time, I can't quite shake my slight discomfort. Nor can I pin it down—my mind slides away from the issue. I can't specify or articulate it.

Gary is looming large, his previously understated presence transformed by his sexual energy. I can't think; I just walk beside him, breathing rapidly, a pulse throbbing between my thighs.

But something dark and sinister skulks into my consciousness, at odds with this desire.

Being shushed. Being directed. Being compliant.

Trying to hide in dark corners. Already not eating, but eating even less.

Because it was best to be small. To be small and insignificant. To be invisible. To hide in the background. To virtually disappear from sight.

I remember wanting to be so small that no one even noticed me.

———

WALKING BACK ALONG THE PIER, Gary tugs on my hand and pulls me from my reverie. As I turn toward him, he expertly steps into me so that the railing is at my back and one of his legs is wedged between mine. He's suddenly less gentle, amiable Gary and more assertive, his expectation of getting what he wants coming to life before my eyes.

Tipping my chin up, his eyes bore into mine before he places his lips on my mouth.

His kiss is expert and possessive.

Without thinking too much, I kiss him back.

30

AARON

Everything has become transparent.

I wonder that no one else can see it.

People wander in and out of my vision and they are naked; they have no skin. Are they even people? They seem to be transcriptions. White shapes with letters everywhere; thousands of characters; black little spindly legs and arms; shapes, blobs, blurs.

These little black arms and legs tell me what is going to happen. What is going to be said. What is going to be felt. What I should do in order to respond in the correct socially acceptable manner. They are the guidelines for the rules and regulations I think I should impose upon myself of how life should be lived and how one should behave.

Is that crazy?

I don't think I'm crazy.

I just think I'm all alone.

31

CLARA

LYING wide awake in my own bed, alone, I try to sit still in my own discomfort.

Write it down, Therapist Clara insists, and though I grumble and protest, I know it's as good an option as any other. Better than tossing and turning and flailing haphazardly all night. *Writing myself sane,* I call it—to myself and to my therapy clients. A way of taking this internal mess and organising it, making sense of it.

Our brains are so attuned to stories. They don't even have to be true. Writing it down is like making a story that makes sense to me, that helps me understand my actions, my motivations, but is it the truth? Sometimes I wonder if I also use it to absolve myself of the uglier things I do. Write myself a story that I like better.

Anyway—I don't want to write in my bloody journal.

I assign it as homework for my clients endlessly, yet I am astonishingly resistant to utilising it myself.

I know so many things in my head, but I am so spectacularly bad at applying them to my own life that it's almost funny. Almost.

So I just lie awake in bed.

I feel like I've got my nose pressed up against the glass,

looking in at the real world. Looking at people caring for each other, loving each other, being invested in each other. Being vulnerable. I can't describe quite what I feel about it. It's somewhere between fascination and wistfulness. I really just can't understand it. With Gary, it's a transaction. He's kind and thoughtful and surprisingly hot—but at the end of the day, this is still a transaction. That I get. That I can do.

But *caring* for someone? Letting someone matter so much that the pain might obliterate you if they left?

I've barely even started down that path and it's already killing me.

So Gary? Gary might just be as close as I will ever get to love. Gary might be good enough if there aren't any other options.

Gary might be *satisfactory*.

Or maybe I just don't care about Gary in that way. So risking his rejection doesn't matter one fucking little bit.

———

SLEEP ELUDES ME.

I wonder if, like Sophie, I'm hustling for my value, being who Gary wants me to be to win approval. Letting what he wants matter rather than what I want matter. To tip the scales back the other way. To counterbalance Lucas and my lack of value there.

I know that Gary isn't the answer. But Gary is easy and thoughtful and unlikely to hurt me. Gary gives me value and cash.

Importantly, Gary didn't turn up in a strip club and make me feel pain.

So while I know he's not the answer, he's doing a damn good job of making the sad, rejected, hurt part of me feel better.

And maybe that is, in fact, some kind of answer in itself?

32

LUCAS

ANOTHER BAR, another whiskey.

It seems to be my new norm.

Ben joins me, late as usual.

"Well, you look like shit," he says. I glare at him.

He throws his hands up in mock defence. "Easy, tiger," he mutters. "What's eating you?"

"Aside from the obvious?" I snap.

He winces. "Of course. Sorry. You just look...worse than I've seen you in a while."

Ben is the only mate I hang out with who knew me before. Before the business. Before the money.

Before I got away from my mother.

Not that I dumped people—my goals just didn't leave much time for socialising. I got busy and forgot about stopping to enjoy myself for a few years there. People fell off my radar, and I fell off theirs.

That's what I tell myself. But maybe I wanted to leave all elements of "before" behind me. There's still something about that quiet kid that makes me cringe.

"There's a girl," I mutter.

My thoughts swirl round and round, not going anywhere useful.

It makes no sense. I don't know the woman. She's elusive and secretive. And my private investigator threw up some concerns.

A couple of stints in a psych ward in her early twenties. Depression, eating disorders. A lot of therapy.

He also threw up some comfortingly normal stuff.

Divorced parents—seems to have a good relationship with both. A deceased stepfather. An older sister now in a management role.

Nothing outstanding about any of them.

A few close friends who are smart and clean.

A homebody, by all accounts.

Two degrees.

Her own business.

A good reputation.

The only blip on her report card currently was working as a stripper.

A convenient blip: it made it a hell of a lot easier for me to accidentally meet her.

But why is she really working at that club?

And if I can't stop thinking about her, why why *why* was I at that other club, ruining things?

I know the answer to that, though.

I was there because I liked her.

I wasn't supposed to *like* her.

That wasn't part of the plan.

"Hello? Lucas?"

Ben jerks me out of my reverie, tapping on his glass like he's about to make a speech, looking half-worried, half-irritated.

"Sorry," I mutter. "I think I've screwed it up."

"How? Who is she, anyway?"

"Clara. She's a therapist. I met her in an...unusual way." I don't want to talk to Ben about that.

"Okay," he says. "Are you going to tell me more?"

"No. Just that...something fucking *weird* is happening to me. I can't stop thinking about her. I want to *talk* to her. I don't know what the fuck is wrong with me." I frown at my glass, then knock it back, the sharp aromas making my nostrils flare a half-second before my throat warms and burns.

Ben grins. "It had to happen one day," he crows. "You *like* her! Lucas, the king of the fling, *likes* a girl. What happened? She knock you back?"

I frown at him, irritated, then wave at the waiter, indicating a refill.

Ben's expression changes, leans more toward worried.

"That bad, huh?"

"I do like her, okay? So I went out with some other women." I don't want to get into the whole strip club thing. "And she saw me."

Ben looks serious. "So, you fucked up." He watches me sip at my drink. "Have you tried to fix it?" He's still eyeing my whiskey.

"I've called a few times. She hasn't answered and she hasn't called back." A few is maybe an understatement. I'm definitely getting into obsessive territory now.

I don't mention that after that, I spent most of the following weeks fucking as many women as I could. I thought I could fuck her out of my system. Prove to myself that there were plenty more fish in the sea, as they say. But I keep seeing her, looking over her shoulder at me, shy, perfect. That ass. Those eyes.

But it's more than that.

Brave. That's what I keep thinking. There's something brave about her. Brave and calm and...contained. I'm drawn to it like a stupid moth to light.

I have this crazy idea that she might truly see me and still stay.

That I actually want to let her see.

But I don't say any of that to Ben either.

"So what did she actually see? How bad are we talking?"

"Bad enough." I'm short, with no inclination to tell him anything further. I can't mention strippers without explaining why Clara might be at a strip club. And I can't talk about that without offering something more about who she is. And in some strange way I feel protective of her—like it might be misunderstood. She might strip, but she's no simple stripper. There's so much more to her than that.

"So," Ben muses. "You really like her. And because you really like her, you screwed it up. And she won't answer your calls. What about texts?"

"Wrote about twenty. Sent none."

"Hmmm." Ben continues to look thoughtful. "So I think you need something big. The grand gesture, as they say. Not grand like you could go. No fucking money thrown at it, okay? You need to explain to her why you fucked up. You need to tell her a bit about that. And if she won't talk to you...well, you either have to show up on her doorstep—without being creepy—or maybe write her a letter. Women love that shit."

He watches me for a moment. Then he adds: "And stop with the whiskey. That is not going to get you the girl, okay?"

"There's something else, though," I say, watching him, undecided about whether to say what's on my mind. But hell, if I can't say it to Ben, then there's pretty much no one.

"It's about my mother."

33

AARON

19TH JUNE 2016

I have taken up smoking.

I am hell-bent on self-destruction. It gives me satisfaction to contribute to my own demise. The feel of smoke getting sucked into my lungs is unpleasant, undesirable, and I can imagine it thickening, turning to tar. There is nothing pleasant about smoking. I dislike it intensely. Which is why I do it. Gulp down some vodka in between drags. Poison my body so that it might collapse before the poison in my head makes me implode in on myself. Punish the rest of my body for creating my mind the way it is. Punish, punish, punish myself because someone has to pay and I'm too nice—or maybe too scared?—to cause anyone else any pain.

I want to hurt someone, something, for doing this to me. Making me the way I am. Letting me feel the things I feel. I feel that if only I could blame something real and tangible and definite, like my body, it will ease the pain or the anger or the frustration I feel. Like if I do some damage, some part of me, somewhere, will be eased.

Or maybe it's simpler than that. Maybe it's just self-loathing and I want to hurt myself for not being someone else.

Someone I could like more.

34

LUCAS

DRIVING BACK from a ride on Rocky, I find myself heading in the wrong direction.

The forest had been calming. Quiet, cool, the hum of forest life reminding me of things bigger than myself.

I'm meant to be going to the country horse auctions, even further out of town. There's always some poor mongrel-looking horses there, unloved and scraggly, wincing when I go to pat them. I buy up any young ones with potential and retrain them, slowly and with more patience than I extend to many of the two-legged creatures in my life.

Train them right, show due care—they are flight animals, after all—and a horse will never surprise you. You can just be with a horse. You *have* to just be—if you're not in the moment with them, that's when they might surprise you. So I find it very calming.

But I'm heading somewhere else, despite myself. I put a quick call through to Zoe on my car phone.

"I'm not going to make the sales today," I tell her. "Can you make decisions for me? Send me pics if you're not sure. And send Joey with the truck when you're done."

Then I keep driving. Knowing where I'm going but not knowing why.

———

CLARA'S DOOR.

It's been nearly two months since she saw me at the other club.

Two months! Ben had shouted, agitated, disbelieving. *I've known you for twenty years,* he'd said. *And I've never known you to truly like a woman. So do something. Like, NOW.*

Do what, though? I don't really have a plan. Just a feeling. Like we could be something.

But is that just what she inspires in people? Because I know I'm not the first to feel like we could be something. Be everything.

Aaron felt that too.

Apparently it was one-sided.

Apparently there's something about her that makes men want to tell her all their secrets.

It makes me wonder, though—what is it that she wants from us?

35

CLARA

Lucas.

The flash of anger that rises in me subsides slightly, observing the fear in his eyes. The hurt, pained, rejected part of me wants to send him away unheard, justify that fear, but even I understand that that is not the answer.

My heart has skipped several beats already, feeling concurrently like it is falling through my abdomen and finishing a marathon. Wild, wild heart.

"I'm sorry," he begins, earnest, his troubled eyes staring into mine. "I want to explain, if you'll let me. I owe you that."

"Okay." I fight with the sentences in my head, jostling to spill out of my mouth. *Yes, you do! What was with that pursue, pursue, then find someone new five minutes later?!! Is it just ego for you?*

I win; I remain silent. But I step aside and gesture him in.

"I'll make tea," I say, busying myself in the kitchen. He sits on the couch, and I can't help but remember the last time he sat there—the lust, the satisfaction. I wonder if he's thinking about it too: why he's here.

I hand him a mug of English breakfast, sit opposite him,

cradling mine protectively between us—something to occupy my hands—and look at him enquiringly.

"I lied to you about my mother."

The sentence hangs between us, unexpected and confusing.

"The truth is," he starts, and though one would hope he's thought a lot about what he's come here to say, he still seems awkward, uncertain. Like he's forgotten his lines.

"My mother," he finally says. "She does live in Melbourne. I bought her a flat in Carlton. She calls every Sunday."

A long pause. At least my profession has equipped me well to sit with this. And wait.

"After...Peaches...I felt terrible. I want you to know that it had nothing to do with you."

He sighs, grips his mug, adjusts himself awkwardly on the couch. Glances at me, then away.

"I liked you. It scared the shit out of me. So I sabotaged it. I was so angry with myself. But..." he trails off, and I keep waiting.

"I wasn't supposed to like you," he mutters eventually. "I lied about that too."

Lies, lies. What lies?

My heart is galloping against my ribs, and I make a conscious effort to breathe deeply and drop my shoulders, trying to calm the flight response already threatening to derail me. Rapid breathing, clammy underarms. My thinking reducing, reducing, reducing to a tunnel I can't escape from. Can't think "big picture." Can barely think at all.

"My mother was not...kind," he goes on. "It's always stayed with me. I try to avoid her, and I have always just gotten on with things. But...my half-brother passed away last year. I have his journals. They're...stirring. Things were pretty bad for him. He sounded kind of...unwell."

Hunched forward, staring at the floor, he stops abruptly and looks up at me.

"You knew him. That's why I found you. Pursued you. I don't

even know why. I was angry. I wanted to blame someone. I blamed you."

My flight-mode thinking is making it difficult to understand him. A brother. Who I knew. Who died. I wrack my underperforming brain, but can't think of anyone who's died in the last couple of years.

I must just be staring at him, looking confused. So he pulls a notebook out of his bag and pushes it across the coffee table to me, opens it to a bookmarked page.

I don't take the book, however.

"Wait, what?" I finally manage to get out. My voice sounds high-pitched, squeaky. "I don't know who you're talking about. I can't just read someone's diary. Are you sure he knew me?"

"It's addressed to you," he says, indicating the notebook lying open between us. "Most of them are. Just read it. Just this one. Please. It explains it better than I can."

Still I balk.

"It seems so intrusive. There must be another Clara Black. It's a common name. Wait—what was your brother's name?"

"Half-brother. Aaron Cooper. He was a client of yours. He addresses you as 'Doctor.' 'Doctor Black' sometimes, 'Clara' others."

The name doesn't ring a bell.

"No. Most of my clients are female. I'd remember a man who died."

Lucas considers me for a while. His face is impassive.

"I don't have my doctorate. I'm not a Doctor of anything," I add.

"Is this some client-therapist confidentiality crap? You can't confirm you were seeing him? It breaches his privacy rights or something?"

"No," I say firmly. "I wasn't seeing him. You've got the wrong person."

36

LUCAS

I'm so thrown by the turn this conversation has taken that I'm not sure what to say next.

This changes everything.

I sought her out because I thought she was his therapist. Her being the wrong Clara Black did not even occur to me.

In fact, as I percolate on this, I realise that I didn't ask my PI to confirm Aaron was a therapy client, or how long he'd been having therapy. Which in retrospect seems pretty stupid. Hard to accuse someone of professional malpractice without some of the basic facts.

Slip-ups like this are new to me. I never slip up at anything. That in itself is just as arresting as the information is, and I sit there, stunned at myself, my mind struggling to move forward. Move anywhere.

While I sit, however, Clara's mind has been ticking over.

"So," she says slowly, the vowel drawn out, the thoughts and realisations crowding her brain completely unnecessary to articulate. I know exactly what conclusions any intelligent person would draw from this.

"You didn't just like me, then? You wanted something from me, believing I had information about your brother?"

"I know how it seems. You have every right to be angry—"

But she cuts me off before I can say what I mean. That I was being a jerk. That I know that. Selfish, focused on my needs, my goals, not caring about anyone else, about her. How she felt. How she would feel, being betrayed like that.

But even as I form the sentences, the truth hits me, cracks me over the head, bursts my heart open in a way that feels like the air has been slammed out of me and I can't get any more back in.

It shatters into my awareness with a clarity that feels like being sliced in half with an axe.

I wanted to blame someone so I didn't blame myself.

I wanted Clara to have failed him, rather than me.

Because I never called him.

I knew what Mum was like, and I never extended a hand to him. I never helped. I left him there with her. I didn't want to acknowledge what I felt back then. I didn't want to acknowledge what we shared. I wanted to be successful, feel nothing, forget it all.

Never, ever, ever think about my childhood or my mother.

And then he died.

It's hard not to feel things when someone dies.

When their journals remind you of every single little thing you have in common.

But I don't have time to process any of this. Clara's voice drags me back to the present problem.

"You're pretty good at faking things, then, aren't you?" she says, her voice even but icy, her eyes freezing cold. There's no depth behind them now—my gaze glances off them like a blunt axe off slippery wood. That door has slammed shut. That little window to her soul has closed.

She stands and moves to the door before I can decide what to say, before I open my mouth.

I feel like I can't breathe, the pain and the thoughts and the regrets burning through my being like a fire. Sucking the oxygen out of me.

"Get out," she says, her voice dangerously low. "And don't fucking contact me ever again."

I want to explain, to scream, to cry. But I can't form any words.

I stumble blindly out of the open door.

37

CLARA

I sit on the couch after Lucas leaves. I keep very, very still.

I don't call Beth. I don't have a bath. I don't go running.

I just breathe.

In, out. In, out. In, out.

This pain. This is worse than choosing other strippers. This is worse than loneliness. This is crushing me, because I let myself believe I might be chosen—despite my fears, my reservations, my attempts to protect myself. I let myself have hope.

But more than that, I feel stupid. That I'm supposed to be good at reading people. That I'm supposed to be good at protecting myself. Yet here I am, wrong and hurt and crucified.

I didn't notice that it was all an act. How did I not notice that?

How will I be able to trust my judgment ever again?

I sink gently onto my side and curl up, hugging my knees, closing my eyes. I don't cry. It hurts too much to cry.

I just breathe.

THE DAY DRIFTS BY. Shadows lengthen on the walls, the light becoming golden and warm. My phone buzzes intermittently.

I feel like I am floundering. How easily my world crumbles, I observe, detached. How carefully I built in the things that I thought mattered. A few close friends, meaningful work, less than meaningful work but plenty of cash, fun. Solitude, reflection. It felt like I was building a life at the time. Just a few short weeks ago. How easily it is exposed for what it is. A nice neat box to live in. Safe. Impenetrable.

Lonely.

I keep coming back to the notion of being broken, trying to sell it to myself. Of putting your life in a frame and hanging it on a wall and saying—*There! Now I have to decorate it.*

You can't just colour the landscape with safety nets and high-rise steel-reinforced walls. Otherwise, what is there? It's just you. And half of me thinks, good! Let it just be me. I can be so happy, so enthusiastic, so inspired.

But at some point you need experiences to pepper your life with.

You need something colourful or beautiful in the frame so that the picture is worth looking at.

Maybe, *maybe* you need to let people close to you so that there are some striking brushstrokes on your painting: love, connection. Heartbreak, even.

But I don't convince myself.

That nice neat box? I'd take it over this, any day.

Staring vacantly, watching the change in light as afternoon creeps toward evening, my eyes settle on something, a faint sense of something wrong crowding in on me.

The journal.

It rests on the table, where Lucas left it. Open to the page he wanted me to read.

A flash of anger rises in me. Did he think he could trick me into reading it? That my curiosity would get the better of me?

That I might skim over a dead guy's journal, like some light entertainment for the afternoon?

Angrily I slam it shut and throw it toward the front door. It lands, pages spreadeagled, bent and exposed, and I feel guilty. Aaron's words deserve respect, whoever he is. I might not want to read it, but it's not mine, and it's not for me to throw or trash. I stumble over to it, pins and needles stinging outwards from the ball of one foot. God, how long have I been on the couch?

Grimacing, I smooth the pages flat and close it gently.

Then I return to my silent vigil on the couch.

The sentences don't come yet. I think in sentences: whole, fully formed. Coherent conversations in my head. I had a friend once who thought in music. We had stared at each other, baffled. I couldn't imagine how one sorted out what one was thinking or feeling without a constant stream of dialogue in one's head. He couldn't understand how one would survive such endless, diverting, maddening chatter. He loved his days being narrated to music. Always fucking masterpieces, too, by all accounts.

Now, on the couch, I want to think in music. Not dramatic music, not a masterpiece. Something beautiful and gentle. Something to wrap around me, to cushion me, to shroud me in soft, misty, ethereal light while I move through this. Instead of moving through it with dialogue, heavy and hard. Music to lift me up, carry me through it. Not words, with their hard, ugly edges, their heavy curves and pointy meanings.

Because I know when the dialogue comes, it will obliterate me. The sentences that will be thrown up, the feelings that will follow. Even with Therapist Clara to ground me, to remind me that just because I think it, doesn't mean it's true. Even with all the tricks and tools in the world to remind me of my worth.

The sentences will destroy me because I will have to feel the pain of them. I cannot flee this time. I don't have the energy. I don't even think I can get off this couch again.

38

LUCAS

BACK AT THE PROPERTY, with no memory of actually driving here, I check the horses Zoe bought, distracted.

Zoe is talking to me, but I'm finding it hard to focus. Everything seems like such a struggle. Usually the horses calm me, but right now they feel like an extra problem that I can't solve.

"You can start on them as soon as you're ready," I tell Zoe, oblivious to whatever it is she's been telling me. "Take one each. Just start with groundwork for now. No riding, ok?"

Zoe nods, looking at me strangely. Probably I failed to respond to anything she just conveyed. But suddenly I want to be alone.

"I'll be back to check on them in a few days," I tell her, the scrutiny of other eyes suddenly invasive and unsettling. The thoughts that are bubbling up in me need silence and solitude. I feel like I can't think straight, can't understand them, can't work them out.

I hurry away from her and head back to my apartment.

———

I DON'T KNOW what else to do. So I start a fucking journal.

I don't think about it, or I'll think I'm losing my shit. I don't think about what any of my friends would think, our words saved for smart-mouthed banter on yachts, over champagne in private jets. Smooth words to win over the sexiest girls. Smart words to win over clients, win contracts, make more money.

They wouldn't believe for a second that Lucas Evans was writing about his feelings in a *journal*.

They wouldn't even think I had any feelings, actually. My life looks pretty breezy on the outside. Girls, toys, travel. Nothing to write home about. Nothing to cry over.

My life was pretty breezy, actually. Until Aaron's fucking journals cracked something open in my heart and let something murky out.

———

Dear Clara,

Of course I'm going to write it to you.

There's some kind of symmetry to that. My brother wrote to you. At least, I thought he did.

He brought us together. Though the word together *is a stretch in any sense of the word. I don't think we have any sort of "together" now.*

He had these big fucking feelings, Aaron. About you, about the world. He always did. Even as a kid.

Now I have these big fucking feelings. It's like his words have broken loose something in me. Something denied, repressed. For all these years.

I don't know anything about therapy. If I had to say anything, I'd say you'd come up with some Freudian shit about my mother. I've never thought about it like that. I never felt like I was damaged. I felt like I was the epitome of success. I ticked all the boxes we were taught to tick.

I just didn't realise how meaningless it all was until now.

I feel so crazy about Aaron. About what he went through, what he felt. It rings something inside me, insistent, unrelenting. Because when I think back, way back, I do remember feeling things. Bad things.

Alone. Unloved. Not good enough.

Is that what he felt when he died? Are they the last feelings he experienced?

I want to kill someone for him.

I don't think he was crazy.

I think her malevolence poisoned him.

But then what did her malevolence do to me?

I pause in my scribbling, the pen poised midair, my thoughts moving too quickly to write them down.

Even I don't know what I'm looking for anymore. I had wanted answers.

Answers of some kind.

Why Clara—whoever the right Clara is—didn't help my brother.

Why he wrote to her obsessively for months. Books and books and books of scribbled thoughts, rambling and incoherent. Contradicting each other. Splashed with tears.

Even an imbecile could see that he needed help. The entries reference a desire not to be here or a desire to die on countless occasions. How did no one see it? Why did no one help him?

But even as I think that, the most painful thing—the thing I don't want to think about at all because it's unbearable, it shreds me—keeps rising up:

Why didn't I see it?

Why didn't I help him?

Where the fuck was I through all of this?

I glare at the pen, shake my head, start writing again:

The pain of all of it got misdirected. I didn't want to think about losing him, leaving him, not being a big brother to him.

Not helping him.

What it all said about my experiences too. If he was that fucked up,
how was I? Was I okay?

So I think I just felt angry instead.

So much easier to feel anger than to feel pain.

He wrote about that, actually. Sometimes his entries seemed so
wise. So together. So much more insightful than me.

Other times they didn't even make any sense.

It seems so stupid now. What a waste of energy. I plotted to meet
you. I didn't even have a plan. I wanted to accuse you of something.
Malpractice. Being responsible. As if, when I placed the blame on
someone else, I would be absolved. Something else would be at stake
here. Not my family. Not my mess. Something neat and external I
could box up. A professional failure. A way to keep it separate from me.
So I could go back to my normal life. Untouched by it.

I stop writing again.

God. This journaling. Thoughts I didn't know I had are
spilling out of me onto the page. Insights. Motivations. It's
addictive, mesmerising. I can't stop, my hand moving over the
page compulsively, barely knowing what I'm going to write before
it's there on the page in front of me, wild and messy and painful
to see.

Is this how Aaron felt, writing? Writing to you?

Afraid to continue, but also afraid to stop, I put the pen tip
against the paper again. It feels like it starts moving of its own
accord.

The anger has fizzled out. Now, just emptiness.

I've been so closed off with people; I've kept my emotions so far in
check that I don't feel like I've actually had any. My life has been on
automatic pilot for so long. Win. Succeed. Achieve things. I didn't even
know that I wasn't happy until I met you. I saw something moving
behind your eyes and wanted some of it. I think it was a FEELING.
How stupid is that. I looked at you and thought perhaps that I might
like to feel something?

Perhaps I am just as crazy as Aaron. Writing shit like this to someone I don't know? Writing stuff that makes no sense? Wanting things that I've invented?

Or have I just caught a glimpse of something that I've been missing all these years—the thing that happens when you get close to someone?

You look at me like you wouldn't judge me for being sidelined by memories of being pushed under a cold shower as a fucking child, for Christ's sake.

But maybe I'm imagining it. Maybe all of Aaron's crazy journal entries are fucking with my mind.

Reading the messy thoughts of an unwell dead person might do that to a man, I think.

———

I FIND myself staring into space again, the pen limp in my hand. I don't know if ten minutes or an hour has passed. My hand feels heavy, writing suddenly an effort.

In the days after his death I could barely focus.

My whole body seemed to zing with electricity. Thoughts didn't carry on along their normal orderly paths. They shot all over the place, confused and blurry. Sparking. Burning things.

Our mother showed up at my office with the photo from when she'd identified the body. (Was that even legal? Are you allowed to do that, if your son is a grown man? Are you allowed to do it at all?) Self-important in other, new ways—now a grieving mother, needing things from me.

Always taking things, our mother.

The boxes. Four boxes, delivered to my home, the address written neatly, orderly. No indication of the disorder and madness inside them. All the things he valued in his life, apparently. Tattered notebooks filled with garbled scrawl. Pages and pages and pages of them. To *Dr. Black*—or *Clara*, when he was feeling more familiar, perhaps.

Some photos, a musty hand-knitted scarf, some awards from high school.

Not much if one was to narrate his life from these boxes.

No note. No explanation. Just the journals.

Sent to me on the day he died.

I start writing again, slowly this time.

I got lost in reading.

It became apparent how much I didn't know my brother.

How desperately I didn't want his life to be tied to mine in any way.

So I blamed you. If I blamed you, then it had nothing to do with me. With my family. My childhood. My memories, tattered and broken and ugly and painful. And suddenly larger, larger than life.

I tried to shut them out and revel in the anger.

Because feeling things? Painful things? I didn't do that. I won at things. All the things.

These creeping feelings? Sinewy and sly and wrapping round me like a deathly, choking vine that you don't even notice until you can't breathe anymore? Painful feelings?

They felt like losing things.

Losing all the things that mattered.

———

As I sit there, thinking and writing, there's nothing for it but to face the truth I've hidden from.

There are many painful truths.

My mother didn't love me and it hurt me. I've never been able to frame it quite so simply before.

But the most painful one, the one that kills me:

She mustn't have loved Aaron either. And somehow we came out differently. I fled and did everything *just so*. If I was brilliant and perfect on the outside, then I was loveable, right? On the inside?

But Aaron did something else. Aaron self-combusted. He needed someone, and I wasn't there. I didn't even notice. I was so busy showing everyone that I was perfect that I let him down.

And all that perfect counts for nothing when your brother dies.

39

CLARA

MY PHONE BUZZES, waking me.

It's dark outside, and my neck and back are aching.

Miraculously, I fell asleep on the couch. I can usually never fall asleep anywhere but a bed in a quiet room. But somehow of late I've been managing it in strange places. The couch. Lucas's car.

Lucas.

The memory of his visit settles back over me, itchy and grey. But I push it aside and check my phone.

Gary.

In the chaos of the day, I'd forgotten all about him. But it's just past ten o'clock and I let it run to voicemail. Despite the way our last date ended—or maybe because of the way it ended—I still haven't worked out what I want to do about that arrangement.

Along with my cricked neck, I feel emotionally hungover. But physically, the sleep has rebooted me. I feel capable of moving. My thinking is clearer, less foggy. Which is good. Because I have some decisions to make.

———

UNDER THE HOT spray of the shower, I close my eyes and lean my forehead against the tiles. The water beats against my back, comforting and firm. Minutes tick by. I feel warm. I feel better.

As I let the warmth and calm envelop me, a memory brushes against my eyelids, hazy and fleeting, and I start backwards, water hitting my face, running into my eyes.

Aaron.

Oh my God.

I did know Aaron.

40

LUCAS

THE LAST TIME I saw Aaron was about eight months before he died.

He'd shown up at my office with a couple of cheap take-away sandwiches and said, "Let's go eat in the park."

My office is opposite the Fitzroy Gardens—a beautiful spot to chat and eat. But it was an overcast day, the air thick with potential rain, the wind swirling outside, blowing rubbish around in that gusty way that Melbourne alleyways are wont to. In the streets below, I could see people huddling into their scarves, hands deep in pockets, leaning into the wind. Eating in the park with my aimless kid brother was the last thing I wanted to do.

"I have a meeting in twenty," I lied. "Let's eat here. Thanks for bringing lunch." I eyed his offerings warily. Five-dollar sandwiches were not my usual lunch fare.

"So, what's up?" I asked, wondering what he wanted. He'd never asked me for money. He'd never even asked me for advice. He was living in a share house, working in a bar. He looked handsome but wistful.

I hadn't seen him for about a year, since I helped him move

into his new house. It wasn't the first one since living with Mum. He'd been share-housing since leaving school. Drifting through life without purpose. But usually he looked bouncy, charming, irreverent. *Bigger*. He usually looked bigger than this.

"It's been a while," he said. "Just thought I'd say hi."

He never asked about my business, my life. I felt like he was a stranger. I couldn't think of anything to say.

"So, any thoughts about your career?" I settled on eventually, sounding more like a nagging parent than a big brother. Though God knows, we both could have used a parent who actually cared.

Ten years younger than me, he and I couldn't have been more different. I never knew his father, a "mistake" my mother had had briefly in between girlfriends. By the time Aaron came along, the air of our childhood home was already thick with hatred and regrets. I was battling my own loneliness. I barely thought about my new baby brother. What life must have been like for him. When Mum's hatred—of the whole world, it seemed to me—had had ten years to flourish. Grow roots and loom large. Cast our entire lives in a putrid shadow.

Now, I wonder about his arrival. The morning-after pill was already around. Our mother had already instilled in me—ten years old, quiet and careful and lonely—just how deeply she regretted my arrival. As I ponder this as a 33-year-old—new to journaling, new to thinking a little deeper about my family—it occurs to me that there was something wrong and damaged and painful in her to choose to continue on with another pregnancy. For all of us. But for her as well.

I'm pulled out of my memories by my phone. It's my PI, Alex.

"I can't be sure," he says. "But I've dug around a little. I can't find anything to suggest that Aaron saw Clara professionally. Or saw any psych, for that matter. At least, not through Medicare. He could have been paying cash."

I thank him for calling me on a Saturday and hang up, stare at the wall for a while.

Wonder what the fuck I should do next.

41

CLARA

THE JOURNAL LIES on the table where I left it.

I know how he died; I don't have to look inside. I don't have to ask.

I pick it up, smooth the cover unnecessarily. The gesture is soothing and I keep running my hands over it, again and again. I imagine I can feel the strength and the pain and the ripples of the words inside. The magnitude.

The air feels tinny, electric. I knew Aaron, but I didn't *really* know Aaron. Yet somehow our lives have become intertwined.

The page is still bookmarked at the entry Lucas wanted me to read. I stare and stare at that little ridge. The corner folded over firmly, crisply. Something strong and manly even about the way he marked the spot. The rest of the pages' edges are worn, ink smudging across them, soft rather than crisp. The folds fat with pages swollen by moisture. Fat with thoughts, feelings.

Pain, I'm guessing.

Heavy with a pain that must have felt larger than life.

I don't know why, but brushing up against Aaron's journal is clarifying. I place it carefully back on my coffee table and sit on my couch. Jasper creeps onto my lap and circles tentatively before curling into me, his head bumping lightly against my hand.

I stroke him absentmindedly, staring at the wall.

My breathing is calm.

My heart is steady.

And by the time I'm in my bed, I know what I need to do about Gary.

———

AFTER HE KISSED me on the pier—it feels like a lifetime ago—he had proposed we go back to his room.

It was the perfect moment to suggest it. The wine, the dinner, the walk on the pier. The summer breeze and the twinkling stars appearing overhead. My body thrumming under his caresses.

He *was* an expert. Kind and funny and sexy. And no doubt knew exactly what to do to a woman's body to make it sing.

But I couldn't do it. I couldn't even understand it at the time. I shrugged it off as *I'm just not ready yet*—because what gentleman can argue with that? I couldn't explain it any further. I didn't understand it myself.

But I understand it now.

As it turns out, I want the very thing I'm hiding from so desperately. So crazily.

I want to be known.

I want someone to see me fully and choose me. Gary didn't feel right because he didn't know me; he doesn't want to know me. He wants to have fun with me, spoil me, have a classy, hassle-free date for his work functions—but his interest is superficial. Glancing off me like a poorly aimed butter knife, a dull and blunted blade.

I have always resisted being known. Waited until someone came in with a sledgehammer. Saw me trying to deflect them, and smashed my walls down anyway. It's not that I *want* to stay hidden. It's not that it's a game to me. It's just defensive: only letting close the people who really wanted to know me. Who *fought* to know.

It wasn't foolproof, I know that. It wasn't even reasonable. But it felt like a small way to protect myself.

But maybe I just missed out on closeness with many people who might have cared an awful lot.

Beth once likened me to a sentry hiding inside a triple-reinforced iron-sealed locked room. "Only there's no windows. And no door. And no cracks. And just in case by a miracle someone manages to get in—you're waiting in there with a double-barrelled shotgun, anyway," she said.

"That doesn't make any sense," I'd replied. "Doesn't sound like I could even breathe in there. Wouldn't you run out of oxygen and die? What would you even do in there?"

"That's not life," I'd complained. "That's death."

She had just stared and stared at me without response.

———

SOME PEOPLE NEED to hear the words; some need to see the actions; but me—I need to feel known.

Feeling invisible is the worst thing.

It's late, but I call Gary anyway. I explain that, as it turns out, an arrangement like this is not for me.

He's disappointed, but not unkind. He refuses to accept the return of any money or gifts. "You enjoy them," he says, gracious as ever.

"What are you going to do?" he asks.

"I'm going to try to be open to love," I say.

Then I put in my earplugs and, despite the whirlwind day, the clamouring thoughts, the sadness and hurt, I somehow fall into a deep and restful sleep.

42

CLARA

When the knock comes at the door, I'm not surprised. I'm not even upset.

I gesture Lucas in again without a word.

The journal is lying on the coffee table, closed now, but pretty much where Lucas left it.

"Did you read it?" he asks, no pleasantries. Just getting straight into it.

"No," I reply, gazing at him steadily.

"You're not surprised to see me," he says. "You're not angry, either."

It's a statement, not a question.

I feel like I've been laid bare to myself. And somehow, vulnerability doesn't seem like such a big deal.

I think of Brene Brown, her research on vulnerability. For the first time, her words make sense to me.

Vulnerability is neither comfortable nor unbearable—it's just necessary.

It's a beautiful sentiment and I have battled and raged against it. And suddenly, now, I don't know why.

"I remember Aaron," I say. Lucas and I stare at each other. He looks raw, exposed. I feel the same way.

"He came into the club a few times. He just wanted to talk. That happened a lot to me for a while," I shrug, the gesture summarising the broad confusion, the incongruence of that. "It was like somehow people could sense I was a therapist in another life."

We stare at each other some more. He has dark stubble accentuating the line of his jaw, his dark eyes. His shiny, winsome, golden boy glow is gone, his veneer stripped from him.

His armour, perhaps.

I wonder if mine is missing too. I feel like he might be Beth; he might be anyone. I don't worry about protecting myself.

Death might do that, I think. Pare everything back to the basics.

I keep talking. Not censoring myself.

"He only came a handful of times. He didn't tell me much. But he looked distressed. He said that he couldn't find any purpose in life. That he didn't know why he felt so bad all the time. Of course I asked him about suicide. He assured me he wasn't suicidal. He had no plans, no date. But I thought he needed to see someone. He wanted to see me.

"You know, in a therapy relationship, there'd be follow up. I'd check in. I'd be seeing him again the next week. I'd monitor his risk. But I met him in a strip club in a g-string. He'd had a lap dance. It wasn't professional. I said no. He pressed a bit, but then accepted it. He didn't hassle me. But he knew my real name because I gave him the names of some other therapists. I said to say that I sent him...and then I didn't know why. It was a stupid thing to say. Maybe I thought he'd get an appointment quicker. Because another therapist thought he needed to see someone. But I didn't think about the circumstances. If they'd ask why he wasn't seeing me. I remember worrying later if he'd out me, tell the therapist that 'Clara Black who is also Zefi the stripper sent me.' I wished I hadn't given him my name. But he seemed gentle and kind. I chose not to worry. I forgot about it."

While I talk, our eyes stay glued together. I can't read Lucas's expression. It doesn't matter. It doesn't matter if he stalked me for some weird reason or if he hates me or if he used me. Or if I dared to hope that he might like me. His brother is dead. Tears prick at my eyes. The sadness of it. The waste.

"He never saw anyone. As far as I can find out."

"I'm sorry," I whisper. "I'm so sorry."

I don't know how he interprets my "sorry." I mean it at face value. I'm sorry your brother died. I'm sorry he's not here anymore. I'm sorry for your pain, your loss. The grief that makes mad men of us all, if we let it. If we dare to let ourselves feel something.

But also if we refuse to feel it at all.

Does he think I'm sorry that I didn't see Aaron as a client? I don't suppose it even matters.

I'm just sorry about all this pain. Aaron's and his and mine and ours.

Everyone's.

————

WE SIT in silence for a long time. I break eye contact first, the intensity of it too heavy, too raw, hanging between us like both a lifeline and a lead sinker.

"Our mother damaged him," he says eventually. He looks angry. "But we both got the same shit. And I'm fine." A tic starts in the corner of his right eye. His wrath is growing. He looks anything but fine.

Those stories that we tell ourselves.

For a while he struggles, thoughts and feelings rumbling across his face, indecipherable to me, though I could take a guess.

Suicide leaves so many questions.

Why did he kill himself?

Why didn't he ask for help?

Why didn't he come to me?

And the biggest ones:

What did I do wrong? Where did I fail him?

I try to short-circuit whatever is going through his mind.

"You'll probably never know the reasons why," I say gently. "We can know a lot of things. We can put together some sort of picture. You probably have some idea from his journals. But grieving a suicide is so difficult because we can't definitively put it to rest. We can't dot the i's and cross the t's. We don't know what we could have done. We don't know what was under the surface. We don't know so many things about what was going on, how it felt to him. How he thought about it.

"If it helps, we *do* know that the majority of people who suicide have a mental illness at the time of their death, whether it's diagnosed or not. And we do know that it's very unlikely that there's just one trigger—not one thing anyone said or did. More the accumulation of many things that felt so bad to him. Made him feel hopeless. Like he would feel like that forever."

I fall silent, letting my words sink in, or not.

"It's no one's fault," I say, meaning, *it's not your fault. You didn't do this.* But a flash of anger lights up his eyes.

"Isn't it?" he hisses, sliding the journal back toward me. "Read that and tell me it's no one's fault. Read all of it."

He stands and starts pacing around my living room. The anger rolling off him is tangible; I can almost smell it. Feel it's dank heaviness slinking around me, curling into me. His anger is alive, and it doesn't want to be alone in this.

"Does it help?" I ask him softly. "Blaming someone?"

He stiffens, clenches his fists. Spins toward me.

For a second I have a flash of fear that he's going to hit me.

And then he crumples to the floor and cries.

SITTING on the floor behind him, one hand gently circling his shoulder blades, soothing him, I feel the change in his body as soon as it occurs. A lengthening, a slackening. Tightly coiled hurt becoming something else.

I tense up in response. Soothing time is over.

He rolls onto his back, stretches out on the wooden floorboards. My focus gets inexplicably stuck on the floorboards. *This is not comfortable. Comfort before the next thing.* It's like a hitch in my thinking that I keep circling back to, trying to resolve, because it's tangible and solvable and everything else seems too enormous and too uncertain for my thoughts to settle comfortably upon.

Our eyes meet. He looks, suddenly, magnificent. Muscles rippling as he moves. Eyes wild with something primal and beautiful and untamed. And suddenly, the floorboards are forgotten after all.

Without speaking, he takes my hand and pulls me to him, certain and slow. And just like that, he's back in control.

I wonder how not being in control felt to him: if this is his armour, perhaps. Is this him connecting with me or disconnecting from himself?

But it doesn't even matter.

My thoughts scatter away in the here and now of this.

His lips are warm and soft. Gentle, even.

He runs his tongue along my upper lip, flicking inside my mouth, not a question but an assertion. His eyes are open, watching me.

Then he pulls back and gently pushes me to the floor, yanking a cushion off the couch to place beneath my head.

"Tell me what you want," he murmurs.

But I can't speak.

I just stare at him. His beautiful jawline. His dark, haunted eyes. The way his shoulders move above me.

"I just want to see you," he whispers, and something opens up inside of me. I don't care how he means it. It's good enough for me.

I sit up slowly, my eyes not leaving his, and push him back so that he's lying on the floor, moving the cushion beneath his head. Then I slowly unbutton his shirt. After each button, I pull the shirt open further, running my hands across the new skin that it exposes. For the first time in my life, I do what feels right to me. What I want. Not thinking about if I am pleasing him. I just want to touch him. Traverse him. Slowly and in wonder.

It's almost like he senses this; he keeps very still. Like I'm a wary deer and any sudden movement might send me bounding away. His eyes flick from my hands to my eyes. His breathing is deepening, his chest rising and falling under my fingers. His hands are laced behind his head.

Slowly, slowly, I keep exploring his torso. His muscles are well-defined, but not huge. His stomach feels hard and smooth beneath my fingers. I trace the lines that run down in a V toward his crotch. It's almost non-sexual, the way I want to touch him. Just marvelling at him. How beautiful he is, and how I can touch him. How I can look. Slowly lingering over each muscle, each groove.

Finally his shirt is completely unbuttoned and I push it off his shoulders. They are so beautiful. I've rarely thought of men as beautiful before. But his shoulders are so toned, so sculpted, the bicep bulging out perfectly beneath them. Maybe it's the juxtaposition of that strength, that beauty against the fragile realm of death and pain and suffering. Tears. He looks more beautiful than I can bear.

Tentatively I lean forward, my hair falling against his chest, and run light kisses down his arm, pulling it free from behind his head. I grasp his thumb, running my finger over and over it. I don't even know what I'm doing. I just want to touch all of him.

I run my fingers from his collarbone down to a nipple, feeling the small hard bud beneath the pad of my finger. Abruptly, I lean forward and lick it, my tongue swirling around it. He groans, his hand gripping mine, his eyes closing. Emboldened, I nibble at it lightly, pulling my teeth over it gently.

He groans again. Louder. Deeper.

I look up at him through my hair, loving that he is lying there, that I am in control of this. I've always thought that I like the man being in control. That I like being possessed, dominated. Knowing that he is doing what he likes so I don't have to worry about whether I'm meeting his needs. But this. This is a revelation. It's a miracle. I can just explore him here, all for my pleasure. Touching, feeling, learning him. Giving him pleasure accidentally. A side effect of my explorations.

Sitting back up, watching him closely, I start to undo his jeans. The button. The zipper. I pull down his briefs a bit, slowly trailing my fingers along the muscles plunging down toward his crotch, the wiry fuzz of hair that I've exposed. And still he doesn't move. Just breathes heavily. His eyes are still closed. Bliss across his face, but something else too. Something intimate. Open.

I don't know what we're doing. Counteracting suicide, perhaps. Affirming life. Affirming closeness. It doesn't even matter what it means. It feels revolutionary. It feels like home.

Gently I lift my leg across and straddle him, my hands trailing up his sides and down his arms. His eyes open again and I pull my shirt over my head, still watching him. Then I unclasp my bra and shrug it off too. His hands stray to my thighs, then my waist. Then he runs one hand from my throat down to my belly button.

"You're so beautiful," he whispers.

"So are you," I whisper back.

Then he sits up so we're nearly at eye level. One hand wraps around my waist and the other snakes behind my head, grasping my neck as he kisses me deeply, hungrily, feasting on my mouth, his tongue running over my lips, teasing my tongue, suddenly possessive and demanding again. Holding me like I am the only precious thing in the entire world.

And suddenly my slowness, my gentleness is unsatisfactory. I no longer want to explore. I want him immediately. I throw my head back as he kisses my neck, my collarbone, finding my nipple and sucking it urgently, deeply. Then we're both fumbling our pants off, coming unstuck as we wrestle reluctant jeans over feet and ankles, crashing back together, the floorboards digging into my knees but it doesn't matter, because I need him inside me, now, immediately, and seeing my need he lifts me up, positions himself and pulls me back down on top of him, his cock sliding into me the most perfect, most important thing I can imagine.

I lean back, my hands grasping his knees, his hands massaging my breasts, then grasping my hips and moving me up and down the length of his cock, urgent and deep, both of us panting and gasping. He's barely started moving me when I fling myself forward, grinding down onto him, letting out a long cry that is almost a sigh. My insides clench his cock deliciously. I wrap my arms around his neck, burying my face in him, letting my orgasm wash over and over and over me. I feel completely exposed and completely safe.

Eventually I pull away from his neck and look at him. He picks me up, still hard inside me, and carries me to my bed. Then he lies on top of me and starts moving again, his fingers brushing against my sides, my breasts, my jaw, his thrusts deep and hard, slowly getting faster, harder. My tits are shuddering with each thrust inside me and he's staring at them, his eyes hooded, lustful. He looks so sexy, so primal. I can feel my excitement building again.

"You. Feel. So. Good." He grunts out with each thrust. "Do you like that? Do you like my cock there? Do you feel how hard I am for you?"

I have never talked dirty to anyone in my life. I love that he wants to talk about hard cocks while he fucks me. It's so raw, so guttural. So honest.

"Yes," I whisper, hoarse, wide open to him, my body, my soul. My openness terrifying and beautiful.

"Harder. More," I say, louder, stronger this time, reaching for him, pulling him into me. Closer, deeper.

He groans, grasping one calf and pulling it up over his shoulder, his hands on either side of my head, the position allowing his cock deeper inside me. It's almost too much. Too much depth, too much closeness.

"I want all of you," he groans into my thigh, then thrusts into me so hard that a cry escapes my lips. His need, his urgency is consuming, pushing me further, higher. But somehow I also want to scrabble away from him.

It's too beautiful.

It's too intense.

———

LATER, I am lying beside him. We are both staring at the roof, not speaking. Both feeling, what? Something. It flows out of him; it flows out of me. Some sort of perfection. It's terrifying. Terrifying that it exists at all; terrifying that it may not last. All it is is air, currents of air swirling from him to me and me to him. How precious, how fragile, how uncertain it seems. I want to box it. Capture it and put a lid on it and keep it where it can't escape. Is this love? Because in a box it would be no good to either of us. It would just be stale air. But if we just let it float around like this— what's to keep it here? What's to stop it from just floating away?

He leans over and kisses me. Languid and deep and slow and perfect. I am filled with pain. I don't know if there is enough room inside of me to feel every feeling that is threatening to overwhelm me. I'm scared that I will drown in it. I'm scared that once I let this feeling into my whole body I will never escape from it; that once receptive to love I will always require it. This feeling, this openness, this knowing what connection is—I will never escape it again. And it will be wonderful. But it might also kill me.

Because I can no longer pretend that I don't need it.

I can no longer pretend that I don't care.

———

I MUST HAVE DOZED OFF, because when I wake, Lucas is dressing.

Watching him jerk on his jeans, his face a mask again, I murmur, "Hey you."

He doesn't respond.

He zips up his jeans with an angry wrench.

Suddenly fearful, desperate to bring him back to being open with me, I blurt out the first thing that pops into my mind, the thing we connected through: his brother, his grief. I ask if he'd like to see someone. His head jerks up and he stares at me in disbelief.

"A therapist. I can find someone who specialises in grief after suicide." Already I know it was the wrong thing to say.

"I don't need a fucking *therapist*," he spits at me and I'm stunned at the hostility in his voice.

"What's wrong?" I ask, my voice a squeak, no idea what has happened in the space of a short nap to warrant his change in demeanour. Reality once again rendered unreal, unstable, useless.

Openness is going to kill me possibly sooner than I'd imagined, I think to myself.

"You tell me," he snarls at me, the man I just spent an hour naked in bed with—naked in my body and naked in my heart— completely vanished. "You tell me about fucking Gary."

But he doesn't give me a chance to. He's walked out the door.

43

LUCAS

I WAS WATCHING her sleep when the text came through.

She looked less extravagant this time, more vulnerable. Young and soft and striking. Something about her sleeping triggered a desire in me to protect her, look out for her. Something masculine and possessive yet somehow vulnerable in me as well. That desire to *care* about someone. To know them.

To trust them.

Then Alex texted. The perfect juxtaposition to my unfurling, tender, baby-shoot feelings. To her "vulnerability."

Found out something else. She's a sugar baby. She has a sugar daddy called Gary Watt through Seeking Arrangement. He's 52, lives in Sydney. They see each other once or twice a month. He pays her 5K a month. Here's a pic.

He looked nice enough. Tan, cheerful, friendly. Not seedy, not gross.

But I feel so duped. Even though I know I went to her. I kissed her. I cried in front of her. She told me never to contact her again, yet I did all of those things. And it felt so right. So natural. We felt so *connected.*

She made love to me like she cared, she touched me like I was fucking *electric*, she moaned my name like I was the only one who'd ever made her feel like that...even though she's seeing someone else. Fucking some old dude for money. What the fuck is wrong with this girl?

Impulsively, I delete her from my contact list, rev the hell out of my car, and burn rubber in my haste to leave her and her stupid weird-ass sexual choices behind me forever.

44

CLARA

STUNNED by Lucas's abrupt departure, I sit naked in bed for quite some time. Curiously, mainly what I feel is irritation.

Who the fuck doesn't wait for an answer before storming off like a teenager?

And sure, I know, the guy's messed up about his brother. I know better than anyone how grief can mess with a person. But, really? The storm off?

Sighing, I text him a brief message—*I'm not seeing him anymore.* Then I get ready for the practice.

———

"I'VE BEEN READING *The Bell Jar,*" Kate tells me.

"Light," I deadpan.

She grins.

"I like the scene where Esther tries to swim out to sea. And then to dive to drown herself. But she kept popping back up. Is it wrong that I found that so funny? But I related somehow. Bloody life. It keeps spitting you back up and forcing you to endure it.

There's no escape. And it doesn't feel bad. It just feels...relentless. And I think I've made some progress and then...I haven't."

"Sometimes it can be helpful to think about better coping, rather than perfect coping. To reward yourself for one choice, one day. Rather than expecting to be 'cured,'" I tell her. "To be 'perfect.'"

Kate thinks about this for a moment.

"I like that," she says eventually. "It makes change achievable. One choice at a time. And being kinder to myself is something I definitely need to work on. But at the end of the day...there's just another one. All these endless, endless days. I have to fill them up, try not to be horrid to myself, try to enjoy myself, try not to destroy myself...even the thought of this exhausts me. Life just keeps going and going and going. The endlessness of it. Where is the joy?"

I ponder her for a moment.

"Where do you find joy?" I ask her. "Is there anything in your life that brings you happiness?"

"Yeah, sure," she says. "But it doesn't last. It's fleeting. It feels like survival is my baseline. Not joy."

"Well. There are two things I'd like to say about that. The first is that life can be hard; we're not supposed to live in joy. Sometimes we're happy, sometimes we're sad, sometimes we're indifferent or angry or whatever. It's unrealistic to expect to be joyful all the time. Certainly we can choose to look at things with a glass-half-full attitude. And try to do more of the things that bring us joy and less of the things that stir up our anxieties or sadness. But they have to co-exist; it's not possible to excise one. And it can be a self-fulfilling thing: the idea that we're failing if we're not happy all the time makes us feel worse. Rather than it just being the reality of being human.

And the other thing I suppose is that there are no quick fixes to any of these things. Some days will be better than others. It's important to not view a bad day as failure. Like progress on many things, it might be two steps forward and one step back for a little while. Even when we know things in our head, we have to allow ourselves to learn them in our hearts and bodies too. Sometimes they're slower on the uptake. And it's hard for people with perfectionistic type personalities, because you want to do it right. But there is no right here. It's a process. It takes time."

I think about this and intimacy. How well my head knows the value of being close to someone; how hard my body fights it.

How dangerous it feels.

And then I think about Lucas's last visit, and how it didn't kill me. And I think I am in fact moving. Forwards and back, to be sure. But moving.

In the general right direction.

———

WHEN I GET HOME, Lucas is waiting on my doorstep. He looks up from thumbing through his phone, guilty and embarrassed.

"I just wanted to say sorry," he says, launching to his feet. "For taking off like a jerk."

"I should think so," I say. And wait.

He seems to be waiting too, however. Sighing, I add: "Firstly, how did you know about Gary? Cause that's kind of weird. And secondly, that approach to solving problems is not going to work for me. If we have an issue, you're going to need to stay and talk about it. Screeching off in a huff has never solved any problems, ever. It just makes me think you're a dick, to be honest. Judging before asking questions and finding out my side of that story. God knows where you heard the other side."

"I know. I'm sorry. I just...I freaked out," he says, shrugging, feigning nonchalance. Then he seems to catch himself and looks me in the eyes, worried. "Usually I can take it or leave it. With you...I don't want to leave it. I don't want you to leave it. I freaked out at the thought that you could just dabble with me. I want you to want me as much as I want you."

Despite myself, my breath hitches in my throat. I want to pursue how he found out about Gary. I want to talk about this. But my eyes keep straying downwards. His white shirt pulls across his shoulders, his pecs clearly defined underneath the fabric. The sleeves are rolled to his elbows. His hair is ruffled and wild, like he's run his fingers through it in agitation a thousand times since this morning. Glancing back up, his eyes latch onto mine and cause a flutter somewhere deep in my tummy.

Whatever idiot thing he does, apparently, my body is prepared to forgive him.

"Again," I mutter, and he looks confused. "Apologising—again. Showing up uninvited—again. Disarming me with your bloody perfect bare arms—again."

I try to hide a smile, but he catches it, a finger under my chin, forcing my eyes back to his.

God, I want to kiss him.

"Playful," he murmurs, the corners of his mouth lilting upwards in that way they do, half smile, half smirk. "More than I hoped for."

"More than you deserve," I shoot back. But I quiver at his touch.

Reading the look in my eyes, he daringly runs a finger from my chin down my neck to my throat, pausing briefly, then slowly continuing down, his eyes not leaving mine. Down between the rise of my breasts, slowly slowly down to my belly button, which he circles, circles, then presses into. It's absurdly erotic. I'm already wet.

Still watching me, he bends down and takes a nipple in his mouth through my shirt and bra, seeing how far he can push me, how badly I want him. We're standing on the balcony at my front door, in full view of the street below. If any pedestrians stopped to look... The only break in their view is the feeble glittering leaves on slender silver birch branches, swaying gently in the breeze.

My heart is hammering in my chest, my breathing ragged.

"Not here," I squeak, fumbling for my keys, but he grips my hips insistently, sucking me through my shirt, his eyes fastened on mine and daring me to push him off.

Laughing, embarrassed, horny as all fuck, I finally get the key in the lock and stumble inside, pulling him with me. His breathing is heavy too, his cock straining against his jeans.

He throws me onto the couch and stands above me.

"Don't move," he growls.

"We should talk," I pant, but am already unbuttoning my jeans, running my hand over my breasts—the wet patch over my nipple where he sucked me. I feel glazed, hopeless, desperate. I want his cock inside me so badly.

He groans, watching me. Then: "Take your pants off."

I oblige, yanking my jeans off in one swift motion, throwing them to the floor, my eyes not leaving his. Then I slip one hand down my underwear, flicking my fingers lightly across my clit. I moan and arch, close to coming already.

God, what this man does to my body.

"*Fuck,* you are hot," he murmurs, watching my hands, his own hands working on his zipper, pushing his pants and underwear down to mid thigh, his cock springing free. "Keep touching yourself. Touch your tits with the other hand."

Eyes closed, I'm trying to stroke myself slowly, draw out my pleasure, when I hear him drop down on the floor next to me.

"Open your eyes," he commands, then reaches for my underwear and I lift my hips so he can pull them off me.

"Come to the edge of the couch. I want to see all of you."

I wriggle down so my ass is at the edge of the couch, my legs on either side of him. He uses two fingers to open up my slick folds, staring at the depths of me, fixated.

"Keep touching. Put your fingers inside," he instructs me, his eyes not leaving my opening.

I slide one finger down the length of myself, thick with my desire, the smooth slickness exciting me further—I'm ready for him already. Then I slide one finger in.

"*Fuck,*" hisses Lucas. "More."

I slide my finger out and then slide two back in, pushing in as far as I can, lifting my ass off the couch for greater penetration, moaning. Then I withdraw them and slowly circle my clit some more.

"Now you," I whisper, eyes on his straining cock. It's inches from my cunt and I want him to push it into me so badly. But I also want to watch him stroke it.

On his knees, he grips it firmly and starts sliding his fist up and down, slowly. His eyes are still on my cunt, my fingers lazily swirling around my clit then disappearing inside of me.

"That's so hot," he whispers. "More."

With my other hand I undo the buttons on my shirt, tease my nipples through my bra, flicking and tweaking them. My lips are parted and I'm panting, trying not to come yet, wanting this sensation to last so much longer. But, aside from our two divine encounters, I've been starved of this—actual, real, hot, sweaty sex—for so long that just watching him stroke himself is enough to make me come.

His fist is moving faster up and down his cock, a little pearl beading at the tip, his breathing matching his pumping fist.

"You have such a pretty pussy," he murmurs, his eyes glazed, the tip of his cock so tantalisingly close to me. I arch my hips up, trying to get closer, panting.

"I want to fuck you," I gasp at him, my voice strange in my ears, my fingers moving faster, inching toward him. He moves away, mesmerised by my fingers, my wet slit.

"Not yet," he says.

"Please," I beg. "Put it in me." I keep edging further off the edge of the couch, trying to get contact, reach the tip of his cock, thinking if he can just feel it against me he'll have no choice but to slide it in; he won't be able to help himself.

"Put what where?" Suddenly he's grinning at me, handsome and teasing and hot as all fuck.

"Your cock. In my cunt. Please. Now."

"How will it feel?" His words come out in little growls, deep and commanding, but a smile is still playing around the corners of his mouth.

"So big. So hard. So perfect. Please." I'm gasping, my fingers rubbing frantically, my pleasure building so much I no longer care if it's his cock or my fingers, when he grasps my hips and thrusts inside me with one hard, deep thrust. I cry out with the pleasure of it, the satisfaction, finally.

Panting, still buried inside me, he lifts me up, my legs around his waist, and lays me on my kitchen table so he can stand, his forearms resting on either side of my head.

"Tell me it's the only cock you want," he says in my ear, licking and nibbling my neck, his breath hitching, his hips still. I push against him, push into him, trying to get some traction, some friction against my clit, but he grabs my hands and pins them above my head.

"Say it," he commands, and I'm writhing helplessly underneath him, desperate for more.

"I want your cock. Only yours," I pant. "Now please. Fuck me."

Still leaning over me, rotating his hips in tiny circles, he grins down at me devilishly. "Tell me you'll take me anywhere. Any time I want to lick you or fuck you. You'll spread your legs. You'll take my cock."

"Oh God," I moan. "Anywhere. Any time. On my balcony. In your car. You just have to touch me and I'm wet. Godamnit will you...please..."

He grins, releasing my hands slowly, his fingers travelling down my torso, tracing the curve of my breasts, my waist.

Then he starts moving and everything else recedes to irrelevant. The table, the kitchen, the world. Words. Meanings. There's just Lucas, moving on top of me, inside me, his breath hot against my neck, in my hair. Our bodies pressed together, moving together, clammy and unrestrained and utterly perfect. I don't even know which sounds come from me and which from Lucas, I'm so lost in pleasure. I've never abandoned myself so fully to sex before. The crescendo is deafening. I can't even distinguish the sounds from the sensations.

Lucas comes with me, thrusting hard and fast, moaning into my hair, his cock flexing and straining inside me, his hands all over me.

I feel possessed, completed, spent.

He carries me gently to the bedroom. Then we sleep.

Entwined. Entangled. Perfect.

———

"WILL you tell me why you really strip?" Lucas asks me.

We're lying in my bed, in the warm, languid, hopeful post-sex glow. Where anything feels possible. Love. Happily ever after.

Oxytocin, I mutter to myself.

"Are you going to tell me how you suddenly knew about Gary?" I shoot back lightly, cocking my head to the side, raising my eyebrows at him. "Also, I don't strip anymore," I add.

I roll away from him, stretching luxuriously, hoping to distract him with the curve of my butt, feeling evasive and kind of irritated. Which is unfair. I'm conscious that he is trying to know me. There's something endearing about his boyish enthusiasm, his desire to show me his life, his horses, his dreams.

I want him to be curious enough to ask the questions that matter. To be persistent. To take the time to find out who I am.

But he did that, and I hid from him just now.

Again.

Is it because I also want him to not take deflection for an answer? To not be quite so respectful of my obstruction? To have sharp enough edges to slice into my armour? God knows, I'm not sure I can dismantle it all by myself.

How can I explain that to him?

I want to be explored; I want to be traversed. I want every nook and cranny to be of interest to him. And I want him to want it *now*. I want him to *burn* with his need to know me.

I want him there with a torch. With that damn sledgehammer. Canvassing my depths like he'll die if he doesn't find out everything.

I need him to know me like I don't even know myself. To know me with his tongue, his hands, his mind, his soul. To paint me with his breath, brand me with his lips.

To read me with his hands so that I don't have to articulate every painful, shameful little thing that lurks inside me.

"I hired a PI to find you when your name kept coming up in Aaron's journals." That sentence brings me back to the present with a jolt.

I roll back toward him in surprise. "Seriously? That's kind of... insane." I feel like I should be angry, but somehow, I'm not.

Another thought occurs to me, though. "What exactly was he looking for?" Suddenly it seems very exposing. Intrusive.

"Where to find you. Basic facts. Your family. Your work. Qualifications. Nothing too crazy," he hastily adds, seeing the worry flit across my face.

"Hmmm. I need to think about that." I watch him for a minute, then add: "I might have some questions about that later."

He nods. "Whatever you want to know. Sure."

I'm half disappointed that he doesn't push about stripping anymore. I wonder how he knows there's more of a story there.

But I don't have time to think about it any further. He's moved on, joyful and lively.

"I have a plan," he says, grabbing me around the waist and pulling me to him. "Can you come away with me for the weekend? Surprise destination?"

His enthusiasm is infectious. The cool demeanour of that man I first met is slipping away; he's like a red setter, buoyant and bouncy and wagging his tail. Turning toward him is turning toward sunlight and away from the heavy, murky thoughts in my head.

I can totally get away for the weekend. With no stripping and no sugar-babying, my availability is wide open.

"You'll need carry-on luggage and walking shoes. I'll need to go home and get some things. I'll pick you up at eight."

What the hell, I think. Better to be bounded all over by a joyful, sexy man than sit at home ruminating about the past.

———

LUCAS HAS BOOKED us flights to who knows where. He insists I don't look at the airport departure signs. How he's going to drown out the announcement at take-off is yet to be seen.

Clasping my hand, he directs me to our seats. First class, of course.

I've brought my Kindle, but he wants to chat. He tells me about how he got into showjumping, how he learnt to ride late— how unusual that was. To have skipped Pony Club, to just teach himself. Once he had the money.

He tells me about the places he's travelled to compete, the money involved if you win.

He tells me about his favourite holidays.

Eventually, his fidgeting stills and he tells me about Aaron.

I don't even notice the destination announcements as we prepare for take-off.

45

LUCAS

SITTING NEXT TO CLARA, just flying somewhere for fun for the weekend, somehow I find myself rambling about Aaron.

Hardly a carefree escape, then.

"He was such a quiet, scrawny little kid. Always so jumpy. He reminded me of myself at that age; that's probably partly why I wanted to forget him. I didn't want to be that guy. Scared and alone. I just focused on getting the hell out of that house. I built up a persona of who I thought I was supposed to be and then I built a life around it. And every time I saw myself in Aaron, I hated him a little bit more."

I'm gripping Clara's hand tightly, but it feels nice, actually, to finally talk about Aaron. After months of trying to evade the thoughts and feelings that came up whenever he did.

"He tried to get in touch a few times after I left home, but I was always too busy. I always said I'd get back to him and I never did. I was a crappy big brother."

I mull over this thought for a few moments, turning it over in my mind, inspecting it. Because that maybe is what it all comes down to. All the rage and the shame and the heartbreak.

Clara watches me quietly. I keep talking.

"I'd built myself such a carefree, light, and happy life. I had money. Women liked me. Everything seemed to be going so well. I even tolerated Mum calling me every week. I told myself she'd probably had a hard life too. To make her so spiteful, so small. I never thought about any of it any deeper than that.

"And then Aaron died. And it knocked me flat. Even before I started reading his journals. Because all the things I never let myself think about were tied up in that. Why he was so unhappy. How we were different from all the other kids I knew, with their mothers who took them to footy or basketball practice, who made them nice lunches, who took them on picnics or to the movies on the weekend. And our house...our house was full of meanness and anger. I can't think of one single time I ever felt loved."

Clara squeezes my hand gently. She watches me steadily.

This: this is what I had thought. That she could make space for these words and they wouldn't destroy me. That I could look at this, roll it around in the open, feel the shape of it on my tongue, in my palm. The shame I feel to have left that kid all alone—so alone, he killed himself. The possibility that I could shine a light on it and still survive.

We both lapse into silence, comfortable, our hands clasped together. I had thought I'd say more, but it feels like enough. It feels like everything.

I lean over and kiss her softly. Then I lean back in my chair, close my eyes. Hold her hand tight.

Much later, she looks up from her Kindle. "The other kids, with their footy and basketball practice... They might not have had it so easy either," she says. Her tone is light, but there's something serious in her eyes. For a moment I think she's going to elaborate, but then she smiles and squeezes my hand. Goes back to her Kindle.

Leaves it at that.

46

CLARA

WE ARRIVE IN CAIRNS LATE.

The heat is still stifling, radiating off concrete, beads of perspiration forming on the taxi driver's forehead and lip.

By the time we reach our hotel, further north in Port Douglas, it's well after midnight. But I feel vibrant somehow. Alive. Shimmering with possibilities. Dark thoughts about difficult childhoods banished once again.

We fall into bed, make slow love on cool sheets, then fall asleep with our bodies entwined in all the right places.

The day is well underway by the time we wake up. For a while we lie in silence, smiling softly, stupidly at each other, the hum of the air conditioner the only sound we can hear. Lucas tucks my hair behind my ear, his thumb then lingering on my cheek, my lips.

Touches lead to kisses, which lead to more lovemaking.

It feels like we have all the time in the world.

When we finally leave the hotel, the sun is high in the sky, the heat beating down upon us.

Lucas is jubilant. I can see how much he loves it here. The heat, the seafood, the snorkelling. He pulls me around by the hand, showing me his favourite haunts. We eat and swim, eat and snorkel, eat and walk. There's something joyous about the heat and the colours. The tastes.

We make love in our room in the afternoon, then drink wine and eat canapés in a restaurant surrounded by palm trees and exotic birds all evening. And the next day he hires a boat and takes me out on the reef, just the two of us, the sun, and the ocean. It's like a magical parallel universe where anything is possible and yet at the same time the sheer joy of it is outrageous. I've never felt so light. So free.

On Sunday morning, we hire a motorbike (*Is their any vehicle this man can't drive?!*) and ride up to the Daintree, the air thick with promise. It's impossibly lush and dense and prolific. I don't want to go home. I want to stay in this heat, this beauty, this abundance forever. Suspended in between worlds. The real world—of work and death and pain and fear, and this other world—of light and laughter and joy and depth.

Love, even.

Shimmering out at us from the tropics like a promise.

47

LUCAS

WHEN I DROP Clara at home late on Sunday night, her face is flushed with joy. From what? The whirlwind weekend, the leftover heat, the time together? I don't know. I don't need to know. It feels so right just to be near her.

It was hardly long enough, but just enough. Enough to feel like there's a future here.

"Can I come in?" I ask her, and she shakes her head. But leans over to kiss me softly on the lips.

"It was wonderful. But I have an early start. I need some quiet time," she says. Then, laughing softly: "And if you stay, I'll spend all night touching you instead of sleeping."

I watch her trot up the stairs to her apartment, my mind brimming with hopes and dreams and feelings. Already I miss her soft skin, her warm lips, her long legs. Her quiet steadiness.

Back at home, I pour a whiskey and sit on my balcony and wonder how soon is too soon to call her again.

48

AARON

24ᵀᴴ JUNE 2016

When he left, you have to understand that the biggest thing that I felt was relief.

That doesn't make much sense from the outside; he'd always tried to protect me, stand up for me. Champion me. Boost my self-esteem. He was popular and kind and thoughtful and should have been an ace big brother.

But give anyone a childhood of comparisons delivered with the ruthless, pointy precision that my mother perfected, and see how much they love the victor of those spoils.

I thought—foolishly, as it turns out—that without him, her love might settle on me. Like a soft flurry of the most beautiful snow. Like a crocheted blanket, made with love. Like a warm embrace, standard from other mothers.

We never spoke about it, Lucas and I. He disappeared. We barely saw each other. Made a success of himself—I never heard the end of that, either. Bought Mum an apartment, so I guess it couldn't have been that bad. Maybe the loved child doesn't break so bad, even with a nutcase for a mother.

Maybe love is all we need, huh?

49

CLARA

SITTING ACROSS FROM SOPHIE, I'm struck by how young she looks when hopeful.

"So, I'm doing well," she beams at me.

She's talking about Dave, the guy she has started seeing. Specifically, she's talking about how she's managing herself within this possible relationship: being the person she wants to be with him. Authentic. Present.

"He wanted to try this position in bed that I don't like. And usually, I just go along with things if a partner wants them. Try not to be fussy, or difficult, or something. I don't mean just in bed. Where to go for dinner. What to do on the weekend. But I told him it wasn't a comfortable position for me. Emotionally speaking, not physically. And it was fine! I didn't go into a thirty-minute funk in my own head about whether I was being this or that or something else. I didn't try to justify it or soften it or make excuses. I just said what I preferred and we carried on. Miracle!"

She pauses for a few moments, then says: "And you know what's even better? That I could say that and actually believe, if it's not okay with him, then he's not right for me, and that's okay. *Not* that if it's not okay with me, then I'm not right for him and I have to try harder to *be* right. I could sit with the idea that I might state my needs and he might not be able to accommodate them and we might go our separate ways. I think that's the first time I've really believed that. It felt really powerful."

I think about our needs, our ability to state them, to stand by them, to not sideline them for other people's needs. How hard that is for some of us. To believe that we are worthy, just as we are. That our needs are just as valid as the next person's.

And the opposite of that: the things that we'll do to feel loveable.

The masks we'll wear to convince others, as well as ourselves.

Look what a good fit I am!

Look how good I am!

Am I loveable enough for you?

WHY DO YOU REALLY STRIP?

After my last client has left for the day, Lucas's question lodges in my brain, uncomfortable and pointy.

I remember smells. More than anything, the smells. Of stale beer on breath, stale sweat on clothes. The constant smell of cigarettes.

Sometimes, I feared that *I* would smell like that, and I would be in trouble for smoking and drinking beer. The irony that *that* was what I worried about.

I remember the words.

"You make me do this. With your short skirts and your smiles and the way you move your body. You want this as much as I do."

I don't remember the touches. The impressions of skin on skin, flesh on flesh. The way that the smells ended up on me, night after night. While my mother was at work. They're absent from my memory logs, and I don't know whether to be grateful or terrified.

But I remember the feelings when the door creaked open. The pounding of my heart. My breath leaving my body; it felt like it didn't find it's way back into my lungs until I was alone again.

I remember every time thinking that my sister would hear the creaking door, that she'd bound out of her bed in the next room to berate me for leaving my room when I should be asleep. That with her bossy voice and determined nosiness she would make everything all right. Put the world the right way up again.

Every time the door creaked, the hope flared briefly, and then died.

"It's our secret. You mustn't tell your mother. She'd be so sad that you would do this to her. She might not survive the sadness."

Children are so vulnerable. So malleable.

And everybody around me had so many needs.

And me, I was so sensitive to all these needs. I was sensitive and compliant and I gave, gave, gave. I shifted and changed and contorted myself, chameleon-like. Meeting all these needs.

I pushed down my own needs because everyone else's seemed so much more important, more urgent, more demanding. What did it matter if I needed not to be touched by my stepfather? My mother needed his love and he needed my body and I needed him to stay so that my mother would be happy. Might somehow know how hard I worked for her happiness. How good I was. How loveable.

Look what a good fit I am!

Look how good I am!

Am I loveable enough for you?

And suddenly I'm sobbing, curling into my client chair, howling at the moon for that girl, and her invisible needs, and her years of hunger, and her decades of pain. My thoughts and my rationalisations and my explanations roll away from me, elusive and brittle and not even important. And all I'm left with is the tears.

50

AARON

27TH JUNE 2016

Dear Clara,

I've been thinking about you.

For a change.

I had a flash of insight.

I always decide so quickly whether I like someone or not. Not just romantically—friendship-wise as well. I mostly don't like people, though I can fake it pretty well. I get along with people. They like me. They think I'm fun. Ha!

Anyway. Mostly it's no, no, no, no, no, no—YES.

You were the YES.

I tell myself that I always just KNOW. I follow my gut. It's never let me down. I didn't expect it to start now. Why would I?

But I don't really know, because all those no's? They might have been wonderful.

I thought that you might have been surprised by what we could have talked about. How connected we could have been. I really felt like we were a good fit.

It's interesting to reflect on the incongruity of this: the feelings of inadequacy and self-doubt on one hand, and the certainty that we were right for each other on the other. There's a kind of arrogance to it, I get that. A stupidity, if you must. Because what do I have to base it on? A couple of nights of your time and attention?

It occurred to me that I don't know you at all. Not the slightest little bit.

So I wrote you a poem. It's not a love poem. It's not romantic. But I hope that you can see the beauty in it. That I've come out the other side of that obsession.

It's not hopeful, no. But it has made me feel better about you. Or about myself perhaps. That I've got my shit together on this one front, at least.

I'm going to stop writing to a stranger.

But I'll leave you with this poem.

WHEN I MET you I decided I would love you.
Not because I particularly liked you;
Just because it was what everyone else was doing.
I decided it didn't really matter who you were.
Just a person
A body
A face.
I tried to talk to you but didn't really have that much to say.
I watched you and waited and thought
The thunderbolt
Might hit, if I waited long enough.
I was so patient.
My patience was faultless.
I waited and waited because with time,
It seemed,
Everyone found someone and made them special.

YOU WERE IRRELEVANT.

But I made you special.
And then I wondered why nothing felt right,
And why the world was suddenly empty,
And why the concept of special became meaningless.

I WONDERED why my head became a voided space
And why you,
In all your specialness,
Seemed voided too.

I WONDERED,
In the end,
If special existed at the start—
Or if we just took mediocre and gave it a new name.

I WANTED something that I could believe in.

THERE WAS NOTHING THERE.

51

CLARA

INSISTENT KNOCKING on my door finally transforms from my father, dressed as a chef, banging pans and shouting about catching sheep to the unwelcome reality that someone is, in fact, at my door.

I blink blearily and sit up.

9:39 a.m.

An empty wine bottle is lying precariously on my bedside table, it's neck hanging over the side. My glass appears to have been cradled in bed with me all night, the dysfunctional adult version of a teddy bear.

I groan and flop back onto my pillow.

Waving off a concerned looking Beth last night, I'd come home, opened a good bottle, and cried as though my life depended on it.

I've so long lived in my head about what happened to me that once I let myself cry for that girl, I nearly drowned in tears. I cried and drank and cried and drank and somehow, despite my thumping head, this morning I feel better.

It's not like I haven't spoken to anyone about it before. Hopefully, no one goes to a therapist for years and manages to not mention being sexually abused as a child. But somehow it all feels different in relation to Lucas. Like opening up to the idea of being with someone has cracked open all the feelings that I've kept buried away.

"Hang on," I shout in the direction of the door, hastily pulling on a dressing gown and trotting the wine bottle and glass to the sink. I imagine it's probably Beth checking on me, but just in case it's someone else, I want to hide the "drinking till I passed out in bed" evidence.

I have a moment of hope that it is Lucas. Finally I feel ready to talk to him about why I really strip. The ugly, shameful, secret parts don't even seem so scary anymore.

Then I open the door.

———

I STAND IN THE DOORWAY, my hands dropping limply to my sides, my dressing gown falling open. And I stare.

The man on my doorstep glances down the length of my body slowly, then looks back up at me and grins.

"Were you expecting me?" he says, and laughs—the ease of it, the merriness, completely absurd.

I stare at him, my mouth open, no words coming out.

"You're supposed to be dead," I finally manage. It's all I can think of to say.

"Not me you were expecting then," he says, still grinning, glancing down again. "Still. It's a nice hello." He cocks his head to the side and I finally catch his meaning, pulling my dressing gown over my underwear, flushing. I pull the cord around my waist, tight.

"Can I come in?" he asks, like nothing is more normal.

"No! What the fuck?" I'm still just staring at him.

He cocks his head to the side, perplexed. He puts his foot—

already raised to cross the threshold, as though I'd agreed to it—back on the ground.

"I'm kind of seeing your brother."

"How the fuck did that happen?" he asks.

I stare at him for a little while, my mind trying to play catch up.

Then, inexplicably, I start to cry.

———

"Hey, hey," Aaron speaks softly, moving to comfort me, concern in his eyes. But I wave him away, sobs escaping from me, everything suddenly seeming too much, too complicated, too painful. It's like all the tears I've kept at bay, backlogged behind my eyes for decades, are breaking loose, refusing to be contained any longer.

Everything hurts. So I just cry.

I can't even talk. I slide down the wall and sit on the floor, my legs no longer able to hold me up.

Gently, Aaron closes the front door behind him and sits down a few feet away, watching me quietly.

Eventually, my tears subsiding, I look back at him.

"Why are you here?" My voice sounds fractured. I sniffle, and he looks around until he spies a box of tissues and brings them to me.

"I'm doing better," he says slowly. "I just wanted to say thanks." He's distracted though, his brow furrowing, the actual thanks lost amidst more pressing concerns. "How did you meet my brother? How did you even know he was my brother?"

Other than confused and concerned, he does look better than I remember. Less shrivelled. Less morose. He's tanned, his hair long and sun-kissed, his body toned. He has an enormous, detailed tattoo peeking out of his shirt, which is unbuttoned one button too many. I can see ink across his bicep, too.

"Why do people think you're dead?" I can't focus on such mundane questions as how I met Lucas when there's the bigger problem of what the hell is actually happening crowding my brain.

He stares at me. "Fucked if I know. Who, exactly? My brother?"

I think about this, trying to sort through my confused half-finished thoughts. I actually don't know.

"Lucas thinks you killed yourself. He has a whole heap of your journals. Apparently you wrote to me a lot. After you died he came looking for me." I use air quotes around "died" to highlight the obvious: that Aaron is sitting in front of me, very much alive.

Very much testament to all the things I haven't quite managed to tell Lucas yet.

―――――

TYPICAL, I think to myself.

Just when I felt ready to tell Lucas everything, the universe throws a Really Fucking Big complication in my way.

Fucking universe.

The reasons I really strip—and the lapse that was Aaron—seem much more acceptable with Aaron dead. Romantic, almost. Like he brought us together.

Alive...Aaron makes things very messy.

I catch myself with this thought, though. It's not a good sign if you need a person to be dead for your relationship to flourish.

"Why are you here?" I ask, realising immediately I've already asked this. But Aaron shrugs and answers again. "I just got back from overseas. I wanted to say hi."

I actually can't think of a coherent line of conversation. Why he wants to say hi to me, why everyone thinks he's dead, how this little omission is going to play out with Lucas. The chaos that is unfolding in my mind is monumental.

"Lucas has been pretty messed up about your death," I say slowly. "About not being there for you. You might want to think about how you're going to get in touch with him."

"We go for a year without talking all the time," he says, irritated. "Why on earth would he think I was dead?"

"He got your boxes. All your journals."

"And he read them? What the fuck?"

"Why did you send them to him?"

"I was going overseas, for Christ's sake! I had nowhere to store them. I told Mum I'd send them to him. He wasn't supposed to fucking read them. God." A look of horror passes across his face. "I should have burnt those fuckers. No one should be subjected to other people's journals. Urghhh."

We're both silent, thinking.

"There must have been a funeral," I say eventually. Then, frustrated: "I have no idea what's going on. I think we need to talk to Lucas. But he's going to want to know why you came here. And it's going to cause some fucking big problems, so let me handle that, ok?"

He considers me for a moment. "What will you tell him?"

"The truth," I say firmly. But my tummy is doing flip-flops and my tone conveys a truckload more conviction than I feel.

52

LUCAS

"We need to talk."

That's a line that no one wants to hear in their fledgling relationship, ever.

I pull on my boots slowly, Clara's request to come over weighing heavily on me.

"I'll come to you," I'd said. So I could be doing something. Not just waiting at home, thinking about all the things she might be about to say.

I'd just read the last entry in Aaron's journal. The day before he died. My Aaron.

Except he wasn't mine. He wasn't anyone's. That was the problem, maybe. He didn't even belong to himself.

———

28ᵀᴴ June 2016

I stood in front of the mirror last week and told myself "I love you." I was told this was a test. To see how far you'd come along the path. Self-realisation and all that.

Someone once told me that until you can do this, you can never be happy.

So I stood in front of the mirror, adrift in this music. I felt I would be lost forever. There was only the mirror, and the music, and these feelings that refused to tie me down, refused to let me anchor myself anywhere. Not in happiness, not in misery. Not in despair. I didn't know. I was lost. I was trying to cling to some concept of myself but every one that I felt just overwhelmed me, and doubled me over in pain, and I couldn't bear it, couldn't bear it. Couldn't bear how little I felt I knew; couldn't bear how small I felt. Couldn't bear feeling anything at all.

I have spent so long detaching myself, I had forgotten what it was to feel something.

But somewhere in the confusion, in the struggle between feeling nothing and feeling everything—somewhere in there I looked at him, in the mirror. So overwhelmed with sadness and the hopelessness of it all. And I realised—how can I not love him?

I wanted to help him. I wanted to wrap my arms around him and tell him that everything would work out all right in the end. We would both know that I was lying. But it would be human contact. Warmth and security and at least the two of us, together, to fight it all. And I would hold him tight to my chest—this fragile, frightened, aching little boy, so naïve yet so much older than his body gives away; and we could cling to each other, knowing that there is no answer and no grand plan, knowing that there is no one else to comfort us; but we would have each other, and we would do the best we could.

And I thought, for a brief and beautiful moment, that everything was going to be okay.

———

IT WAS SO BEAUTIFUL. Possibly the most beautiful thing I've ever read. Maybe just because I know what happened after he wrote it. And just when I was waxing all lyrical to myself about his death having some meaning—that it was some fucking gift he left me which allowed me to finally be honest with myself, finally be brave enough to feel something real—because I have to believe that his life meant something, that it wasn't all for nothing—I get the phone call with the sentence of doom.

Slowly, slowly, I drag my feet toward my car.

53

CLARA

"I wasn't honest with you the other day," I say, pretty much as soon as Lucas walks through the door.

My underarms are clammy, my heart thudding in my chest.

I want to flee. I want to go for a run, read a book, have a bath, a glass of wine. Or maybe a bottle. Push these thoughts down the way I always have. Pretend they're so far in the past they don't matter anymore.

But they're not in the past.

They just landed on my doorstep, back from the dead.

God. What a mess. And where do I even start? What is the true story?

It's hard to find truth, in memories.

The truth is I was a child, and someone with greater power than me abused me. And on the surface, I could leave it there. There is enough there to damage someone. Enough to make them crave smallness. Enough to make them wary of men. Enough to cause so much havoc that throwing up felt like calmness, felt like peace.

Enough to locate stripping within, if damage was what you were looking for.

Why do I strip? I could say.

I strip because men feel dangerous.

I strip because there, I can control them.

I strip because if men are going to stare anyway, at least they're bloody paying for the privilege.

I strip because there, I can define how they see me, if our bodies touch.

I strip because I want to learn to let myself be noticed. Not the real me. Not the truth. But still: I want to let people look and experientially understand that being seen does not equate to death. Taking up space will not kill me. Thighs and breasts and butt will not make me self-combust. And I couldn't seem to manage visibility in baby steps. I just continued to hide in the shadows.

Stripping, I am thrust into the light.

But they're more half-truths.

The truth is slippery and dark. The truth is hard to look at, hard to accept.

The truth might blow my newfound love life into a million little pieces that I'll never patch back together into something good, ever again.

I take a deep breath and edge toward the precipice.

———

As I TALK, Lucas is clenching and unclenching his fists. A vein is pulsing on the side of his forehead. And I've only just got through the Darren part of this story.

"There's more," I say. "Please. Just listen."

"Okay," he nods, but I can see it costs him something. He looks ready to explode. But he takes a deep breath and stills himself to listen.

"I think what I've learned throughout my work is that it's so common. It's so common for children to be injured in one way or another. And maybe that's sexual abuse, maybe it's emotional abuse, maybe it's physical abuse. Or maybe it's parents who did their very best and their best was just not good enough. And I listen to you talk about your mother, and it seems so much worse. So much more legitimate to struggle when that was what you got in lieu of parenting. Because my parents tried. They helped. They did what they thought was best. And I was still so damaged. Long before Darren. I was not eating long before Darren. I was throwing up long before Darren. I was trying to be the person my parents needed me to be long before Darren. So how I handled Darren, well, that was a product of how broken I was already. He didn't break me. He just pressed on the bruise.

"I didn't tell my mother because even then, even at twelve, I knew she wasn't capable of helping me. If anything, I felt I had to protect her. Because that abuse—it wouldn't have been about me. It would have been about her. A measure of her worthiness. I didn't believe she would survive. And it wasn't because Darren was telling me that. And it wouldn't have been sadness for me that destroyed her. It would have been about her sense of worthiness. It would have been proof that she was unlovable. And that was seeping out of her long before then. Long before Dad left, even.

"So I need you to know that the abuse, I've come to terms with that. I've had therapy. I can forgive that girl. She did the best she could. She coped the best she could. Darren's been dead for ages, and Mum, well—she'll never get it. There's nothing to gain from talking to her. That's not the problem. The problem was how I tried to make myself feel better *later*. I haven't forgiven *that* girl. She hurt people. She knew she was hurting them and she couldn't stop."

I talk in the third person, as though that will help—as though I can separate myself from her. When really all I think is that I managed to control her. Not that I managed to change her or excise her from my being. I just found a way to keep her darkness where it belonged: in the dark.

Bad choices are one thing.

Hurting people—that is quite another.

"I had affairs. Affairs with people I shouldn't. It was like I constantly needed reinforcement that I was valuable and worthy and desirable. So I seduced everyone. I lost friendships. My best friend. And I couldn't stop.

"So if you want the ugliest, ickiest truth about why I strip, it's that I decided it was somewhere I could get this desperate, insatiable, out-of-control need for sexual affirmation repeatedly fulfilled. Where I wouldn't hurt anyone. Where I could have it reiterated, over and over again, that I was desirable. I know how stupid it sounds. But there. That's why I strip."

For a moment I stare at Lucas defiantly, daring him to judge me. The way that I have judged myself. But then something crumples inside me. And then I can't talk anymore; I'm crying too hard.

Lucas moves to comfort me, and for a moment I let him. He smooths my hair and kisses my temple.

"You were so young," he says, gentle, soft. "You were trying to feel loved. You did the best you could with a bloody shit hand."

I lean against him. Breathe in his smell. Let myself feel cocooned by his strength, his apparent understanding.

But then I move away. Before I lose my nerve. Before I let his warmth and kindness shroud my judgement. Lull me into thinking I could just leave it there. Move forward. Be a better version of myself.

Exactly what I had intended to do before Aaron knocked on my door.

But now, I have to tell him everything.

Feeling like I'm about to free-fall from a very considerable height, I say, "There's something else. About Aaron."

54

LUCAS

"So. We seem to have built this relationship on lies."

Clara stares back at me levelly.

"So you did see him. But not in the way I thought. Not professionally. Unless you call sex part of your stripping profession."

"Don't, Lucas."

"How many times?"

"A few."

"How was it?"

"For fuck's sake. How will that help?"

Another thought: "You said you didn't go home with clients. I specifically asked you that."

"I didn't go home with him. I dated him. Sort of."

"Semantics," I scoff. "You knew what I meant."

"No. I thought you meant, did I go home with clients after work because I felt horny. For casual sex. Which I never did. A couple of clients I did go on a few dates with. I see that as different."

"A couple? So, two?"

"Yes. Two. Not that it's any of your business, Lucas."

"Of all the people in the world. One of them had to be my brother."

We're both silent, Clara watchful, me wanting to punch a wall.

"I can't believe you didn't tell me. We had a whole conversation about this. You said he'd had a lap dance. What were you even thinking as you failed to mention everything else he got a taste of?"

For the first time, Clara looks pissed. "Firstly, we weren't dating when I was seeing Aaron, so you can't be pissed that I dated him. Secondly, it was all bloody messy and I wanted time to think about it. You stalking me. Lui Bar, that was no coincidence, right, you being there? I just wanted to work it out in my own head. I didn't think, 'I won't tell Lucas that.' I just needed to get it all clear myself first."

"Did you know, that first time that I told you? Told you his name, and you denied seeing him?"

"No," she says, exasperated. "I don't know why. I'm sure I must have known his surname. But we went on like three dates! You brought it to me as part of my therapy world. It just didn't twig. I was so used to keeping those worlds separate. I didn't think about people I'd met stripping. It didn't occur to me. It probably should have, but it didn't. I'm sorry."

"I'm sorry," she repeats, softer, trying to reach me, searching my eyes, lifting a hand toward me. But I can't stop. I *want* to stop. But the questions just keep coming. That familiar feeling of wanting to blame someone.

"So you should have seen how unwell he was. You could have helped him."

She hesitates. Her hand drops.

"What?"

"Lucas. I have something else to tell you. About Aaron. I only just found out. Today."

"What? He sent you some fucking love letters before he died?" I'm snappish, brutal, and I hate myself for it, but I can't help it. Everything that looked so beautiful three hours ago is turning to shit before my eyes. How much worse can it get?

"It's good news, I think," she says softly, watching me closely. "But I don't understand it, and you probably won't either. But he's not dead. He's alive."

The next tirade I've started in my head is shocked into silence.

What the fuck is she talking about? I've seen the picture. I've read the journals. But then another thought sinks in: "You've spoken to him?"

"Yes." Again, that hesitation.

"Did you see him?"

"Yes."

"Did you fuck him?"

"Oh, for fuck's sake! No. Of course not."

I have no idea what to think.

We glare at each other.

I need some air.

I walk out without speaking and slam the door.

55

AARON

"Hello, Mother."

When she opens the door, she doesn't even have the courtesy to look guilty.

"I didn't think you'd come back," she says. She doesn't miss a beat.

"So you knew I wasn't dead, then?"

She doesn't say anything, just watches me, expressionless.

"Why does Lucas think I'm dead?"

Probably I should have gone to Lucas first. It's unlikely I'll get any truth out of my mother.

"It was just a silly joke," she says, shrugging disinterestedly. "I thought he'd know the picture wasn't you."

I stare at her for a long time.

"You showed him a picture of a dead person and told him it was me?"

"You sent him all your journals like a parting gift," she shrugs again. "Like an explanation." She says it like it was a joint project, like we collaborated on this deceit together, a giant joke that Lucas would learn about and laugh over.

Like she thought he wouldn't grieve me, or that she simply doesn't know how that might feel.

"You were meant to ask him to store them somewhere for me and send me the bill!" I shout at her, suddenly enraged. I always knew she was awful, but this was insane.

"You were leaving," she says coolly. "Going on your fancy *explore-the-world* travels. I wanted him to know it was just him and me now. We were all the family that was left."

I want to shake her. Slap her. Ask her all the questions. What she thought would happen when I came back. How she pulled off a funeral without a dead son to actually bury. What she expects to happen next. How she continued with this insanity for a *whole fucking year.*

But I know there's no point.

I turn around and walk away.

56

AARON

LUCAS PULLS me to him roughly when he opens his front door.

He has tears in his eyes. I've never seen that before.

But as he hugs me to him I can smell the whiskey on his breath. Leading me inside, he offers me one too.

"Sure," I say. Then: "How did she do it?"

He pours my drink, glancing up at me.

"She told me they'd already had the funeral," he shrugs. "Your boxes had already arrived. I thought you sent them as an explanation. I didn't even question it."

"Didn't you think that was odd? That she didn't make sure you were at the funeral?"

It feels surreal, discussing my pretend funeral.

"Is there anything she's done over the years that wasn't fucked up, malicious, or downright insane?" he counters. "Being considerate of other people has never been her strong point. I thought, *fuck you,* of course. But it wasn't surprising, by her standards."

"Can we charge her with something? Emotional damage? You were damaged, right?" I try for teasing, but I miss the mark. He looks angry.

"Yes," he says. Short. Throws his whiskey back in one smooth motion.

Pours another.

"I'm glad she lied," he says eventually. "I mean—." A pause. "I'm glad that you're back."

"What about Clara?" I'm tentative, unsure. I don't know what she means to either of us.

He throws back his glass again. I wonder how many he had before I arrived.

"What about her?" he says, looking at me with hard, glittery eyes.

"You like her or what?"

"Why? Do you?"

"Sure," I say lightheartedly. "Got a bit obsessed with her before I left. But I was a mess back then, man. You've read my journals, I hear. So you know that. She was the only person who listened to me. Scared the fuck out of her, I think."

"You slept with her."

"Yes."

"Don't you think that's a bit fucked up? How will we hang out at family gatherings?"

"We don't have family gatherings."

"You know what I mean."

We watch each other warily.

"Look, I did a lot of thinking while I was away. A lot of shagging too, if you must know. I feel like I've got my shit together. I really just went to see her to say thanks. For showing some care. Pointing me in the right direction. I feel like she helped me when I felt pretty fucking all alone. I had no idea you knew her when I went there."

Lucas stares into his glass.

"I kind of stalked her a little bit after I found her name in all your journals."

"So I brought you together then," I grin, trying to lift Lucas's mood. "I'm kind of like your fairy match-maker godfather."

For the first time, a hint of a smile.

"You look better," he says. "More like yourself."

"More like myself than someone else's dead body, you mean?"

He actually smiles, shakes his head. I always could make him laugh. Even when I felt like shit.

"God, where did she get that picture? Poor dude. You know, it really bothered me that she took a picture. Went to identify you and did that. You know how we have no pictures of us as kids? That picture really got to me. I don't know if this makes it worse or better."

We sip our drinks for a while.

"Clara's a good person," I say eventually. "I'm cool with being the third wheel, you know. If you like her." It's a lie, but I want my brother more than I want Clara.

Lucas considers me for a while.

"You sounded pretty messed up, you know. Those journals."

I roll my eyes. "No one was supposed to *read* them. I was depressed. I was drinking too much. Smoking too much weed, too, actually. I didn't know where to get help. It was Clara who convinced me I could feel better."

"But you didn't get help," he says, then looks guilty. "I had a private investigator check."

I let out a low whistle. "Wow. You really did let loose with your stalker side, huh?" Then another thought: "How did he not notice I was, uh, alive?"

Lucas ponders that. "I guess I never asked him to look into that. He was checking for psych records, I guess. Medicare. And finding out about Clara for me."

Suddenly he laughs. "God, this is so messed up. But I'm so glad you're...alive." His laugh dies in his throat and he chokes on the word, his eyes tearing up again, his hands tight around his glass, his shoulders rigid.

"I felt so shit about your death," he chokes out. "Not just that you were gone. Thinking about you choosing suicide. How bad you must have felt." He stops, struggling to gain control, gulping air. I reach out a hand and touch his shoulder gently. But he shakes his head, indicates I should wait.

Eventually, when his breathing is steady again, he says: "And on top of all that, I realised what a shit big brother I was to you. I knew better than anyone what our mother was like, and I didn't help you. I didn't get you away from her. I just left you there."

Eventually he raises his eyes to mine.

"It really did a fucking number on me," he says.

"It's okay," I tell him. "I don't know what you could have done. By the time you were old enough to help, the damage was well and truly done."

We sit in silence for a while. Then I knock my knee against his gently, smile at him.

"But, you wanna make up for it anyway?" I ask, teasing. Laughing. "Cause I'm kinda stuck for a place to stay."

57

LUCAS

LIVING with Aaron is maddening and enchanting.

At its most basic, it's like having a complete stranger move in with you who you can't ever sever ties with. Can't ever kick out.

It's amazing how little we know about each other. For instance, I never knew that he has a nut allergy. He's laidback and funny and energetic and seems to have the short-term memory of a goldfish, but when it comes to food he's thorough, decisive, and a walking encyclopedia.

Who knew so many things had traces of peanuts in them?

I bet that our mother didn't help him with that very much. He's probably been managing it himself for most of his life.

But I guess you pay attention to that shit if you don't want to die.

And then there's that: every time I think about death it's like my stomach drops half a foot away from me. Like I can't quite believe this place we're in. After the utter madness of the last year.

He sleeps in until after ten every day, he leaves clothes strewn from one end of the house to the other, his showers seem to go on for the whole day. He finishes my beer and my muesli and only ever grins when I shout at him about it. Waves me away, says he'll buy more later.

But he sits with me in the evenings and makes jokes about our childhood. All the things I've run from, denied, repressed— he pokes fun at them and somehow makes me laugh about it. We both know it's not funny. But somehow he makes it seem okay.

So if I want to shake him half a dozen times every morning, I also want to crush him to me in the tightest, most unrelenting hug half a dozen times every night.

———

"YOU KNOW, if you're going to stay here, you're going to have to cook sometimes," I tell Aaron, as he gulps down mouthfuls of pork belly, moaning in bliss.

It's Friday night, a couple of weeks after he's moved in, and I'm half-teasing but half-serious. I really am not going to be the cook and cleaner in this relationship.

He grins at me. "You asked for it," he says. "Remember that when you're choking down my spaghetti for the fortieth night in a row."

I roll my eyes. "Get a recipe. Buy the ingredients. Follow the steps. It's not that hard."

"Probably not," he agrees. "But haven't you heard the clichés about students and living on spaghetti and beer?"

He's enrolled in a Bachelor of Fine Arts at the University of Melbourne and seems, strangely enough, happy. Serene, even. I watch him for a little while, tucking in to dinner, larger than life.

"How did you get your shit together so quickly?" I ask him. "Those journals weren't written that long ago."

Aaron takes a long drink from his beer, regarding me thoughtfully.

"I did see a therapist while I was in London," he says. "And I'm seeing one now, actually."

I bristle, immediately thinking of Clara, feeling a thud of despair in my chest at the thought that he might be seeing her when I am not.

"It's not Clara," he says, observing me once again with more insight than I had anticipated. For all his fun exterior, he sees a lot, my brother.

"Why haven't you called her?"

I frown. "I don't know. It all seems so fucked up. I don't know where to go from here." Then I look at him sharply. "How do you know that I haven't called her?"

"Well, you're all moody and down. I bet you'd be a lot cheerier if you were banging her occasionally." He grins, but ducks before the bottle top I chuck at him has even left my hand.

Then he looks serious.

"Also, I want to be friends with her. She was, like, important to me. I feel like I might have kept floundering for much longer without her being so thoughtful and so candid with me. She bothered to listen when it really wasn't her job."

I open my mouth to make a cutting comment about that, but he holds a hand up, giving me a warning look. "I know you feel messed up about that at the moment, and I know it's hard for you. So, to be clear: I don't want to be with her. I'm not going to be a pain in your ass about her. But I would like her as a mate, and I think we can do that." He's watching me warily. "But we need to be honest with each other about it. So—I know you haven't called her because I've spoken to her a couple of times."

He's looking at me like he's both worried about me and like he's going to stand his ground about this.

I wonder just how honest he thinks we can be. How forthright *I* can be when the thought of anyone touching Clara, *ever*, makes me want to fucking kill them on sight.

"I think you should call her," he adds, his attention shifting back to his pork. He attends to his next mouthful studiously. I get the sense that he is giving me some privacy to react rather than avoiding my gaze.

"Oh, yeah? And why do you think that?"

"Because she's important to you. Whatever you might say to me, I'm pretty sure if you're honest with yourself, you'll find that there are not that many people who'll come along that you really connect with. So don't throw it away because it's awkward and you're being all alpha-dude, I-can't-believe-she-slept-with-my-brother. She's a good person. She's into you. Work it out. She's worth it."

He raises his eyes to mine again, calm and contained. My twenty-three year-old little brother, fresh off a year so messed up I believed he had suicided, offering me wise counsel.

But somehow I feel like this is a gift he's giving me. That he's pointing me in the right direction.

And that I'd better fucking move on it before he changes his mind.

58

CLARA

"JUST GIVE HIM SOME TIME," Aaron keeps telling me.

But I'm practically exploding with waiting for Lucas to get his shit together and call me.

So, I slept with his brother previously. Who I like an awful lot. But he's not the one I want. He's not the one who I've opened up to. He's not the one who makes my heart skip beats and my breathing ragged.

I feel like we're all tied together in some crazy, fucked up way. And sometimes crazy and fucked up is where the beauty lies. So as wacky as it seems, I want to try to make it work.

Aaron and I already are. He calls me and tells me about his day, about his travels overseas, about his mother. We've fallen into this easy camaraderie that feels intimate and solid. Dependable. Important.

But he won't tell me anything about Lucas. Just to "be patient." That he thinks Lucas will get there. That that is our stuff to work out and he doesn't want to interfere.

So I'm waiting, drinking with Beth, chatting with Aaron, working hard at the practice. I've opened up another day there. I'm taking as many referrals as come my way.

I'm working on letting myself feel hurt, and scared, and vulnerable.

Sitting with the reality that I want Lucas, and he might not choose me. And it matters.

And it's terrifying.

I sit with all of that and wait and wait and wait.

59

MAUREEN

Maureen stares vacantly at the television. It's black and white, and she doesn't understand what is happening on the screen. She's not watching it for entertainment, anyway. It's just something to look at, to occupy her mind. Pretend she's doing something so no one talks to her.

She's at the first of many foster homes that she will be sent to from the orphanage during school holidays, to "experience family life."

Her foster parents hover behind her, anxious and attentive. At ten, she's older than most of the children they have fostered before. It's been over a week and she still hasn't spoken to them. She will nod or shake her head. Pick at her food.

Stare at them with a blank expression that they find hard to face.

They know that her stepfather was violent.

They know that she has witnessed the abuse of her mother.

They know that she was neglected, is small for her age, and is slow to respond when spoken to.

In Australia in 1974, they know nothing about childhood trauma, how damaging witnessing violence to her mother is for her development, how she might have tried to protect herself psychologically, or how they might help her.

Unsettled, they will say they can't keep her, and she will go back to the orphanage.

During the next holidays, she will be sent to another foster family.

If she could form coherent thoughts about it, she would wish that she were back at the first one.

Of all the ones that come after, the first one was the most benign.

But she doesn't form coherent thoughts about her circumstances. She protects herself as best she can.

She stares vacantly and doesn't speak.

————

May 1976

Maureen has learned to move faster.

Backhanders to the face enough times will teach a child something, at any rate.

When her current foster father tells her to do the dishes, she moves quickly. She does not stare at him vacantly.

When her foster brother tells her to shut up as he climbs on top of her, pushes inside her, she quiets her cries. She turns her head to the side, pretends she is at the park she remembers going to sometimes, with a woman who was kind to her, who brushed her hair, kissed her temple. Sang to her softly with a lilting voice.

So she remembers the park, and the swing, and the kindness, and stares out the window. She is so far away from this room, this day that she doesn't even notice when her foster brother finishes his grunting and leaves the room.

When she goes back to the orphanage, she hasn't spoken a single word for nearly two years.

During the next holidays, she will be sent to another foster family. Then another.

And on, and on, and on.

————

AUGUST 1986

It's Maureen's 22nd birthday, though she doesn't know it.

It's Maureen's 22nd birthday, though she doesn't know it.

The baby is crying.

My some miracle, Maureen did not fall pregnant until she was nineteen years old. Working as a cleaner, renting a room from her employer, she found herself in some sort of relationship with her neighbour. He was living with his father and working as a casual labourer. He took her to the local diner for pies and chips and believed he took her virginity one of these nights after dinner, when his father was out at the pub.

Now, Maureen bounces the baby on her knee absentmindedly. She is in the cramped room she shares with John in his father's house. Lucas is in a cheerful blue jumpsuit with stains around the chest, but he looks bright and plump and well-looked after.

The crying is new. The noise is grating on her nerves.

John should be home by now. It's Friday: his payday. She needs the money to go to the butchers in the morning. They have meat on Saturdays only. Maureen has found some kind of joy in her simple routine. She walks Lucas to the park, sings to him shyly in a low voice, cradles him on the swing with a tenderness that feels familiar. Cooks for John and his father and keeps their house clean.

She rejoices that she is not on her knees scrubbing houses seven days a week.

But John has been coming home later and later. Especially on Fridays. On this night, John does not come home until very late. Lucas has only just settled, and John's clumsy entry wakes him again. He starts to cry.

In the way that people with few options and little insight do, when John's work starts to dwindle, his visits to the pub start to increase. His shame at not being able to provide for his small family is interpreted by him as irritation by the crying of the small boy and his wife's failure to keep him quiet so that John can get enough rest.

Labouring is hard physical work.

John is always so tired after work.

He just wants some peace and quiet to wind down.

He starts coming home later and later every night.

The pay that he hands to Maureen gets smaller and smaller.

His breath becomes a shade of stale that also feels familiar.

Later, Maureen will always tell Lucas that his father left her. But that is not strictly true. In fact, he told her to leave. He didn't have enough money to support them, he said. When she cried, and protested, his temper flaring with booze and shame, he slapped her a few times. And when she clung to him, terrified, he shoved her backwards all the way down the hallway and out the front door.

She screamed for Lucas, banging on the door, until she heard his cries from the rear of the house. When she reached him, he was sobbing only from the shock of being left outside by himself in the dark. His meagre supply of clothes was on the step beside him.

Maureen went back to the cleaning job.

She and her colleagues took turns minding the children while the rest of the team were sent out to houses to clean. She worked 7 a.m. until 7 p.m. six days a week.

The very small, very fragile part of Maureen that remained hopeful of a better life—intact despite the unimaginable years in orphanages and foster homes, nurtured by her relationship with John and being a real family—shatters in the way that it does when you have absolutely nothing left to hope for.

And Lucas will feel the reverberations of that for the next three decades.

———

BUT IN MAY 2017, Maureen doesn't think about any of this.

She never thinks about it, in fact.

She feels angry that Aaron is back in Melbourne. Though she doesn't understand it, she's angry because she is afraid. Afraid that her two sons will be closer to each other than she is to either of them.

Afraid because her last relationship is long over, and she is alone.

She wants someone to love her. But she doesn't think about that either. These yearnings are not something she can put words to. They come and go as feelings that she doesn't understand.

With Aaron believed dead, she felt hopeful that Lucas would turn to her, his only family left.

And even though that didn't happen, she feels angry that Aaron is back. Because now that hope is dashed.

Holding on to hope—even in the face of overwhelming evidence that it is futile—is maybe the only human part of Maureen left.

And it's always easier to blame someone than to feel hurt, or sad, or lonely.

Or unlovable.

60

LUCAS

I DON'T KNOW what I was expecting.

But when I can't stay away any longer and knock on her door —with absolutely no idea what I want to say—Clara barrels into my arms with the tenacity of a long-lost Jack Russell and enough momentum to throw me back against the balcony's rails.

Standing on tiptoe, she's nuzzling into my neck and kissing my collarbone before I've even said a word.

If I had any thoughts at all about what we needed to talk about, they fled my mind at her first kiss.

Groaning into her hair, my arms find their way around her waist, holding her against me, breathing in the smell of her. Completely lost in the feel of her breasts pressed against me, the curve of her waist, her fervent kisses.

I close my eyes and hold her tight.

Eventually, resting her forehead against me, clutching my arms, she mutters, "What took you so long?" into my chest.

I don't say anything, because I have no idea.

Sighing, in a way that sounds like contentment rather than frustration, she leads me inside and puts on the kettle. I watch her in the kitchen, fetching teabags, reaching for cups, her hair trailing down her back, her feet bare.

Watching her is a kind of contentment for me, too.

Occasionally she glances at me, sees me watching her, holds my gaze. And when she turns back to the cups, my eyes linger on her ass.

Unable to help myself, unable to think of anything except touching her, I move behind her, sweep her hair to the side, kiss her neck. Pull her ass into me. I know we should talk, but touching her feels like talking. Like my need and my passion might say it all better than my words ever could.

She turns into me, raises her face to mine. Kissing her is like solving problems. My fears and doubts about how this could work seem incomprehensible, irrelevant. Her lips, her hands, her kisses say all the things I need to hear.

I want you.

I'm listening.

I'm here.

———

NEVERTHELESS, I want to give her my words too.

"I'm sorry I walked out on you," I start, running my fingers up and down her arm, feeling the skin tighten underneath my touch.

We're sitting on the couch, my tea going cold on the coffee table, my hands incapable of being anywhere but in contact with her.

She shivers, turns toward me, her face wary, her eyes trained on me, unflinching.

"I know I keep doing things that are shit. Not talking. Storming off. Despite everything, when you told me you'd been with Aaron, I still found it so hard to risk showing you how much I cared about you when you might not choose me."

Clara opens her mouth to say something, but I put a finger gently to her lips.

"Let me finish before you say anything. I want you to hear this first. Because I want you to know: whatever you decide about us, I choose you. I've never felt like this about anyone in my life. I feel like you are essential somehow. I know it sounds so cliché and sappy, but you are everything I've ever wanted. I feel like I can be my real self with you. I don't have to hide. And the last time we spoke I got scared, and I forgot that I don't have to hide with you. I trust you with my heart. I want to be with you. I want you to be able to trust me with your heart and know that I will treasure it. And you can take all the time that you need to figure out what you want. I will wait. I will be impatient and it will kill me to stay away from you, but I will do whatever you need. And if you choose Aaron, I won't make it hard for either of you." I think to myself that I will probably punch holes in walls and want to rip someone's head off, the pain of losing her feels so devastating to even consider, but I carry on: "I will find a way to be happy for you both, however hard that will be for me. And believe me, it will just about kill me. But I feel so lucky, so amazed to have a second chance to be a big brother to him. I will make it work. And I want you to really know that before you make any decisions."

My heart is hammering in my chest. I'm saying the words, but I'm terrified. Terrified that she won't choose me.

But she reaches over, her fingers trailing softly along my jawline, wonder on her face. She edges closer, creeping in slowly, slowly, until she is pressed against me, her eyes wide, not leaving mine. Her painstaking advance across the couch into me is the perfect passing of time. Because I see it and I know what it means.

Finally, when she is flush against me, she kisses me. It is a slow kiss, a deep kiss, soft and warm and delicious, with the faintest hint of sex in it. But mainly it is a kiss of ownership.

She is not giving herself to me.
She is not asking me a question.
She's owning us.
Declaring us to each other.
She doesn't need to say a word.

61

CLARA

Two months later

When I wake up, stretching lazily in silky white sheets, Lucas is sitting in his armchair staring out the window. A gentle mist has settled in the valley, green hills poking out above it like dreamy islands in a sea of rolling waves.

He turns to me and smiles.

"Morning, sleepy," he says. "Will you look at this view?!"

It's our first morning in his new house in the hills.

Our new house, I correct myself. Relish in being a *we*, an *us*.

If his staff are working the horses below, we can't see them. We're high above the arenas, everything lost in swirling white.

"I have something for you," he says, as though the last few weeks haven't been enough.

He took me for a ride in the forest, my first time on a horse. The silence and the beauty of the bush tracks made my heart sing, Rocky quiet and obliging beneath me, a pair of wedge-tailed eagles bursting out of a tree above us.

"They're often here," he'd told me. "Do you know they mate for life?"

He took me on a surprise hot-air balloon ride over the bay

one morning, dragging my ass out of bed way earlier than I ever like to be up, but it was so worth it. Again with the silence, the beauty.

He took me hiking and camping around Wilson's Promontory, our tent on his back, the ocean freezing and ferocious and beautiful.

Given our short time together, he's caught on to the silence and solitude theme remarkably quickly.

Now, he hands me a little rectangular frame.

I turn it over in my hands.

It's a tiny sketch of a wedge-tailed eagle, floating on a slash of blue. Alone. Magnificent. Self-contained.

We can love ourselves the way we wish to be loved, it says, in small, fine lettering underneath. *A Cooper* is scrawled across one corner.

"Nevertheless," he says, lifting my chin with a finger, "I'm going to be loving you pretty hard the way I wish to love you, too." He smiles at me wickedly, lowering his lips to mine. Possessive. My tummy flutters in response.

Then he's serious again. "I just wanted a little something to remember. Aaron's...non-death. Where it brought us. My mother is fucked, and I'm not going to thank her. But..." He trails off. I know what he means.

How all this wrongness led to something right.

I prop the frame up on my bedside table, cocking my head at it.

"He's doing his art, then," I say, and Lucas grumbles.

"Fucking hippy, painting rainbows instead of getting a real job." But he's smiling. "He's coming up for dinner tonight to see the house," he adds.

Then he pulls me onto his lap, pulls my hair across one shoulder, runs kisses across the other.

"So how much insatiable loving is required to satisfy that girl you can't forgive yet?" he murmurs, his hands already wandering.

His cock already pressing into my ass. "Because I think I can handle it. It'll be tough. You'll owe me," he says, his breath, his murmurs delectable against my skin. "But I think I'm the man for the job." He licks my neck slowly, tantalisingly.

I crane around to see him, his face solemn. Committed to the difficult task of boning me—endlessly—ahead.

I laugh and wrestle him backwards onto the bed.

Kiss him deeply.

Tell him that he's the man for all my everythings.

Put my trust in him.

Then—forever—hold him close.

PERFECT

EXCERPT, BOOK TWO

Catch a cameo of Clara and Lucas in Perfect, Book Two in the Beautiful Ordinary series.

Praise for **PERFECT**

"It's rare to read a romance that does intrigue so well and has such unforeseen plot twists." **Amazon review**

"...a haunting romantic thriller." **Amazon review**

"...entertaining, captivating and...sexy read. I could not put it down. Wonderfully written with strong, intriguing characters." **Amazon review**

"Sexy and full of suspense, PERFECT is a complex and layered story about love, family and our perceptions about ourselves. I was sucked into it from page one." **Saffron A. Kent, Amazon Bestselling Author**

"This book is oh, so entertaining. Not an easy, relaxed read. But...pay attention and enjoy. It is so well written and clever. I highly recommend." **Amazon review**

"...a breathtaking read. You will love all the suspense and angst this thrilling read has to offer. Go one click today." **Amazon review**

"...surprisingly and pleasantly different from the "norm". This author was able to successfully weave romance, suspense, angst, turmoil, love and sex...a really good read that kept me on the edge of my seat." **Amazon review**

"Wow! Loved this book! ...kept me captivated from the first to the last page. No ones life is perfect...the author did a wonderful job portraying the complex thoughts we all have trying to be our best." **Amazon review**

"Amazing romantic story with spice. Superb." **Goodreads review**

"What an interesting read! Well presented storyline; characters that kept you guessing; some creepy twists and turns with lots of the unexpected...If you like books a bit off kilter... Perfect by Fen Wilde belongs on your TBR Lust." **Goodreads review**

"Great story, complex characters...amazing, gritty and emotionally charged." **Book-Lover Book Blog**

"Perfect! There isn't one thing I didn't like about this book..." **My Girlfriend's Couch Blog**

"This was a wholly original book...Ben is a kind, warm and emotive soul who balances out Ada's frosty exterior.... his character was a great at exposing the fun and carefree side to her character. Their scenes and interactions together were beautifully constructed and filled with chemistry and passion." **Bubbles The Book Pimp**

"So much more than a romance. There is family conflict, suspense, many kinds of emotions and lots of hot, explicit sex..." **Goodreads review**

"This amazing book is so very well written. It is always surprising the things that a person can withstand and the heart can cope with." **Goodreads review**

BLURB

Two years ago, perfect Ada Cosgrove made one mistake—and narrowly escaped with her life.

Gorgeous, clever, and the editor of the sexiest magazine on the racks, she dealt with it in her usual efficient, solitary manner —then carried on as she always had. Working hard, following the rules, and winning at everything she turned her hand to.

Mistakes weren't part of her identity, and she didn't care to linger on—or share—the nightmarish details.

Except now, threatening letters start appearing.

Someone knows something they shouldn't.

And in trying to work out if she's in danger, Ada is forced to relive that night and question everything she's worked so hard for.

Did she really leave the menace behind her that night?

Trying desperately to understand her past, she unearths more secrets than she bargained for...but coupled with an ex who's determined to protect her, they just might be the truths she needs to save herself.

A dark, sexy suspense that has it all—complex characters, family drama, scorching sex and endless intrigue.

Ada

October 2015

Waves lap gently at the hull of the boat.

The sky through the small window beside the bed is almost black.

Two champagne glasses on the tiny bedside table list and clink gently with the swell.

The naked man on the bed lets out a long sigh.

He's too drunk to take in the flawlessness of the scene.

The scene that—even by my exacting standards, even on short notice—is utterly perfect.

On the surface.

If you ignore a few crucial underlying details.

But I push them out of my mind, gather my things, scurry onto the pier, and walk away.

I stumble on the uneven surface—the finality of the moment marred by my awkwardness in my impractical heels.

But I leave. That's the important thing.

That should have been where our story ends.

Perhaps I should have slapped him.

Stabbed him, even.

Because then the story really would have ended there.

But stories don't always end the way you want them to.

Chapter 1

Two years later—November 2017

Ada

"Well. This is awkward."

Ben turns toward me, blue eyes twinkling, amusement oozing out of every damn perfect inch of him. He's lounging backwards, one well-defined bicep tantalisingly close, hanging over the back of the stiff-backed chair as he turns toward me.

The man is imperturbable.

"I can't believe that being seated together at a wedding is the thing that springs to mind as 'awkward' for you," he murmurs. "I could think of a few more blush-worthy examples."

He watches me beneath his ridiculously long black eyelashes, the corners of his mouth curling slightly in the hint of a smile.

"We agreed not to see each other anymore. So, yes, this is awkward, if you ask me." I observe him with a blank expression, tilting my head slightly to the side, as though mildly disinterested in his failure to understand. An expression that I know for a fact he finds equally as intoxicating as I find the amused grin he is throwing my way.

It pitches his competitive streak into overdrive.

He always wants to plant some emotion on my blank expression. Overlay it with something more spontaneous. Something that offers a crack into my soul.

His lips curl slightly more, and he leans in toward me, the smell of his aftershave enough to make me inhale sharply. I want to close my eyes—partly to lose myself in it, but also to gather some resolve to fight the swell of longing it induces. But I hold my expression, the angle of my head, and watch him innocently.

It's hard to stop the games with Ben, whatever we've agreed to.

Whatever I know is for the best.

"As I recall," he drawls, deliberately letting his hand brush mine as he reaches for his champagne glass. I jump inadvertently. His skin feels more alive to me than any other texture on the planet. I feel his touch in my very core, every time.

He clocks my reaction and allows himself a tiny victory smile, his eyes telling me exactly what he's thinking: *I can win this. You know I can.* Then he continues: "We didn't agree to anything. You told me what was happening. Via SMS. Classy. Surprising, even for you."

I keep my face deadpan. I haven't actually spoken to the man since my curt text message three weeks ago, pointedly ignoring his calls. He's right—I didn't give him any right of reply. But it's not like we haven't discussed this before.

"It was time," I reply, my voice calm and cool, betraying nothing of the feelings underneath it. The uncertainty, the desire. The regret. "You knew it was coming. It's been fun. But let's leave it at that."

"*Funnnnn,*" Ben repeats, his parted lips lingering on the *n,* watching me with an unreadable expression. "That's not the word that I'd have used to describe it."

"Really? What would you choose?"

I can't help myself; I want to know what word he'd choose. What word he'd wrap around us, exult us with.

I know ending it is the right decision. I know it's all wrong, Ben and I. But my heart still soars at the possibilities this unknown word choice offers. Like one right word could melt my heart.

He sips his champagne, watching me closely. He knows I'm hanging on his damn word.

That's the problem, when you know each other as well as we do. When you've known each other for most of your lives. There's no hiding. He can see me like I can't even see myself.

"One word?" he asks, stalling, his eyes fast on mine, his long fingers curling sensually around the stem of his delicate glass, his full lips aggressively tantalising just by their mere existence. But he presses them together slightly, nonetheless, watching me watching them.

He smooths his napkin, dragging this out, his face a mask— but I know exactly what he's feeling.

Satisfaction, at me hanging on his every word.

Hurt, that I put an end to us.

Longing. Hoping to seduce me with his eyes, his mouth, his fingers. Hoping that I'll change my mind.

Hope: that's always the killer for me. Ben, with his huge, hopeful eyes, full of all the feelings.

He looks back up at me, a deliberate blink, his eyes dark and brooding, saying all the things I love to see. How much he wants me. How well he knows me. How the whole world stops and slows when we're together. It's like being on some kind of slow-motion fair ride. Or maybe a movie trailer with special effects: bright lights, seductive music—the whole nine yards. Just us, in the middle. Everything else fading to a blur around us, a dull roar of inconsequential sound and colour. Where the only thing that matters is us.

In this space with him, I feel my most alive.

He speaks slowly, intentionally. Unflustered as ever. And as he speaks, he lets one hand drop under the tablecloth, sliding it up the inside of my leg, slowly, provocatively. Dangerously.

His fingers are light, brushing against me, his touch so familiar: warm and masculine and possessive and promising. His eyes don't leave mine, and he leans in even closer, his next words a caress against my cheek, the corner of my lips.

"If I only had one word?" he says, "I'd choose...*perfect*."

I inhale sharply, at his fingers as much as his word, though both are exhilarating. One hand automatically flies to his arm, my fingers curling around his bicep, the gesture at once both intimate and grounding.

My rock.

My one true love.

His eyes continue to hold mine, languid, satisfied.

Ben 1, Ada 0, they say.

Then he withdraws his hand, downs his champagne, raises his eyebrows at me, and stands up and walks away.

Chapter 2

Ben

"Chloe." I try to keep my voice light, but a fool could hear the resignation in it.

"Ben," she replies brightly, her social cheer grating after only one damn word. "Enjoying the wedding? Such a gorgeous bride! Spectacular dress. Those shoes! Makes you all woozy, doesn't it?"

There's no point trying to clarify—a conversation with Chloe is like being caught in a tornado. None of it makes any sense or is at a pace you can decipher until the punch she's been trying to camouflage under all her niceties hits you in the face, full force.

It's an attack by sheer confusion.

"So nice to see the family! Everyone together—happens so rarely these days. Your dad looks very fine. Did you help him pick the suit? No, of course not. He's a grown man, no help required!" Her sentences run together, falsely bright, with an undercurrent of agitation. I've learnt to just wait for the point, not get sidetracked by the reams of spewing chatter.

"God, how many of these have we been to over the last few years? I'm sure it will be your turn soon! Seeing anyone special at the moment? So hard to meet people these days, isn't it? Thank God I met Trevor before all this godawful Tinder and Twitter and internet dating! Just a regular old meeting for us!"

I watch Chloe with a kind of scientific interest. She's actually an incredibly successful woman. It's hard to pick exactly what her high-speed interactions are all about. She surely could not be this scattered and wired in managerial meetings? It strikes me, once again, as almost adolescent in its nerviness.

Being Ada's sister, and someone I ideally want on my side, she is someone I usually humour. But today, I feel pissed.

"Is there something you want to discuss, Chloe?" I ask her pointedly. "I was on my way to get a top up." I hold up my empty champagne glass and wiggle it for effect, highlighting the importance of my errand. Doubly important now. If she wants to chat, I need a bloody drink in hand.

Her eyes fasten on mine, stern and piercing. "Yes, actually," she says, her voice suddenly evening out. Sounding adult and firm. Like she might dictate some terms and expects, through years of experience, for the recipient to listen.

Ah, I think to myself. *There's a manager I can better imagine.*

"Now that you mention it," she adds, as though her next sentence is an afterthought. As though it wouldn't have come out without my prompting.

"It's about Ada," she goes on, her eyes like a vice against my own. She's not going to let this go, whatever it is, without something from me. Inwardly, I sigh deeply.

Chloe knows about my history with Ada. She doesn't like it, but she's never said a word about it directly. She frowns at me occasionally, but that's the extent of our interactions on the subject.

So I wait with interest to see what she's going to say now.

"It's about Kingston." She watches me carefully.

That stops me short.

"What about him?" I ask equally carefully, my face deliberately blank.

Kingston is the last reason Ada called off our...*thing*, a few years back.

Last reason before now, I correct myself.

Then I frown, irritated that I can't think of a better word to describe us. Our relationship? Affair? Neither one is quite right.

Chloe continues to watch me. She seems on edge. Sharp. Less fluttery and full of nonsense. It's so unusual that my tendency to dismiss her is sidelined. Something is up, and my focus sharpens too. So I wait, giving nothing away.

I'm not afraid of what Chloe thinks of Ada and me, but I don't want her to know how little information I have about the competition.

Chloe speaks slowly, searching my face.

"She got another letter."

————

BACK NEXT TO Ada for the speeches, I drum my fingers on the white linen tablecloth impatiently.

She elbows me discreetly, frowning.

"Shhhh," she hisses. But I can barely wait for everyone to shut up so I can turn my attention to more important conversations. Eventually I hiss back, "We need to talk. Now."

She stares rigidly ahead, not giving me any eye contact, pointedly smiling and nodding at Aunty Kate's longwinded rendition of how the happy couple met. Her speech is laced with relief that her eldest daughter finally, *finally* (age 43) found someone, though of course she doesn't say anything of the sort.

You don't have to say everything out loud in families. Sometimes everyone knows it all, all too well.

Usually I'd be in my element. Champagne, family, laughter, dancing. A cousin's wedding—sitting next to Ada—would be high up on my list of enjoyable ways to spend a Saturday. But between the breakup via SMS and Kingston's letter, I'm not in the mood for fun or romance anymore.

Finally the speeches are over. But when I turn to Ada, she's pointing to the dance floor. The newlyweds are standing awkwardly alone up there. The band are still fiddling with strings and microphones and appear to be in no hurry to start the music. And neither bride nor groom is comfortable in the spotlight. Everyone is facing toward them, waiting for their first dance. They look absolutely petrified.

Without thinking, I stand. Raise my champagne glass. The guests cheer loudly; they're all half-cut already. I barely have to say anything—propose a toast, talk about that time I first met Kate, some admirable quality she displayed. An anecdote that highlights her cheerfulness, her thoughtfulness. Unconsciously, I compare her to myself in that instance, self-deprecating and silly. The crowd laughs appreciatively. They all know me so well anyway.

I sit down when the lead singer coughs into the mike.

When I turn back to Ada, she looks warmer. She smiles at me with genuine affection. She's grateful for my intervention, and I pounce on the advantage it affords me without missing a beat.

"Ada. Chloe tells me there's a problem with Kingston. Tell me about these letters she's so worked up over."

For the briefest second, I see something I'd call fear pass across her face. But it is immediately replaced by a frown, a flash of anger. Her whole body stiffens.

"That's not any of your business. And Chloe had no right talking to you about it, either."

"She seems worried about you," I counter. "We both know I'm not her favourite person in the world. So if she's reaching out to me, it makes me think maybe I should be worried, too."

Ada remains stiff and on guard.

"She's overreacting, as usual." There's a hint of scorn in her voice. "Kingston wants to be 'friends.' There is no chance, ever, of that happening. Zilch. So both of you can leave it alone."

"Is he why you broke it off with me?"

She looks startled.

"Don't be stupid. You know why I broke it off. This can't go anywhere. We both just need to get on with our own lives. The longer we drag it out, the harder it will be."

I study her for a moment. Her coldness—aloofness, even—is so at odds with her appearance. Her fiery auburn hair is beautifully styled, the long tresses falling across her shoulders just so, bouncing off her glorious breasts in perfect loose curls. But even with the most careful styling in the world, her hair hints at something wild. Or maybe I've just seen it across a pillow too many times. The fullness of her lips, the shape of her eyes, the curve of her waist—she screams sensuality. Her mouth is for kissing, her body for touching. For pleasure. It's incongruous with this stiffness, this unease in her own skin.

"You're worried about something. And you broke up with me like a teenager." It's meant to be a barb, but as well as I know her, Ada knows me just as well.

She softens, squeezes my arm. "Don't worry about me. I'm fine. Let's just enjoy the party, okay? We can talk another time."

"Good. Monday. We can grab a meal after work. I'll drop by at six."

Ada opens her mouth, to protest no doubt, but our conversation is cut short in my favour. My dad and stepmother swoop in, elegant and poised. Dad claps me on the back, a little too heartily.

"Hey, kids!" he shouts, way too loud. He must have had more champagne than usual.

"Hi, Dad," I respond brightly, smiling broadly at Ada. *Ben 2, Ada 0,* my smile says. "Hi, Janey."

Ada smiles weakly. "Hi, Bill," she says. "Hi, Mum."

Chapter 3
Ada

All day Monday, I curse him.

His hands, his lips.

His bloody kindheartedness and decency.

It would be much easier to break up with a psychopath.

That thought sobers me. *You did that already,* I correct myself. *And it wasn't actually very easy at all, was it?*

I pull open my top drawer and stare at the envelope inside.

Kingston.

This letter.

It makes no sense.

I'm interrupted by Tracy, an eager intern, and sigh inside. At least, I thought it was on the inside. But she stops her advance toward my desk, her eyes wide.

"Is it a bad time?" she squeaks, looking ready to flee.

"Yes," I tell her. "But you're here now. What is it?"

"Ah, I just wondered if you could help me with the formatting for the sex therapy article. I'm having trouble with the layout."

I tilt my head to the side, observing her impassively.

"You're probably best to speak to Sam or Kasey about that," I tell her. I want to shout at her that there is absolutely no possible reason for her to disturb the CEO about an everyday issue that has nothing to do with management and everything to do with design. But Jason has appeared, leaning against the doorframe and looking at me meaningfully.

After Tracy scurries away, he raises his eyebrows at me.

"Last week you were pulling her up for not running a layout past you. Today you don't want to know about it?"

"Helping format an article is different from casting a final eye over it. You know that. She ought to know that. Or someone in this office needs to teach her," I tell him crossly. "It's a waste of my time, and I have a lot to get through today."

"Hmmm," he says, pushing off the doorframe and coming closer. "You have a lot to get through every day. And that's false economy if you're going to get her to change the whole layout in the end anyway. You might as well have given input now to save everyone some time down the track."

I frown at him. It would be a whole lot more useful if Jason were as terrified of me as everybody else in the office seems to be.

"If you want to change the process, bring it up in Friday's meeting. I'm sure everybody will be delighted to hear your thoughts about it then," I say, smirking slightly, turning back to my desktop.

Jason grins at me, and I sigh again and try to focus on the article I'm reviewing. Written by my favourite freelancer, it's bright and fun and delightful. The photography is stunning. It oozes charm. It's my lead article for the month and I've been reading and rereading it all morning. The closing sentence just isn't quite right and I can't yet find an enhancement.

"Send it back to Harlow," Jason advises. "She'll come up with something. Or ask the team for input." He stands behind me and reads over my shoulder. "Or, just leave it, Ada. Jesus. It sounds great." He blows out a breath in frustration.

"You haven't even read the article," I snap at him, my eyes glued to the screen. "It doesn't quite tie in all the themes. It's quite genius—all the threads running through this one, but they don't all wrap together at the end. I'll just go over it again and see if I

can come up with something better." I wave him off in a type of
dismissal, already reaching for my thesaurus and the notes I'd
given Harlow prior to her interview.

"What about the team lunch? You've skived off the last five of
them. You were the one who wrote all that stuff about team
culture and being approachable. Jeez, some of the new staff
haven't said more than hi to you."

Jason moves toward the door, but stops at the end of my desk,
rapping his knuckles against it, his expression aggravated. My
second-in-command of five years, he is probably the only one in
the office who'll complain to me about my leadership.

"Go ahead without me," I say breezily, not looking away from
my computer. I know I ought to go, but frankly, I'd rather work on
this article. Partly because I can't bear the thought of a single
sentence going out into the world any less than just right—but
also because I prefer working to chatting.

"You mean, 'go without me,'" he corrects me, terse. "As an
editor, I would think you'd be more precise with your language.
Don't pretend you're going to come later."

"Okay, fine. I'm not going to come," I say, finally looking at
him in irritation. "This is how I work, Jase. You know that. Stop
hoping I'll change."

He sighs heavily and leaves without responding.

———

IT'S 5:30 p.m. by the time I'm happy. Although I've read the article
so many times I'm not sure it even makes any sense anymore. But
I've approved it for design and opened the next one.

A niggling sense of something urgent, not dealt with, keeps
troubling me though, and I remember Kingston's letter with a
jolt.

I pull it out of the drawer and smooth it flat on my desk.

Chloe would have a fit; she wants fingerprinting and rubber gloves. But police involvement is the last thing I want.

It's a simple typed note, only three lines long. Different to the earlier ones, which rambled for pages, nonsensical and vaguely threatening.

Threatening in their complete disconnect from reality, rather than making threats against me.

My mind flits back to our early dates. I had been desperate to move on from Ben, our pointless on-again, off-again romance. I loved him, sure. But our family would never accept us being together. So I threw myself into the first relationship I could find.

Stupid. How did I miss it? I wonder for the fifteen-hundredth time. Every other aspect of my life is attended to obsessively—pros and cons weighed, decisions agonised over—but I threw myself into that relationship like my life depended on it.

"Ada!"

My thoughts are interrupted by a shout from the reception area.

Startled, I hurriedly shove the letter back into my top drawer.

Ben pokes his head around the door as I pretend to fuss with papers on my desk. He might know about the damn letter, but I sure as hell don't want him reading it.

"Ready?" he asks, his hair flopping across his eyes, his mischievous grin clearly conveying his belief that he's winning something here.

I roll my eyes and attempt to convey right back that he's only winning because I'm letting him. I could just as easily have locked my door. But Ben's grin only widens. He's impossibly cocky and self-assured.

Sighing, I tell him that I only have an hour and slip on my shoes.

———

DESPITE MYSELF, it's impossible not to enjoy time spent with Ben.

He keeps up a steady stream of entertaining chatter as we wander down charming Melbourne laneways until a table takes his fancy. Perched outside on bar stools on the cobblestones, we sip wine, and everything feels just the way it always did. Even Ben's wandering, appreciative eyes don't disrupt my sense of comfort.

"Are you trying to flirt with me?" I ask, tilting my head.

"No," he shakes his head earnestly. "Absolutely not." Then he grins again. "I'm just enjoying your tits in that shirt."

I roll my eyes, and he smirks, his gaze travelling slowly downward again. Something clenches deep in my tummy.

If only he wasn't quite so sexy, damn him.

Glancing pointedly at my watch, I wonder if I should dive right in or try to distract him. But I suddenly feel exhausted. I lean forward on my elbows and close my eyes.

When I open them, Ben's expression is serious.

"Tell me about the letters."

I ponder him for a moment. If anything, I feel embarrassed.

"That guy I dated for a while. Kingston. God, even his name is stupid," I mutter, distracted, thinking that anyone who went by the nickname "King" was bound to have some issues.

"And?" Ben prompts.

"He got a bit stalker-like when I broke it off. Kept turning up. Wrote some pretty weird letters. Creeped me out that they were hand-delivered all over the place. Places he shouldn't have known I was going." I shudder, remembering.

"Jesus. Ada. Why didn't you tell me?"

"Why do you think?" I snap, irritated.

"We're friends first. That's what you bloody want, isn't it? To be *friends*." He lingers on the last word, and I can't quite tell if he's trying to embrace it or if he's hoping to obliterate it from the English language.

"Did you talk to the police?"

"Yes. Nothing ever came of it. There were no actual threats. No history of violence. Nothing really to go on, according to them." There's a trace of bitterness in my voice. Nothing but my terror. Which apparently didn't rate at all.

"Did you think he'd hurt you?" Ben's brow is furrowed, his eyes intently upon me. I shift uncomfortably under his gaze.

"I don't know. He seemed deranged. I think anyone who's deranged could be dangerous. It was like he had invented a whole narrative around our relationship that bore no resemblance to reality, and he truly believed it. That was scary."

"What happened?"

"It petered out. It took forever. Maybe eighteen months. Contact got further and further apart. I moved. I changed my mobile number. Hand-dropped notes vanished first. I guess I was harder to find. And security at work all had his photo—there was no chance he'd get into the office. Emails took the longest. I didn't want to change my work email at first. But whenever I blocked an email address he'd just open a new one. Eventually I redirected any unknown contacts to go to Chloe automatically, to screen for me. She took it out of my hands."

"That was good of her." Ben ponders this for a moment. "It can't have been easy. She must have worried."

"She was fine with it. She liked having input." *Control, more likely*, I think to myself, and then feel ungrateful. But I'm sick of this subject already. I don't want to give that fucker one more pathetic, shrivelled-up, stale crumb of my attention.

"And now?"

"I got another letter. It was hand-delivered. To work."

Ben shoots backwards in his chair.

"Christ! Ada. You need to get security back on it. Jesus." He's running his hand through his mop of hair, all traces of flirtation long gone. There's something sexy about his agitation, his focus.

His protectiveness? I wonder to myself. *His love, even?*

"It didn't say anything concerning. Some bullshit about how

happy he is. And I should get in touch now before he forgets about me for good if I want to stay connected to him." I laugh, a mirthless bark. "See? Nuts. The guy is fucking nuts."

We're both silent for a moment. Then I say, "Look, I don't want to talk about this anymore. I should never have been with him. It was—" I stop myself abruptly, remembering exactly what it was.

Ben watches me carefully, waiting.

"I need to get back to work. I have articles to finish proofing before tomorrow."

"Like hell you are going back there tonight with no one there. Absolutely not."

I glance at him sharply.

"I can look after myself, actually," I snap. "I'm not going to rearrange my whole life for one idiot. I'll be fine." Then, relenting a little, "I'll lock the doors. And I'll call building security to escort me to the tram stop. And I'll fish out that damn photo. Happy?"

"Not even a little bit," Ben mutters. "What's to say he's not on the tram?"

But I'm already standing up, slapping a ten-dollar note on the table. Ben waves it away in irritation.

"What about dinner? You can't work on a glass of wine."

Chapter 4
Ben

Despite her protests, I grab some takeaway and follow Ada back to her office, knocking on her door only minutes behind her.

She's already engrossed in whatever is on her computer screen, a pen in her hand and a thick notebook beside her.

I think about the work waiting for me at my office, but brush it aside. Nothing that can't wait until tomorrow.

Ada works harder than anyone I know. She's cold and prickly

as a boss—she has a terrible reputation. Junior staff scatter when she so much as raises an eyebrow at them. Never has disdain been so successfully conveyed with such a minute gesture.

But she's also brilliant and dedicated and a force of nature. She can work ninety hours a week without even noticing. She can guide a staff of over eighty people to produce a magazine in which there is not one corner cut. She loves getting everything perfect. So it irks her to no end that I run my magazine in the completely opposite fashion. My staff are relaxed and no doubt working at significantly less than capacity. The odd typo sneaks through into print. Sometimes a photo gets mixed into the wrong story. But there's laughter and friendship and cavorting in my office, which is just how I like it. I don't mind a few cut corners if everyone is having a good time.

"Are you going to bring that food over here?" she asks, not looking away from her screen.

Behind her, the sun is bouncing off the other skyscrapers in central Melbourne. From her corner office I can see the bay, white sails dotted across it. A giant cruiser is docked at Station Pier. Pink clouds streak across the sky, reflected in the buildings around us.

Wordlessly I pull the noodles from the bag I'm carrying and hand her some chopsticks. She's pulled her hair into a rough bun and kicked off her heels, and is concentrating on the double page spread in front of her. Her head is slightly lowered, the curve of her neck tantalisingly close to me, her full red lips pouty with deliberation. Occasionally she chews on her bottom lip absentmindedly.

Her breasts swell in her shirt magnificently, her plunging neckline revealing an inch of pale blue lace bra from the angle I'm standing at behind her. Her skirt has ridden up her thighs and hugs her hips suggestively.

Without even thinking, I reach out and run a finger along the back of her neck. Her skin is so soft. The short downy hair there is glinting golden in the light. Her bun looks like it's about to fall out, letting her glorious red hair fall down her back. I have the urge to shake it free, grab a fistful of it. Pull her head back and press my lips to hers.

She goes very still, her eyes not moving from the screen.

"What are you doing?" she says, her voice controlled, not an ounce of feeling in it. But I know there's feeling underneath.

"Trying to win you back," I murmur, sweeping my fingertips across her shoulders and down her arms, dropping a soft kiss in the curve of her neck. I ache with how badly I want to touch more of her.

I can see goosebumps spring up across her arms, hear her breathing quicken. But she says, in that damn flat voice, "Please, Ben. Don't."

My chest squeezes painfully as my hand drops away from her skin.

I drop a kiss on the top of her head and walk away.

FROM THE AUTHOR

Thank you so much for reading my debut novel!

This story was supposed to be a racy romance to entertain me in my (hopelessly optimistic and mostly nonexistent) spare time at home on maternity leave. But somehow—even away from my day job in mental health—dark themes kept creeping in. And I love, love, love where it ended up.

What I have learnt from my work is that everybody has a story. You really can't judge anyone by the parts of themselves that they choose to show the world. It doesn't excuse bad behaviour, and it doesn't make it okay—but I really believe that sharing stories is the first step to healing. Being brave and being vulnerable and sharing ourselves is necessary to connect with other people...and connection is where the magic happens.

I love that Clara and Lucas were brave and went on that journey and found each other. And it breaks my heart that there are Maureens out there who didn't.

If you enjoyed this book, please please *please* leave me a review! As a new author, reviews really do help. Many people buy books based on the reviews, and it helps persuade other readers to give a new author like me a shot. I would appreciate that so, so much.

ACKNOWLEDGMENTS

There have been so many generous, thoughtful, and slightly wacky people who have helped this novel on its journey to publication.

A huge thank you to Catherine Deveny and her marvellous Gunna's Writing Masterclass—"not judging the omelette mix" and your Love Party posters made all the difference whenever I got stuck working on this project.

Julie Postance's Gunna's Self-Publishing Masterclass, for making self-publishing seem like an achievable goal.

My beta readers, Julie Guay and Victoria Colotta—thank you for your honest and invaluable feedback on early drafts.

To my beta readers-slash-besties, Sarah and Steph—as above, *plus*—thank you for the laughter. Your notes in the margins made me laugh when otherwise I might have cried.

To Alessandra Torre for being the dash of inspiration that started this whole venture. I read an article about you in someone else's magazine in the lunchroom at my work. I'd been toying with the idea of writing a novel for a while, but had not, at that point, managed to start. Then I read about you, read most of your books, and wrote 20,000 words. Since then I've done your classes and found your Inkers. Thank God someone left that magazine there that day!

To the above-mentioned Inkers—what a wonderful group you are. I have been so lucky to find so much wisdom and kindness in such a short time. Whenever I have questions, you guys have the answers. Thank you.

To Brene Brown, whose work and values always remind me why I do the work that I do. Everyone in the world should read your work.

To Glennon Doyle for reminding me that we can do hard things.

To my husband, who never once complained about my late nights, my obsession, my falling off the radar to write a novel that I refused to let him read. Your belief in me is the steadiest, most comforting thing in the entire world. Thank you.

To Erica Russikoff from Erica Edits for her thoughtful comments and sharp eyes. It has been so lovely to have you correct my errors while feeling you understood my story and my characters.

To Elizabeth Mackey for my gorgeous, gorgeous cover.

And to all of you for reading this book—thank you for taking interest in it. I really appreciate it, and I hope that you enjoyed it. x